LITTLE MOTHER

GLOBAL AFRICAN VOICES

DOMINIC THOMAS, EDITOR

LITTLE MOTHER

A NOVEL

CRISTINA ALI FARAH

TRANSLATED BY
GIOVANNA BELLESIA-CONTUZZI
AND
VICTORIA OFFREDI POLETTO

WITH AN INTRODUCTION BY ALESSANDRA DI MAIO

INDIANA UNIVERSITY PRESS
BLOOMINGTON AND INDIANAPOLIS

This book is a publication of

Indiana University Press
601 North Morton Street
Bloomington, Indiana 47404-3797 USA

iupress.indiana.edu

Telephone orders   800-842-6796
Fax orders   812-855-7931
Orders by e-mail   iuporder@indiana.edu

Originally published in Italian as *Madre piccola*
© 2007 Edizioni Frassinelli
English translation © 2011 by Indiana University Press

⊖The paper used in this publication meets the minimum requirements of the American National Standard for Information Sciences—Permanence of Paper for Printed Library Materials, ANSI Z39.48-1992.

Manufactured in the United States of America

Library of Congress Cataloging-in-Publication Data

Ali Farah, Cristina, [date]-
[Madre piccola. English]
Little mother : a novel / Cristina Ali Farah ; translated by Giovanna Bellesia-Contuzzi and Victoria Offredi Poletto ; with an introduction by Alessandra Di Maio.
    p. cm.
ISBN 978-0-253-35610-9 (cloth : alk. paper)
— ISBN 978-0-253-22296-1 (pbk. : alk. paper)
I. Bellesia, Giovanna. II. Poletto, Victoria Offredi. III. Title.
PQ4901.L475M3413 2011
853'.92—dc22

                                        2010047863

1 2 3 4 5 16 15 14 13 12 11

FOR

GIULI,
INTERTWINED TENACITIES

"A man ain't nothing but a man. But a son?

Well, now, that's somebody."
—TONI MORRISON, *BELOVED*

"Still I must ask what becomes of a man or a woman if no moth taps at the window to the universe of his or her creativity?"
—NURUDDIN FARAH, *YESTERDAY, TOMORROW: VOICES FROM THE SOMALI DIASPORA*

"I say: Reality is not found at the start nor at the finish: it presents itself to people along the way."
—JOÃO GUIMARÃES ROSA, *THE DEVIL TO PAY IN THE BACKLANDS*

CONTENTS

TRANSLATORS' PREFACE

THE ACT OF TRANSLATING IS AT ONCE a linguistic and a cultural challenge. In the case of *Little Mother* the challenge we faced was even greater. Cristina Ali Farah, born of an Italian mother and a Somali father, lived her early years in Mogadishu and occasionally spent her summers with her maternal relatives in Italy. When she was in her midteens she fled the civil war in Somalia and journeyed from country to country until she finally settled in Rome. Although Italian is the first language Ali Farah used as a writer, her voice was profoundly shaped by the African oral tradition. This is clearly reflected in the novel, which is, in essence, a long conversation between various protagonists of the Somali diaspora, the threads of their lives intersecting at various points and in a variety of unexpected places.

Most of the conversations are informal in nature; some are not. We felt strongly about respecting the formality or informality of the various speakers. Since English does not make a linguistic distinction between the formal and informal "you," we sought to highlight the difference through our use of vocabulary and register. Following the original text, we have left certain keywords and expressions in Somali, including many Somali words coined during the Italian colonization of Somalia (see the glossary).

Toward the end of the book, Domenica Axad, a character whose very name reflects her dual identity, comments on her experience when, as a child, she had to act as translator between her Italian mother and the extended family of her Somali father. She felt a strong responsibility to "ferry across voices that were entrusted to her without the speaker making any effort to adapt them to the receiver." We, the translators, also felt the challenges of "ferrying across" the reader between the author's idiosyncratic use of Italian and an English text that in a way would be readable and yet would bear the stamp of the original, bicultural language.

Believing, as we do, that this work should as much as possible evoke the same response in its English reader as it does in the Italian, we resisted the temptation to produce flawless English prose that would have betrayed the cultural and linguistic duality which lies at the very core of Cristina Ali Farah's work.

We hope we have succeeded in conveying to the English reader the richness, the poignancy, and the complexity of Ali Farah's storytelling genius.

GIOVANNA BELLESIA-CONTUZZI
AND VICTORIA OFFREDI POLETTO
NORTHAMPTON, MASSACHUSETTS

ACKNOWLEDGMENTS

I WOULD LIKE TO THANK:

The scattered voices of the Somali diaspora that are woven throughout this book.

Giuli for having supported me every day with the love I needed to make it through to the end.

My past and present loved ones.

Motherhood and its gems: Harun, Daud, and Yasmine, my anchors and guides.

The magazines *Scritti d'Africa* and *el Ghibli* for having given me life as a writer.

Alessandra Di Maio, my invaluable friend and a fellow dreamer.

Anna Pastore, a kindred spirit.

Carola Susani for having told me: In the meantime write this book.

Lastly, the Rome library Enzo Tortora, near my children's preschool, for having given me permission to work there outside regular hours.

CRISTINA ALI FARAH

INTRODUCTION:
PEARLS IN MOTION

"WE ARE A NECKLACE THAT BROKE off whose pearls have been scattered all over the world." This is the image that Somali-Italian author Cristina Ali Farah often uses to describe the Somali diaspora, which is the implicit protagonist of *Little Mother*, her first novel, originally published in Italian in 2007.

Cristina Ali Farah is an offspring of the very same Somali diaspora that plays a central role in all her works—fiction, poetry, theatre, and journalism. Born in 1973 in Verona, Italy, to an Italian mother and a Somali father, she was raised in Mogadishu, where her family moved when she was still an infant. Her parents met when her father was studying in Verona, her mother's hometown. In those years, students who attended the Somali National University were allowed, and often encouraged, to spend one or more terms at an Italian university. But why Italy?

Today, not everyone remembers that Somalia—or rather its coastal southern region, whose economy has traditionally revolved around the capital, Mogadishu—was once an Italian colony. This was the case from the end of the nineteenth century, when Italy embarked on its colonial enterprise in Africa, until the post–World War II Paris Peace Treaties in 1947, according to which Italy, having lost the war, was to renounce its African territories. However, after a two-year spell during which it remained under British administration, Italian Somaliland became a United Nations Trust Territory under Italian administration from 1949 to 1959. Britain, which had in the meantime won the war, was the other major colonial power ruling the Horn of Africa, together with France, which controlled Djibouti. Italy's role was to help make the country's passage from a colonial to an independent nation as smooth as possible.

On July 1, 1960, Italian Somaliland combined with British Somaliland, and together they became the independent Republic of Somalia. Aden Abdullah Osman Daar was elected president and led the country until 1967. That year, when his former prime minister, Ali Shermarke, was elected to succeed him, he made history as one of the first leaders in Africa to peacefully hand over power to a democratically elected successor. But democracy in Somalia was short-lived. In October 1969, Ali Shermarke was murdered. Only a few days later, Major General Muhammad Siad Barre, who at the time commanded the army, led the coup d'état that would assure him absolute power for twenty-one years. In 1991, his regime was overthrown and a disastrous civil war broke out. Fighting still rages, despite several international peacekeeping operations.

Somalia is currently not recognized as a sovereign state by the international community. Having produced over a million refugees, the civil war is the product of a complex political process which needs to be considered in its entirety if one wishes to comprehend the contemporary political situation in Somalia. Prominent Somali writer Nuruddin Farah explains in an important work of nonfiction, *Yesterday, Tomorrow: Voices from the Somali Diaspora*, that, unlike what the mass media seem to suggest, the civil war cannot be explained merely on the basis of tribal violence and warlordism, nor exclusively by referencing clanism. Rather, it is the ultimate result of a historical process which began with Europe's prolonged colonization, continued with a brief independence, and was followed by Siad Barre's oppressive regime (which received backing from powerful players in the international arena) until its eventual downfall. In other words, the Somali civil war, like other civil wars in Africa, epitomizes the collapse of the postcolonial model. After decades of colonial oppression, independent Somalia has experienced increasing levels of economic and political devastation. Periods of unprecedented drought and famine have only exacerbated its precarious state of affairs. More recently, the country has experienced a turn toward fundamentalist Islam, and today it appears in the news predominantly as an alleged Al-Qaeda safe haven or because of its befuddling stories of piracy. The Transitional Federal Government, on the one hand, and the Islamic courts, on the other, fight constantly over national control. What is of even greater significance, particularly in the context of the novel *Little Mother*, is the fact that there are currently more Somalis living abroad than in Somalia itself.

Cristina Ali Farah is one of them, one of those "pearls" that the Somali civil war has scattered across the world. Her life story contains in a nutshell the complex history of the country in which she grew up. The firstborn daughter of a father from formerly Italian-colonized Somalia and a mother from the former colonizing power (a reversal of the typical colonial white man–black woman liaison), she is a genuine "postcolonial child" who has always made an effort in her life and art to combine her two native cultures into one common home. After spending her childhood and youth in Mogadishu, in 1991, when the political situation was disintegrating rapidly, she joined the large number of compatriots who were fleeing the country. Her escape as an eighteen-year-old woman carrying her newborn baby is lyrically evoked in one of her first poems, "Red", "Foamy dawn, you stole upon us, alone in the obscurity, as we were leaving forever. / Me, in the dirty little truck, with a precious bundle in my arms. / I stared, stunned, at the rifles resting on shoulders. Somali rebels accompanied our farewell." Since then, Ali Farah has never returned to Somalia. She first moved to Pécs, in Hungary, where she spent the first two years of her exile; then she tried, unsuccessfully, to settle in Verona, the town of her birth. Finally she moved to Rome, the former colonial metropole recently turned into a hub for global migrants, where she has lived since 1997.

In Rome, while studying for a university degree in literature, she soon became a professional writer. In *Little Mother*, like in the majority of her works, Italy's capital city occupies a privileged space. Cristina Ali Farah's alternative, poetic map of the "eternal city" includes historic landmarks as well as ethnic neighborhoods, the monumental capital complex where state funerals are celebrated, the Somali and Chinese shops all around Termini railway station, the abandoned Somali embassy with the elegant villas and palaces surrounding it, botanic gardens, hospitals, private residences, markets, and subway stations where the faces and voices of an increasingly multiethnic twenty-first-century humanity encounter each other on a daily basis.

Cristina Ali Farah writes in Italian, one of her two native tongues—that of education and of formal schooling, and of her literary studies. In Somalia, Italian was the main language of instruction in the colonial system and remained so for many years after decolonization, even after Somali (until then an oral language) was finally transcribed in 1972. Until not long ago, Italian was also the language spoken by the Somali elite, by the "been-tos" like her own father, by the "proper gentlemen" who would linger around the Italian Cultural Center in Mogadishu and elegantly drop one or two Italian words into their conversation as "classy men" were expected to do. Taageere, one of the novel's protagonists, describes this phenomenon. In today's Somalia, however, Italian remains only as the old colonial language spoken by a dying generation, and is largely ignored by young people.

Cristina Ali Farah's use of the Italian language in her prose is remarkable: in this novel, as well as in her multi-award-winning short stories, such as "Punt Rap," "Entirely," and the novel's namesake "Little Mother," she dominates, transforms, and enriches the language imposed by the former colonizer by bending it to her own cultural and artistic needs, thereby effectively inverting the original colonial power relations. Thus, language becomes not only the chosen terrain for significant creative interventions but also, ultimately, a site of resistance. In *Little Mother* we find the tongue of the former colonizer transformed into the language of postcoloniality through creative manipulation and *métissage*—or, more accurately, *meticciato*, in Italian. An example is offered by the recurring interspersion of some Somali terms in the original Italian text referring to concepts and objects specific to Somali culture: *abbayo*, an endearing term for a close girlfriend or sister; *catar*, an oriental perfume; *jinni*, a demon; *fasakh*, the annulment of a marriage according to Islamic law; *iid*, a religious holiday; and many others. Moreover, some of these Somali terms—faithfully left in the original by the translators, who for an explanation refer the reader to the novel's glossary—are words with Italian origins that entered the Somali language during the colonial domination, such as *barbaroni* (from Italian *peperoni*, bell peppers), *fasoleeti* (from *fazzoletto*, handkerchief), *farmashiiyo* (from *farmacia*, pharmacy), *kabushiini* (from *cappuccino*), and *draddorio* (from *trattoria*). Cristina Ali Farah's use of these expressions in the text is a successful attempt to confound and possibly overturn the interior workings of the relationship between language and power. Even the title of the novel testifies to the author's artistic intent, making it manifest: the idiom "little mother" (*madre piccola*, in the original Italian title) is a loan translation of the Somali *habaryar*, the term for an aunt on the maternal side.

The novel, however, accommodates more than Somali, including as it does the various languages and voices of the diaspora's protagonists that Cristina Ali Farah portrays. Set in the present—the action, which is nonchronologically ordered, spans the period from the late seventies to around 2004—*Little Mother* is about the friendship between two cousins, Barni and the *mulatta* Domenica Axad, whose mother is Italian. The two girls grow up together in Mogadishu, once a cosmopolitan pearl on the Indian Ocean, and are torn apart by the war, eventually reuniting in Italy as adults. In Rome, Barni, who works as a midwife, helps Domenica Axad have her baby, to whom she is a "little mother." The baby's father,

Taageere, is an old, long-lost acquaintance from childhood whom Domenica Axad, after meandering for ten years, eventually meets in one of the diaspora's multiple sites, a unidentified North American city (Toronto, in an earlier version of the novel, the metropolitan center with the largest Somali population in North America). In the projects outside of this city, where Somalis live side by side with Ghanaians, Jamaicans, and other communities from the black diaspora, Domenica Axad is filming parts of a documentary on the daily life of Somali refugees. Her partner on this project is a friend she met in Germany, Saciid Saleebaan, who turns out to be one of Taageere's old buddies from Mogadishu. Taageere's first-person story alternates with those of the two cousins in the novel. The three narrating protagonists—Domenica Axad, Barni, and Taageere—alternately take the stage, three times each for a total of nine chapters—nine is a recurring, symbolic number in the text. Contrapuntally, each of them gives an intensely lyrical monologue, Domenica Axad nostalgically reminiscing about her childhood in the prelude, Taageere commemorating Mogadishu in the interlude, and Barni wishing for a happier future in the epilogue. On two separate occasions they converse with different interlocutors, who appear only in absentia in the novel but who, because of their ambiguous presence and inquiring spirit, help the reader to appreciate different facets of the protagonists' personalities and to collate bits and pieces of their private histories.

By interlacing the broken threads of their narratives, moving back and forth in time, the three main characters recreate their interwoven personal stories and those of their shattered, displaced community. The metaphor of the diaspora as a tangled net that is to be unraveled and stitched back up recurs through the novel. Moreover, they offer themselves as resonating chambers, amplifying a variety of additional voices, most poignantly those of some of the best-known contemporary Somali poets and singers—Cabdulqaadir Xirsi Siyaad, Maxamuud Cabdullahi Ciise, and Axmed Naaji—whose evocative verses blend in with the protagonists' monologues. In particular, the finale of the interlude, when Taageere's voice duets with that of Axmed Naaji in the heartbreaking mourning for beautiful Xamar (a local name for Mogadishu), constitutes one of the most lyrical, melancholic passages of the novel.

A considerable number of secondary characters also move in the background, materializing and then disappearing with equal ease. They are all linked through different circumstances to at least one of the protagonists, and often to all three—Shukri, Taageere's former wife, "as sweet as sugar"; his beloved friend Xirsi, who dies in his arms in Mogadishu; his younger sister Luul escaping war, finally landing on the little Italian island of Lampedusa; their uncle and aunt Diriiye and Safiya in Rome; Maxamed X, the "mute," and his mates occupying what once was the Somali embassy in Rome; Barni and Domenica Axad's parents; their first cousins Libeen and Shamsa; their much-loved, older uncle Foodcadde; Ardo, Barni's friend whose filigree earrings and "earth" name remind her of her own late mother; Ayaan, "the wild one, an armored leopard" whom Domenica Axad befriends in Holland; Maryam, "slightly touched in the head," because, Taageere explains, "people who are in exile for a long time end up going mad"; the already mentioned Saciid Saleebaan, who "acts like an American," calling his Somali compatriots "brothers and sisters," in English, and addressing them as "ladies and gentlemen"; and a significant number of children, among them newborn Taariikh, Domenica Axad and Taageere's son, named after his maternal grandfather. Dislocated in parts of the world as different as the Netherlands, Finland, Kenya, Australia, and of course North America and Italy, these minor characters, whose abundant presence might occasionally challenge the readers' attention and lead them temporarily off-track, represent the individual strings that, all together, constitute the web of the Somali diaspora. As it so happens, the more we proceed into the story, the more we realize that their role is not minor but in fact pivotal to the development of the plot. Their life stories are strictly associated with those of the three main protagonists, with whom they share a history of trauma, exile, nostalgia, a desire to keep their country alive through collective memory, and, in most cases, hope for a better future.

The result is a choral, self-questioning (interrogative clauses abound in the text), fractured yet accomplished narrative offering a compelling portrait of Somalia and its diaspora, whose structure it reflects. The author's intention is to recompose the fragments of a nation through the eyes and voices of a younger generation whose experience of that nation has been mainly its collapse, and for whom "home" has mostly been a vexed concept. The search, in this novel, cannot be conducted individually. Somalia's national identity has been torn apart and it takes an entire dispersed community to knit the threads back and overcome family and clan hostilities (in this sense, the story of the friendship between Barni and Ardo, from a rival clan, appears emblematic). Similarly, the three protagonists of this novel need each other in order to find themselves and their place—their paths, rather—in the world. However, individual identity remains difficult to figure out, and throughout the story remains a work in progress. This is true especially for Taageere, because, this story seems to suggest, men have an extremely hard time finding a new place for themselves in the diaspora, while women emerge as the bedrock of the community. Again, power roles appear inverted in this novel. Women assume all kinds of responsibilities. While Taageere struggles to define his role as a husband, father, son, friend, and devout Muslim, Barni and Domenica Axad, whose mothers already paved the way for equality between the sexes, propose an alternative model of family that can do without the physical presence of a father. In the diaspora, a mother and a "little mother" can, and indeed often must, join forces to raise a child together. In conclusion, the final message of the novel is an optimistic one: despite chaos, uprootedness, disempowerment, and a sense of general demise, birth remains possible, and reconnections are not only plausible, but vital.

Cristina Ali Farah's novel swells the ranks of Somali literature—a literature singularly characterized by the fact that, perhaps more than many other national literature, it is written in the multiple languages of the diaspora. Suffice it to mention, for instance, Nuruddin Farah, Somalia's literary patriarch, who writes in English; Abdourahman A. Waberi from Djibouti, writing in French; Ayaan Hirsi Ali, in Dutch; and other Somali-Italian writers, such as Shirin Ramzanali Fazel and Igiaba Scego. These authors' works offer an important contribution to African literature and to the cultures of the African diaspora worldwide. Cristina Ali Farah's *Little Mother* adds to this legacy by contributing to an alternative remapping of the diaspora which incorporates Italy as one of its fundamental, albeit often overlooked, territories. By offering a portrait of the contemporary Somali world as it is perceived by the younger generation, *Little Mother* points to a world in which national borders appear increasingly blurred and problematic, where old identities are constantly renegotiated in the process of crossing, and new, yet inscrutable ones come to birth. It is the world of the contemporary, global African diaspora, where individuals and communities must learn to share space and live side by side. For this reason, it appears particularly appropriate that Cristina Ali Farah's first novel finds its home in the English-speaking world in this new, important, aptly named literary series, *Global African Voices*.

ALESSANDRA DIMAIO

LIST OF MAIN CHARACTERS

Ardo (1)   = *Mother* of Barni
               Wife of Sharmaarke
               Aunt of Domenica Axad, Libeen, and Shamsa

Ardo (2)   = Young Somali woman Barni meets in Rome

Barni   = *Cousin* of Domenica Axad, Libeen, and
               Shamsa
               Daughter of Sharmaarke and Ardo

Caasha   = *Sister* of Taageere and Luul

Domenica =   *Cousin* of Barni, Libeen, and Shamsa
/Axad   *Daughter* of Taariikh and his Italian wife
               Second wife of Taageere and *mother* of his
               second son

Foodcadde =   *Brother* of Sharmaarke and Taariikh
               Father of Libeen and Shamsa
               Husband of Xaliima

Libeen   = *Cousin* of Barni and Domenica Axad
               Brother of Shamsa
               Son of Foodcadde and Xaliima

Luul   = *Sister* of Taageere and Caasha

Shamsa   = *Cousin* of Barni and Domenica Axad
               Sister of Libeen
               Daughter of Foodcadde and Xaliima

Sharmaarke = *Brother* of Taariikh and Foodcadde
             Father of Barni
             Husband of Ardo

Shukri   = *First wife* of Taageere and *mother* of his first
             son

Taageere   = *Husband* of Shukri first and Domenica Axad
             later

Taariikh   = *Brother* of Sharmaarke and Foodcadde
             Father of Domenica Axad
             Husband of Italian woman

Xaliima   = *Wife* of Foodcadde
             Mother of Libeen and Shamsa
             Aunt of Barni and Domenica Axad

LITTLE MOTHER

1

PRELUDE—DOMENICA AXAD

SOOMAALI BAAN AHAY,[1] like my half that is whole. I am the fine thread, so fine that it slips through and stretches, getting longer. So fine that it does not snap. And the tangled mass of threads widens and reveals the knots, clear and tight, that, though far from each other, do not unravel.

I am one thread in that tangled mass and my beginning belongs to the multiple one.

My beginning is Barni as we eat together from the communal dish. We are sitting on the ground next to each other and the boys are laughing at the position of my legs. On the mat my knees are touching, one leg going this way, the other that way. How come they don't break, *dalbooley*? You

---

1. *Soomaali baan ahay:* "I am Somali," 1977 poem by Cabdulaqaadir Xirsi Siyaad, also known as "Yamyam."

should see how funny she looks when she runs with her calves flapping left and right.

Barni: even the boys are frightened of her. She gets up, grabs them by the neck, and scratches them, you should see how she can scratch. Don't you dare joke around. The plate, almost full, tips over, and there goes my Barni, with that heart-shaped birthmark right in the middle of her forehead, running off to complain: Not a day goes by when you can have a meal without having to get in a fight with these bullies. I'll show you who's stronger. I tried once, I wanted to be like her, but there is only one Barni.

My beginning is the two of us slipping into the kitchen, we see the papaya split wide open with its perfectly round little seeds and so, some for you and some for me, then we run into the courtyard and we make a deep hole in the red sand; tomorrow we'll come back and perhaps, who knows, something might have sprouted. Barni telling me to be brave the day when they set the trap for the cat, the one that always stole meat from the shopping basket, and now that they've caught him, they're beating him so hard that I can't bear to look. They threw him out onto the street, but he came back; now he no longer steals the meat, one of his eyes is shriveled up. Perhaps he has come back to remind us that our prophet Mohammed loved cats; they say that once a cat fell asleep on his arm and that the Prophet, so as not to wake him up, decided to cut off his sleeve.

My beginning is Barni when it's my turn to tell stories, she asks for the ones from the books I'm reading and translates the words that I don't know, like that time when I wanted to tell the story of the little mermaid and I was saying a woman half fish half woman, how do you say that? *Gabareymaanyo,* says Barni, that's how you say it. I'd like to be a *gabareymaanyo* too, but I don't know how to swim, at the beach I wanted to join her in the water, but there was a hole; luckily Barni is taller than I am, she came over right away to pull me out, wow, was I scared, I can still taste the salty water.

My beginning seems to break that day when Barni is combing my hair in preparation for my departure: So that your grandmother will see how beautiful you have become! She rubs coconut oil in my hair and parts the strands, and I say, Barni I can't see anything, it's like a black cloud in front of my eyes. Suddenly I can't breathe, I can only feel the cold water dripping from my forehead onto my chest, she's fainted, they say. Domenica, Domenica! And while they are calling my name I begin to see Barni's eyes again, staring at me right up close. Then I say to her: *Abbaayo*, I no longer want to be called by this name that makes everyone laugh, and she says: Don't worry, from now on your name will be Axad, like the beginning.

My mother faints too but she's a grown-up. At the beach they call me: Your mother has fainted, she's fainted. It must be because of the heat. I run through the crowd and I see her lying on the ground: Don't worry, she tells me, everything's fine. Meanwhile, in the background at the Café Lido there's a *waddani* voice on Radio Mogadishu.

Time goes by, a chain of days, think of the seasons too, and if you are someone who has lived, tell me: Who is Somali?

Barni and I move off hand in hand, cousins "of the first degree," as they say in Italy. My father and her father, Taariikh and Sharmaarke, are sons of the same father. They left at the same time, one for Bardheere and the other for Ceelbuur.

If you know, teach, if you don't know, learn, so the saying goes. Two young students sign up to serve the nation in order to get ahead. Two years far from home to forget that by nature they were camel riders, men separated from their own kind, joined from afar by exceptionally strong and intertwined threads.

You were luckier than me, but you won't fool the Bedouin, I won't accept your gifts, my conscience is vigilant, I am Somali.

Teaching our children to write their own language, communicating from afar using the words of the father and the mother, that is what will allow us to stay solidly united, without the flow of someone else's language separating us. Learn the Somali alphabet, brothers: B T J.[2]

When school lets out, the streets around take on a bluish-white hue just like our uniforms. Each one of us with her small schoolbag walks toward home. I wait for my aunt who is late. Today she is dressed European style, with bell-bottom pants, a fashion that my mother doesn't like, but they were the only ones she could bring her from Italy, there was nothing else in the shops. Her hair is loose, Afro style, says my aunt, and she looks at herself in the mirror with the metal comb in her hand. We get home, my aunt says: Sit here on the step and I'll put your hair in two braids. Tight, close to my head, the way I like it because that way it seems that I have long hair even though it's short. But where are they, why aren't my mother and my father back yet? Something has happened, my aunt is more worried than usual, I overheard her whispering in the kitchen, she's saying something that she doesn't want me to hear: This time my brother Taariikh has gone too far, especially after they have already taken Sharmaarke.

Uncle Sharmaarke is Barni's father, but I have never seen him; they say you can tell right away that he's her father, because he has her same heart-shaped birthmark. One evening he came to our house to meet me, because apparently he is always very busy during the day, too bad though, when he came I was asleep. Here they are, they have arrived: I hear them, the sound of car doors opening and shutting, and voices in the background. My mother is wearing her tortoiseshell glasses and in her hands is a transparent plastic container full of spaghetti and meat sauce. My eyes are drawn to my father because Uncle Foodcadde and then Gaandi, his friend, seem to be holding him up.

---

2. The first letters of the Arabic alphabet, approximately transcribed in Roman letters.

I may even be poor, but my pride is intact, I don't stretch out my hands to beg, the man whose friend I am, I do not equate him with the enemy, soomaali baan ahay.

Uncle Foodcadde has his own car, that's why. Not everyone has one, having a car is almost a luxury. Sometimes Foodcadde drives us inland to drink camel milk. It's beautiful there, the sand goes on forever and the sun is hot. By contrast, the inside of the hut is cool and the milk is in large vats. They pour it out, a tin cup for each of us children. Drink it up, the camel drivers live on this and nothing else, and that's all they need to grow as tall and slim as they are. The milk tastes sweet and is a bit thick. The first time I drank it I got a stomach ache. My father thinks my mother spoils me with Italian delicacies, and that's why I don't have the stomach of a nomad. I say: In time I will get used to it. To camel milk, I mean.

I also got used to my father being in and out of jail. He was at school as usual and was talking about certain things. Then some guys arrived, perhaps someone squealed on him, and they told him that if he didn't tone down what he said, next time they would put him in jail. My father Taariikh replied that he can teach what he likes and so they put him in jail. Because he says that it's not right that there are trucks that take people to wage war. War against Ethiopia. Everybody is frightened, and when they come round recruiting, they hide. One of my aunt's friends says that her husband is fighting in Ogaden and she is at her wits' end with all her children. Sometimes she calms down when the radio reports that we are winning the war, that we must remain calm. My father says that's not true, you can tell from all the people who are running away. My father didn't return home for a long time. Together with him they arrested his brother Sharmaarke, a professional soldier, and a lot of other people. No one even knows where some of these people have ended up; they secretly shot some of them.

No man can stroke my head, nor tie me up with ropes, nobody can persuade me, deception for me is a container that leaks water, soomaali baan ahay.

Sometimes mom takes me with her to the prison. We go there on her red Vespa and I hold on tightly to her waist, my little hands touching. Once, while we are going around the Rotonda, the one where there's the monument to the fallen soldiers, a truck closes in on us in a curve. Mom loses her balance and we slide onto the edge of the road. The driver of the truck is very kind, he helps us retrieve one of mom's wooden sandals that has fallen into a shallow manhole, then he asks me if everything is all right. I am shaken up, you don't have an accident every day, so I say that actually, I think I hurt my arm. Not good, because when mom hears me, she immediately says that there's nothing wrong although I insist that there is and I even get a bit mad.

The truck driver continues to apologize to my mother and calls her *dumaashi*, like everyone does. *Dumaashi*, sister-in-law, they call her that because her husband is Somali, so all Somalis are her brothers-in-law.

They call her *dumaashi, dumaashi,* and she isn't always happy, especially when the sentence is: *Dumaashi,* you who are *dumaashi,* please help me; when this happens, I slip quickly behind her and my face assumes an expression that says: This has nothing to do with me, thank goodness I'm a little girl.

I share my name with equality, no living creature can be superior to me, I do not conceal an ulterior motive if I invite a guest, soomaali baan ahay.

But ever since dad went to prison I spend much more time with Barni, the only one who believed the story of the accident, and Aunt Xaliima, the wife of Uncle Foodcadde, often comes by to keep the *dumaashi* company. She is very generous because we don't have much so sometimes she brings us *ootkac,* the dried meat from the nomads, sometimes a *diric* for mom, another time it was a lobster glued to a purple particle board. Mom hung it in my room and at night, if I wake up suddenly, it frightens me a bit with all its little claws.

Actually, the best present was two little gold rings, my first earrings. I begged so much to have my ears pierced that in the end they took me to a lady, all the neighborhood little girls had their ears pierced by her. This lady slipped the needle with the thread right through my ear and then tied it with a little knot, making a kind of loop. It hurt a lot but I didn't scream because I promised Barni to be brave and she was kind enough to hold my hand. The lady who pierces ears said to me: Don't forget to put oil on them every evening, and even if it hurts move the thread around. In a week's time I'll put a thorn through each ear, I get someone to bring them to me from the bush just for that, that way the hole gets bigger.

The thorns made my tonsils swell and then, when I got better, the little gold rings arrived. So at long last all that suffering ended in what I wanted.

Aunt Xaliima is very different from the young aunt who braids my hair and who used to sleep next to me before Barni arrived, because she smiles very little. They say that a few years ago something terrible happened to her. On October 21 some planes were making loops in the sky with different colored smoke. At a certain point two of them collided. Pieces of the airplane fell on the houses and killed many people. My aunt was seriously injured, it took a really long time for her to begin walking again. Poor thing.

My Uncle Foodcadde has a store right near the Ceel Gaab market where each day trucks and buses stop. He always brings us a little rice, a little flour, a little sugar, because otherwise we have to stand in interminably long lines for government vouchers, and ever since my father became a political prisoner they give us fewer and fewer of them.

One day mom slips the two pounds of sugar in her white cloth bag, the same one in which she keeps her wallet, her glasses. and her Russian camera. She comes to pick me up at school and then she takes a photograph of me on her red Vespa with my schoolbag slung across my shoulder. Perhaps the sugar got into the film, because we ended up with a photo of me smiling surrounded by giant shapes of trapped ants.

My path is dictated by fate, my resources are a poison, my borders are certain, my blade is a scourge, my soul is hanging from a tree, soomaali baan ahay.

The one who is closest to us above all is Gaandi, my father's dearest friend. He loves children very much, otherwise he wouldn't be a doctor. Sometimes I think that when I grow up I want to become a doctor like him. They call him Gaandi because he always dresses like an Indian. He has a very thick beard, so thick that we children call him Leo. He always laughs loudly, in a way that makes everybody else laugh, and he likes to take us to the cinema. Sometimes he carries me on his shoulders and I feel as if I'm way up high.

Gaandi got hold of powdered milk for me and all the other children who weren't getting their mother's milk, therefore, says my father, I should consider him like a second mother.

The only time he made me angry was when he told my cousin Libeen that he was sick and I wasn't. We were both having difficulty breathing, and at times I felt like I was suffocating, but Gaandi, you know what he said? That Libeen has asthma, while I am only faking it. Instead, I think that Libeen tricked us all once again.

Usually mom goes to the jail at lunchtime when everybody else does. She takes food to my father but since they don't let anybody in, there's Aweys to take the baskets back and forth. Actually, Aweys is also in jail and they say that the moment they let him out, he tries to steal some small thing because he doesn't know how to survive on the outside. So this is his job, he takes food to the prisoners and in exchange they give him a tip. He is also kind and generous because if you can't give him anything he does you this favor all the same. Once we met him on the street and my aunt said to him: Aweys, what are you doing on the outside? And he began to laugh and said: Actually, I'm thinking of stealing your necklace!

Aweys is the only person who smiles in there, the rest are soldiers with those scarily long guns. Only once have I ever happened to hold one. My young aunts were doing their military service at that time and when they came home Barni and I had our picture taken together wearing their uniforms.

*He who threatens me will have no peace, he who finishes me
off does not exist, I have not abandoned victory, I do not support the
abuse of power, I recognize him who has right on his side, soomaali
baan ahay.*

I don't know how much time my father spent inside.
It seemed like a very long time to me, but calculating it in
days, months, years, is something I cannot do. It's easier for
me to think of moments, one at a time. For example, Barni
and me going to check if the papaya plant had sprouted.
Sand is not good for growing things, but that's something
we don't know. We continue to plant little seeds but nobody
tells us that nothing will ever grow.

Then another moment, in the pool. They tell me that
it is easier to swim in a pool, that the sea is more scary. I
think that if I learn to swim my dad will be happy when we
go to the beach together again, because he is the one who
always throws me into the deep water and then says that
I'm a scaredy-cat.

I discover that in fact pool water is also deep. Barni and I
are on our way home together, she is all excited because she
has been swimming, I'm hopping from one side to the other
wrapped in my *guntiino*. From the road someone greets me
with a chuckle; I say to Barni, but why are they smiling at
me? Because your *guntiino* is torn, *abbaayo*. I run off toward
home, red with embarrassment.

But the biggest event, the one event my father has never forgotten, was my grandfather's death. The adults say
grandfather is almost a hundred years old, and they rarely
let us into his darkened room. All of us little children feel
scared and ashamed because of our grandfather who hardly
speaks, but all his children love him so much that he almost
seems like a king. He is very big, his skin as light as amber;
every day Uncle Foodcadde washes his entire body with a
cloth and warm water and then he feeds him the food he
has minced up for him.

My father's grief is not just because of the death of my
grandfather who lived such a long time, it is above all because he cannot attend his funeral. So there is only mom

and me in his place, dad's entire family. The government will not grant him permission to attend. I know very little about grandfather.

My grandfather for me has always been the child who managed to escape with his brother and his mother after they had assassinated his father. My grandfather who was strong and courageous, an expert butcher of animals, my grandfather, the firstborn son, who carries his younger brother on his shoulders, leaving behind the remains of his mother who was devoured by the lion.

I am the frontrunner of peace, I am disturbed by hostility, I do not turn around in battle, I don't await the hand of the man who strikes the blow, soomaali baan ahay.

For the funeral, my mother wears her light blue *diric* that she was recently given. It is not very common to see her wearing a *diric;* after all she is Italian and Italians dress like Italians even when they are *dumaashi.*

Uncle Foodcadde says that when mom and dad were on their way back to Somalia he immediately ran to my grandfather and told him, *Aabbe,* father, Taariikh is coming back home and he is bringing a wife with him. So my grandfather said to him, and what's so special about this wife for you to be out of breath? So my uncle answered, nothing, just that she's Italian, and grandfather, oh well, what do you expect, he was in Italy and he married an Italian!

I am the possessor of ideas and I will not accept his, I am different from the others, I will not bring anyone his shoes, soomaali baan ahay.

I say, thank goodness my father went to Italy to study. And should I say, thank goodness he wanted to return? He learned many things in Italy and all those things that they taught him, all those beautiful things about revolution, about brotherhood, all those things that he heard and he learned and he breathed, he did not want to keep them all for himself. All those things that some say brought him bad luck. They also brought bad luck to Uncle Sharmaarke, they brought bad luck to many people. But, for once, I say that if he hadn't gone to Italy, I wouldn't exist. And I say that what happened has happened and there is nothing we can do about it, except stop, listen, and change direction.

I am the slashed skin, slashed while I was shepherding my animals, the one who slashed me is that man, but only one branding remained, the duty of unity remained, soomaali baan ahay.

2

BARNI

I DON'T HAVE MUCH TIME. But if an hour is enough, OK, I can stay. You'll work around that? Great, then let's go out somewhere, we'll look for a café. This is a good time of day, they won't be too crowded. We can talk in peace. Give me all the details. My friend told me on the phone that you are writing a piece on the Somali community. The Somalis who live in Rome, right? I'm the first person to be interviewed? Good. Don't let yourself be sidetracked. Everyone has their own version of what happened. I've heard good things about you, I trust you. I am not the kind of person who would talk to just any journalist. Plus, you are a woman, you know what I mean. You'll certainly be more insightful. Do you need to use a tape recorder?

Good, let's start. With my name, sure. My name is Barni Sharmaarke. Careful, spell it correctly. No, it's not difficult. You just have to pick a linguistic code. Yours or ours. They

always make such a big mess on official documents. They
don't just have problems with the transcription: the big
problem is with last names. It seems so simple to me. You
see, we use the patronymic instead of the last name. Family
names? You want to know if we have something similar? It
depends on what you mean. Our elders know their family
trees by heart, all the way back to their very origins, at least
that's what they say. But this is something I'd prefer not to
talk about; it's an issue that deeply divides people. Leave it
out. In my opinion it's all conjecture, all those bloodlines,
family trees, roots.

See, I have already started to ramble. You prefer that?
An outline, questions and an outline would be useful for
me. Please pull me back on track, anytime you think it appropriate. This is an urgent issue for me and urgency can
undermine clarity.

You're impressed by my Italian? I've spoken this language
since I was a child. I started studying it in primary school, together with my cousin Axad. But you probably already know
that we Somalis can almost always speak Italian. At least my
aunts and uncles did, people of that generation. I was able
to practice with my Italian-Somali cousin, Domenica Axad.
Anyway, I'd prefer not to talk about myself. I have so many
things to tell you. One story in particular that I think would
be suitable for your project.

Forgive me if I start in a roundabout way, but do you
remember the shipwreck that happened a month ago? The
bodies of those nine Somalis that were taken to Rome? The
funeral that took place in the famous Campidoglio Square?
I think that funeral struck a chord in the hearts of people.
I don't think that I'm overstating your role, the role of the
press. But all week long newspapers and TV stations spoke
of nothing else but that shipwreck. There was no way anyone could have missed it. Who can fathom out why certain
events attract interest and others don't? After all, that shipwreck might have been just one of many.

Boats have been coming and unloading illegal immigrants along Italian coastlines for a long time now. The tides

go in and out and the beaches keep filling up with garbage: tomato cans, shards of green glass, small tubes of medicine, clumps of tar, and plastic bags, more and yet more plastic bags. And, carried by the sea, lifeless bodies, wearing tattered clothes, their purplish skin blotched with white salt. That day—the afternoon of the funeral—I felt all churned up inside. I thought: It must be because my period's due. I was alone, going there on my own. Once there I would meet many people I knew. I was climbing up the steps to the Campidoglio Square, feeling dizzy, I don't know how to describe it. Almost on the verge of falling. Have you ever noticed those steps? They're crooked, they seem to slant the wrong way. It was as if a centrifugal force were pushing me in the opposite direction. I was trying to go toward the center and gradually I began to see the nine coffins, one after the other, all lined up, and covered with the pale blue Somali flag. I felt as if I couldn't breathe, as if I were losing my balance, although I was anchored to the ground. I climbed slowly. And I heard the muffled voices of the officials that were offering their condolences. At last I got there and I saw everyone standing in a semicircle around the bodies. Everyone holding hands. Everyone wearing contrite expressions. But, in the middle of all that confusion, in all that coming and going, I managed not to miss a single word. Do you remember what they said? I warn you, I have a selective memory. I remember what I want to remember. And what I want to remember is one of their voices urging you Italians not to forget your emigrant past. History repeating the story of poor people spurred on by yearning, such total yearning that it uproots you, it defies sea storms. You know, dying of dehydration, gasping for air, is no small matter. I imagined those rickety boats, and the list of the things they found in the hold. Handbag, notebook, photograph, leather shoe, baby bottle, shirt, backpack, watch, shoelace. Details that tell a story.

Clapping, everyone was clapping. Even if they did not understand the meaning of what was being said. For example, the significance of our ambassador wishing for what? That this would mark the beginning of future cooperation between Somalia and Italy. What do you think? That deluge of clicking cameras and all, absolutely all the newspapers talking about us. Suddenly, with the lights focusing on those ashen faces. Have you noticed how red their eyes are, the eyes of the people who have just gotten off the boats? It is the red of all the blood that they have seen.

Everyone was crowded around the statue of Marcus Aurelius. My ears were buzzing, as if deafened by incessant weeping. As if the frogs had started croaking again. Ribbet, ribbet, ribbet. You don't know the legend? Perhaps it's only an anecdote they put in travel books . . . The story about how, in the hollow part of the statue, some stagnant water had settled, and that there—in the pool—some frogs had hatched. Ribbet, ribbet, ribbet. Was the emperor telling us something?

But I didn't want to be disrespectful in the presence of the bodies. Our women were crying, drying their eyes with the corners of their *garbasaar*. One of the women even managed to get close to the mayor: Mr. Mayor, you must do something for my country, followed by the clicking of many cameras: ribbet, ribbet, ribbet.

At the end, a part of the crowd moved toward the Theater of Marcellus. Somalis for the most part, I mean. Three buses were waiting, like a cradle: *huwa ya huwa*, but it wasn't a lullaby, rather the wail of a prayer. Until we reached a large mosque. It wasn't either a Friday or an *iid*, an Islamic feast day. But all the same, there were market stalls set up here and there. Caramelized sweets filled with honey, almond and coconut cookies, grape and cabbage leaves stuffed with meat and almonds, sesame and nut crunch, *seytuun* and mango juices, tamarind syrup, mint and cardamom teas. My stomach was in knots.

I followed everything from a distance, fighting against that sensation of solid land under my feet that seafaring people call land sickness. In front of us, on the mats, the men were bowing their heads, bending their bodies, getting up again, like a single wave, all together. They were praying, we were not. I saw the pale, streaky blue sky. And the coffins, with their light blue flags, constantly in front of us. Then once again unload, load, get off, get on: the dead in a Mercedes, the rest of us on a bus. It's a long ride to Prima Porta. A few people watched the progression of that solemn convoy from their cars. Once at the cemetery, the drivers grew impatient. It was already past the end of their workday and they were doing overtime for us. We had to hurry. Not that I cared that much; women are not allowed to approach burial sites. We were only there to watch the coffins being loaded onto shoulders, to smell the wet earth, and the cypress trees. Now and then, there was a sudden outburst, a woman began crying. Tears and salt. You'll see, she would say, we, too, will end up like that, beneath wet earth that is not our own. But the boatloads of illegal immigrants did not stop coming, even after that solemn funeral. And what about the living?

Me? I've lived in Rome for years now. I like it. My home is here, my friends, my profession. There is little left of my past. Sure, I miss having a husband, my own children, but if I think of those guys with whom you can't even drink a glass of wine, or who say: When you become my wife, don't think you can go around wearing those tight jeans. No, I'd rather hear people say: Westernized, you've become Westernized now. Westernized, Allah, preserve us from that! To me, what matters is to be able to work. Intensity helps you think less. Working as a midwife is like living in a constant state of emergency. Sure, if I wanted to, I could limit my work to my regular hours, but if you have just a scrap of conscience, it's a very different story. The fact is that after that official funeral, things changed. Perhaps that's my take on things, I'm not sure. Something shifted. Perhaps because people were aware of the tragedy? My colleagues heard about it on the news, they offered their condolences, asking me for details about the civil war: Is the situation really that terrible? I didn't realize that . . . you never told me anything! And your family? Everything OK? Do you still have family down there? What's the situation like? Are you in touch with your folks?

You have no idea how many questions a pricked conscience can come up with. And here's where the story begins. It was just after the funeral and my colleagues were all taken up with the events in my country, when it happened. One evening, it must have been around eight o'clock, Samantha, a nurse on my ward, calls me at home: Barni? Is that you? Without stopping to take a breath, she tells me that, well, she didn't want to disturb me, but after everything that had happened she certainly couldn't ignore it. They had brought him into the hospital in the afternoon. Yes, she knows, she knows that it's my day off, I deserve my rest. But when she saw that there were policemen present . . . Why the police? She was hardly in a position to ask questions: they had admitted the guy to another ward. He had been brought to the emergency room just as Samantha was about to begin her shift. Clearly fate had intervened. Otherwise, how could one explain the fact that, as they were moving the stretcher, his identity card had fallen onto the floor? Probably one of those cards they give out at the soup kitchens run by Caritas, the Catholic charity organization. The name was right there on the card, Maxamed X, and, below it, nationality: Somali. So Samantha had followed the stretcher to give the card back. And my compatriot, in answer, had made a sort of noise with his throat, a rasping sound that meant nothing. The police had intervened right away; Go, go, they had said, pushing her back. But Samantha had seen that man's eyes, his beseeching eyes. That was why she was calling me. Otherwise she would have never dared to call, had she not known that I hold my country close to my heart.

Do you understand the meaning of this sentence? My country close to my heart. I asked myself about this word. A word that is so heavy, so pregnant with meaning. Does country encompass people, does people encompass country? Are they the same thing? These are questions that come to mind when you meet a certain type of person. Just be patient, OK, and I'll explain.

One evening I was out for dinner. One of the people present was an acquaintance, a friend of friends, who kept talking and talking about his trips. Everyone was listening in admiration. He kept on talking, never stopping, describing carved altars, buildings with wet marble facades, seawater with purplish hues; not to mention the red-orange butterfly fish and goats with golden horns. This guy was convinced he was the ultimate traveler. The more he told his stories, delving deeply into the heroic epic deeds of the ancient inhabitants of those places, the more I bristled with impatience. I mean, didn't those countries have people, or was he, the traveler, the only person around? Countries, territories, do you know what I mean? And what if I were to tell you that there is no one place that is close to my heart? Only when I'm by the sea does my heart tremble. That's why I felt a shiver when Samantha said: I think he's one of the ones who arrived on the boats. Come over, if you can; no one here can talk to him. Poor guy, he's in really bad shape.

Now, if I began my story from way back, telling you about the funeral, there's a reason. The reason is because if it hadn't been for that impressive ceremony, for the news on TV, for those speeches about shipwrecked people, Maxamed X would have ended up like so many others, poor devil. Samantha, who is a goodhearted soul, would not have gone out of her way when confronted by that soup kitchen ID card. Neither would she have called me at home sounding like an accomplice. What I want to tell you is that I have been really stunned by what a short column in the daily paper can do. You might tell me that this is a subject that has been done to death in movies and books. How the printed word can build and destroy! Nevertheless, I can assure you that until it involves you directly, you don't really comprehend it. What's more, life is already complicated enough without the need to muddy the waters further by starting to question the importance of the news.

Do we get involved in all the events that intersect our lives? Making choices is imperative—so then, we are limited beings, one size fits all? What I believe is: the criteria we use to make our choices cannot be measured each time. Because beyond this story of Maxamed X that is relevant to your project, today I know that there were still many things left hanging, knots to untie, treasures saved from the shipwreck. I know that everything that happened was meant to happen. Perhaps it's because of my cousin Axad. But that is also a part of my story. Who could have ever guessed? We're scattered all over the world, each one of us surviving as best as we can. Hours spent at the phone center, using up dozens of phone cards; I might well love you deeply, my darling, but I don't even know where you ended up. Later, however, we resign ourselves, and our relationships also become like us, resigned. Oh Axad, you were the one destined to cross my path again.

Forgive me, I let my emotions run away with me. I have to rewind the thread and go back to the beginning. Go back to that evening when I had rushed over to tie back the curtains that were flapping inside as if blown by the sea breeze, holding them back in order to avoid letting the lighted burners of the stove set the house on fire. I was saying it was around eight PM. I had organized a dinner for my friends on my little terrace. My guests were wandering in and out. My hands were covered in spices and my hair was tied back in my *fasoleeti*. It was early summer, this dinner was a luxury for us. And then, the phone call came, suddenly. Samantha from the hospital. She wasn't calling because one of my patients' waters had broken. And I wasn't even on call. So why? My colleague's heart had been touched and she had responded. Was I meant to do likewise? I had to leave everything just as it was. Rub my hands with water and lemon, give instructions on how to cook the basmati rice: don't stir it, always keep the lid on, the rice must be crunchy; as for the meat, we are almost there, add the *barbaroni* and the onions, cover it for another ten minutes. My friends could continue to sip their Prosecco out on my terrace, while I drove off, yelling from my car window: Go ahead and start, I'll be back soon.

Can you understand? From the very start, I was already investing more than necessary in that story. Why all this hurry to rush to the hospital? Samantha herself would have understood, all I needed to say was: I have guests at home, he'll make it until tomorrow. It wouldn't have been cynical to answer that way. Instead, there I was, alone in my car with my house full of people and me still smelling of food. Did I stop to question my actions? Not at that point. I considered it a temporary absence, like a person leaving the room to go to the bathroom. A necessity.

But then it came as a shock to see Maxamed X. As if he were a person I had always known, who had remained there, locked up in my mind, until something happened and the memory resurfaced. Irrelevant details tease the mind and make a buried familiarity re-emerge.

I used a special corridor that took me straight to the patient. Samantha was waiting for me with all the people she had alerted: nurses, psychiatrists, policemen. Maxamed X seemed almost relaxed: the bed was tilted up and his eyes were fixed on the white wall in front of him, his hair long and disheveled, his lips dry and his hands bandaged in gauze. What did I do? I sat next to him without breaking the silence. It was right then that I thought I saw him: my Uncle Taariikh, my father's older brother. A likeness taking me back to the time when Axad and I were little and we lived in Mogadishu. I must have been three or four years old.

I was sitting in the courtyard on a low *gambar* of crushed leather, in my hands I had a magazine that I kept leafing through. So many colored pictures! Until something finally catches my attention: a crunchy cone filled with cream and black cherries! The picture is so lifelike that I can taste it on my lips, the sweet coldness exudes from the page, and the ice cream becomes the object of my desire. I began to stamp my feet, hammering my request home: I want this ice cream, Aunt Xaliima, I want this ice cream . . .

Children are a nuisance when there are too many of them. Too many of them demanding things. Only Uncle Taariikh never got annoyed, with his chapped hands and shining eyes. With his blackened teeth, with his sweetish breath. Alcoholic! Drunkard! Assassin! At dusk a swarm of screaming street urchins followed him along the sandy streets that led to the house. They were chanting words that had no meaning for them, words learned who knows where. While I was sobbing out of desire for the unattainable cone, here comes Uncle Taariikh, quick as a flash: Don't cry, don't cry. I have a solution. With these words, he ran to get a small blade. He came back and together we—Uncle Taariikh and I along with Axad who had run over to help—ripped the page out and spread it down on the concrete so that Uncle Taariikh could go round the borders very slowly with the cutting edge of the blade. There it was, in his hands, the cut-out cone: This is for you, my dear Barni.

My dear Barni. But Maxamed X didn't seem to recognize me. He looked me over and over again with an absent gaze, not a quiver, his brow still. I'm not sure, some time must have gone by, perhaps twenty minutes or so. This might have been the reason why the doctor, growing impatient at the delay, came into the room, calling me back to my task. He wanted me to try and talk to the patient. Because, he said, they couldn't understand if he didn't know Italian or if he was actually mute. If it were just a matter of language, then it would have been easier. I can't tell you what snapped inside of me. In that moment my senses seemed to expand, as if sounds and smells were entering me directly without having to go through my skin. That's probably why I had the feeling that the doctor was speaking loudly, that he was gesturing too much. Anyway, Maxamed X must have sensed the danger, the threat that I might leave, that they might scold me. Or perhaps he was mad at me. He suddenly got up—I was convinced that it was really hard for him to move—and then I saw him in all of his towering height. He took a chair as if to throw it at us. Even I was scared by such a reaction. My colleagues ran over to stop him, asking me to leave the room.

What did I do? You know, I could have left at that point. Instead, I felt as though I had a thorn in my throat that pinned me to that place, gluing me to the glass window and forcing me to look at Maxamed X, who was now calming down and keeping dead still. I waited and then I asked to be let in again. It even looked as though he had fallen asleep. So the idea came to me of telling him a story. Not that it had much to do with this whole business; it was only to justify my tenacity.

You want me to tell it to you? It might be useful for your article? Yes, you are right, since this is an in-depth article, you have more space.

So, as I was telling you, I was sitting next to him, very near, almost as if nothing had happened. His eyes were half closed. And, despite the state he was in, he could not have been older than me, so I said: *Walaal*, my brother. I didn't know who had reduced him to such a sorry state. They had called on me to talk to him although it wasn't part of my job. I had chosen to stay because my soul, my *qalbigeyga*, commanded me to. I was free to choose whether to stay or go. I knew he was asking himself the question: Why was I still there, why hadn't I already left? And I was going to answer his question with a lesson that I had preserved in my mind in spite of the fact that time, all too often, erases memories. Here is the story: It is said that one day the Prophet discovered a pile of rubbish, thorns, and excrement in front of his house. It had been left there by a neighbor who was envious of him and who had dumped all his garbage in front of his door. The Prophet, without turning a hair, bypassed the obstacle and went out. Later he took care of cleaning up the area in front of his door. But the following day the same thing happened. This went on for several days. The Prophet continued to behave in the same way, without complaining about his guilty neighbor. Some time went by, and one morning the Prophet woke up to find his doorstep immaculate, free of all garbage. He was very surprised and asked his wife and neighbors what had happened to the man who, day after day, out of sheer envy, had defiled his door. And so he came to find out that the poor man was sick. He decided to go and visit him and went to his room. But how could it

be that the very man who made him so angry, having noticed his absence, was concerned about him? It is said that
the sick man, moved by such great benevolence, converted
and became a Muslim that very same day.

I told the story to the very end. It wasn't clear to me
whether Maxamed X was listening or not. He wasn't moving, and his eyes were as impenetrable as fog. But then, it
was when I stopped narrating the story that I realized something: Maxamed X had looked up very slightly. Then he
raised his fists, rocking noisily in the bed. The male nurses
intervened, again, brusquely.

You know, I think they reacted correctly, the way I myself
would have reacted had I never experienced salty seawater
in my mouth and never heard gurgling sounds in my ears.
Watered-down kind of sounds. Consequently, their reaction
was like a jolt to me, just like when you faint, and they put
a vial of vinegar under your nose—an abrupt reawakening. I
immediately went to see the doctor. I must admit I was being
aggressive, accusatory: About the patient, they were stressing him too much, they should let me handle him, I knew
what I was doing, they just had to be patient. That is, if they
wanted to get results. Did anyone have the slightest idea of
the traumas that man might have suffered? I could certainly
envision them, even though they had been rude to me and
no one had wanted to tell me anything. Privacy? The doctor
put me in my place by saying that my linguistic competence
was not psychiatric competence. I was supposed to be a fa-
cilitator, not an improvised therapist. That the problem with
people who offer to help of their own accord is that they
always think they can do things their way.

It was really too much for me at that point to be able to
understand that I was obsessing over something that didn't
have anything to do with me. Was this perhaps what got me
mad? No, it was that I was lacking in objectivity. Simply put,
I felt deeply offended. Offended and badly treated: I who
had left home in the middle of dinner, I who had run off
abandoning my guests, I who had offered my skills free of

charge. There really was no reason for me to stay; let them get on with it! I had already wasted too much time, it was time to go back home.

Where do I live? Right now in a street off Via Giolitti. Before, I lived in the Casilina area, at Torre Angela. But I have lived in many places. My home? My home is always a port of call. A few essential pieces of furniture. I have never had much money, nor the desire to spend it on furniture. In the end, what do you need in a house? A table, some chairs, a wardrobe, a sofa, a bed and refrigerator, washing machine, television and CD player—things that can be shared with others and easily replaced. My approach is to keep things to the bare minimum. After all, this is the way we do things. A cousin comes to visit from Canada: *Abbaayo,* your shoes are to die for. There, they're already on her feet! Then you go to a friend's home and she has a skirt that, hey, she says, is too tight for me now, and come to think of it, there are also these boots that I bought on sale, but they're a size too small, luckily—I knew it!—they're just your size. Old photographs, jewelry, perfume bottles with gold filigree, flowered shawls, petticoats edged with precious lace, scarves with velvet embellishments, videos of one's wedding, the only copy I have of my favorite music, everything circulates chaotically so much so that in the end no one remembers who has what.

My home has always been full of people. That is why when everyone left, some for London, some for Ohio, some for Australia, I felt the need to fill it up by having parties. I like noise in the background, the idea that everyone is happy, finally all together again. And when it's time to leave they say: We should do this more often. And what prevents us from doing so? Distance? Our busy lives? Our commitments? Or the idea itself that we have of this distance, of these busy lives, of these commitments?

One of these parties was in full swing the evening I am describing. I had been gone for over an hour by the time I got back. My friends bombarded me with questions. Friends I had picked up along the way, school friends, who lived in the same dormitory where I lived for a while, work colleagues, fellow members of the Ishtar volunteer organization. They were full of questions, but I preferred not to think of anything. The food was still warm.

I am telling my story like a wave rising up and down, up and down. I hope you can follow me anyway. I have a request—I hope you don't mind—when you are done with your research, when your article is written, I would like to read it. I mean read it before you publish it. Is that possible? It's not that I don't trust you, I think you understand that by now. The problem is, with interviews one never knows: you tell one story and a totally different one comes out. I might make a casual remark. Or a subject pops up which has nothing to do with the rest of it. No, let me say it again, it's not because of you.

It's the writing itself I do not trust.

But let's go on, I want to help you, it's no small thing that you're doing for us. Despite nine years of war, who cares about the Somalis?

I don't think one can write about the Somali community in Rome without starting from the Roma Termini train station, the crossroads, the scene of our longings. I even tried to convince myself for a while that it was a seedy place, only fit for tourists and refugees, a place where you had to hold on tight to your purse and gold chain. Preconceived ideas born out of my resentment. Who could not long for that buzz that hit you, in the central concourse, next to the train tracks, as soon as you got close to the café just like any other, the Somali café. Not that there was a sign outside, or that it was run by a Somali, but simply because there were always a whole lot of Somalis in that café.

Especially at the peak of the exodus, nine years ago. All you had to do was go to the Termini train station to meet the world. The atmosphere vibrated in the expectation of news, everyone waiting, close to each other. We thought, soon we'll be going back. Who could have ever imagined. In those days we went to the *draddorio* to eat rice with goat meat, we got a *defreddi* at the stand, we bought *bajiiye* with fresh hot pepper and *rummay* from the young girls. People provided us with documents to rescue everyone, absolutely everyone, in our family. We sought out a courier who would take the money to its destination.

At the Termini station you could bump into the very guy that you had lost touch with, you could find a small job, and if you were a young woman and you felt like smoking, it was better for you to hide the cigarette in case you met an uncle who had arrived unexpectedly. Nine years ago I felt unconcerned and I thought the war would end quickly and we would go back home happier than before. This was at the beginning, when I thought that all of us would make it.

Now many things have changed: the central concourse has been refurbished with flashy shops, Benetton, Nike, Intimissimi, Levi's, Sisley, fast-food places, phone centers, pay-for-use public baths, automatic ticket machines, escalators, maxi-screens with advertisements, updated train boards. A truly modern station. Those few remaining Somalis continue to meet in those places. Especially since they started arriving on those illegal boats. They land along the Sicilian coast, they are crammed into temporary reception centers. A few are allowed in for humanitarian reasons, they are released with very little money and no place to go. Before the Italian government started that business of the fingerprinting, they all tried to go north or northwest. Toward one of those mythical countries that offer you a place to sleep and a plate of food. *Ingiriiska, Norwey, Holand, Swidish.* Even after they started that fingerprinting business, they still try anyway, trusting to luck. Those who didn't make it are easy to recognize, the ones who were sent back. They roam around the station with a dirty backpack, a bundle filled with sorrow. May God take pity on them. Now Roma Termini train station is so full of pain. But when I feel the urge to plunge my arm again into the burning pools, the pools of memory and separation, when I feel that need, then I go there. Just to breathe the air.

And often at Termini train station amazing things happen, worth noting. Our places, old and new, rotate around that axis: Qamar's store, Xassan's Phone Center, the *drad-dorio* and the area around it.

Qamar's store: I can give you the address if you're interested. They sell everything a Somali woman could ever want. Brightly colored s*haash, garbasaar* made of lightweight cotton stamped with flowers, *diric Jibuuti,* satin petticoats embroidered with pearls, long *goonooyin, guntiino* made of hand-spun raw fabric that once everyone turned their noses up at, but which today are back in fashion—the more an object is hard to come by, the more precious it becomes. And still more: yellow amber necklaces, silver bracelets, Johnson Baby Oil, incense burners, *catar* of all fragrances, hair-straightening lotion, egg-based hair conditioner, rose water, lotion for dry hands, *cillaan* powder, stencils for decorating the skin, colored rubber bands. And music, always more music, music, especially modern music. When they find something particularly special, or a woman brings a video of a wedding or an engagement, the young women gather together around the small television set to watch it, to chat and to pass comment. You also go to Qamar's to look for work. Or to change dollars. Or to receive a phone call. However, for these last two things Xassan's Phone Center is better, although all the women say he is a dirty old man.

Well, one day I went to Qamar's to buy *uunsi.* Myrrh and incense crystals. The straw racks that we use to lay out linens that are to be scented had just arrived. My sepiolite incense burner had broken; I wanted to buy a new one. Things you are nostalgic for are expensive. Even if she says she's very homesick, Qamar hasn't lost her sense of business. I was chatting with her when some Chinese arrived. Just picture the scene. The streets around the station are now filled with Chinese stores. Qamar and her friends, as if suddenly aroused, began to chase them away with fabric in their hands, shoo, shoo, as if they were flies. I froze, stunned: What's wrong with you? Did they answer? Hey Barni, don't start preaching. They come here every day. They never buy a thing. They only want to see what we have. And when they've done that, you find their stores filled with our stuff! They copy everything, absolutely everything! Shoo, shoo.

An anecdote, a mere touch of color. But there's a reason why I remembered it: it's because we were talking about the Chinese at that very moment when I heard about this event that I think might interest you. I was saying, we were talking about the Chinese when some people arrived making a lot of noise. A group was also talking animatedly. I knew everyone by sight. Like that girl, Shukri, at the center of the discussion. Shukri who always brings her son with her, a quiet little man with a comic book under his arm. His hair was cut like *elfis* and he was swimming in a pair of light blue shorts much too big for him. Somali children are all either skinny or fat. Nothing in between. His mother, as I was saying, is a young woman I really admire. Strong in her simplicity. And she has her own style of dressing. She makes the *diric* seem comfortable and modern by adding a thin pearl belt and wearing her slip wrapped over, her *guntiino,* the fabric tightly draped around her small bust and the *garbasaar,* the shawl, around her neck, the exact way women used to wear it when I was a child. Today women do not dress like this anymore. They cover themselves as much as they can with long, dark coats. Our dresses? We often wear them for weddings or celebrations, when there are only women present.

All right, I am about to tell you about the fact that was worth noting. Shukri was furious. So furious that she didn't even care that her son could hear her. She had just been to Xassan's Phone Center to talk to her ex-husband. Something needed to be done to resolve the situation. Shukri wanted to put her affairs in order. That's why the previous year she had paid the holy man all of five hundred dollars. The holy man had said that for five hundred dollars he would take care of everything. Her husband, Taageere, doesn't live in Italy. He's never provided for her or the child. According to Islamic law, this is sufficient reason to ask to be repudiated by your husband and be free to marry again.

Shukri had gone to the holy man with her justification and he had told her that it was simple, a matter of a few phone calls. The holy man wanted to convince Taageere by phone. For sure, Shukri had her part to play as well, she had to be persuasive. It is not easy to get someone to say "Yes, I repudiate you" three times over the phone. Three times as prescribed by Koranic law. In the end—rather quickly, I might add—they had managed to bring about this telephone divorce! Shukri, to her satisfaction, had obtained her document, on the required A4 paper, entitled "Divorce between Shukri and Taageere," with their passport-size photos attached to the corners. At the bottom was the signature of the holy man and of the witnesses to the telephone conversation. But at the Registry Office at City Hall in Rome they had not the slightest intention of accepting that sheet of paper.

In Qamar's store, Shukri kept pronouncing aloud the two words imprinted in her memory: "decree" and "act." They told me that in Italy divorce is a decree, not an act; that is why they cannot recognize my document, even if it is on the correct A4 paper. The point is that Shukri is an interpreter by profession. However, after days of running around and stressing out, she finally resigned herself. In her heart she had come to the conclusion that what mattered was to be in compliance with our own laws.

What was the use of a certificate that wasn't recognized in Italy? Don't ask me. Shukri, at least up to that point, had not asked herself that question. Up to that point, what mattered to her was to be able to say that she had done the *fasakh,* that she was divorced from her husband. But now, that shameless Taageere, her ex-husband, had the nerve to demand that the divorce be valid for all intents and purposes. Not only according to our law, but also according to yours here in Italy.

Interesting, isn't it? What happens to laws and conventions without a government, without a legal system? They remain in our minds. Vague principles that we no longer know how to use. They seem to matter only to us Somalis, scattered all over the world.

I, too, was married once a long time ago, and I decided not to register my marriage. How could I trust a system that didn't recognize ours? But, you see, this is my story too. A troublesome chapter. It's so difficult for our men to invent a role for themselves. To redefine themselves. To adapt. To accept themselves. To humiliate themselves. Because you see, for us women, in the end, those fixed points, our home, our daily life, motherhood, the intimacy of our relationships, they are like little signposts that save us from getting lost.

And for someone like me, who is not a mother and who hardly had a mother—more like a mother fragmented among many women—nurturing, caring for others, is a way for me to remain grounded. It is like a feeling of omnipotence, it makes me feel invulnerable. When you take care of someone, you have the upper hand. You're the one giving solace. You're the one who decides how to do things, your own way. It's the others who depend on you, they need your solace. It's the others who accept things done your way.

I think I know what you are thinking. Mine is a round-about way of telling a story. Do I seem crazy to you? No, I'm not looking for reassurance. I want—most of all—for you to continue to be on guard, for you to focus. Everything I am telling you is deeply connected. If I talk to you about caring for other people. it is also to make you better understand why I went back to the man in the hospital who was mute. I didn't do it for a particularly noble reason. It was me who needed to feel useful. It was me who was fighting against my compassion.

The day I went back to him I had finished my shift at work. I'll go by to see how he is feeling, I told myself. And my colleague—no, not Samantha—told me: He has a high fever. The burns—lesions I was unaware of—instead of healing were becoming infected. They even feared it might be gangrene. And then, since he was delirious with the fever, it was impossible to understand what he was saying, if he was even saying anything. Strange laments, meaningless sounds, who knows. So I asked for permission to sit next to him.

Maxamed X was lying under the snow-white hospital sheet. It made me think of the sensation we have as children when we fall asleep and our parents lay us down on the bed and cover us up. Yes, it must have been because of this. It must have been for this reason that I began to talk to him again. Telling him that I didn't know he had been involved in a fire. And upon hearing my voice, a sound from home, he stopped moaning, so I kept going. I said that the story I had told him—the one about the garbage—had been told to me by a very dear friend of mine. And that this friend had also been involved in a fire, that was why she was so full of faith. This very close friend was her mother's only daughter. Mother and daughter were like sisters. The father was almost always away and then he died unexpectedly. This event deeply saddened my friend's mother. She often looked into the distance without speaking and she rarely took care of the household chores. Luckily for my friend, they lived in a big house with aunts and uncles and many cousins. So the sense of melancholy was dissipated in the air.

One evening just like any other, her mother was in particularly good spirits. She cooked a delicious dinner for everyone and even remembered to prepare a jug of iced Tang, powdered orange juice. When everyone had eaten, she put all the children to bed and told them a story. Which story? The one about the three bulls and the lion. She wanted them to learn to always stick together. Did Maxamed X also know that story? About how the lion, taking advantage of the terrified bulls, was able to separate them and then eat them one by one. Here they say there is strength in numbers. Too bad that the Somalis, like the bulls, have forgotten that. Well, back to my friend. At night, in the houses, people used to leave a burning ember under the ashes in order to relight the fire more easily with kerosene the next morning. Coals to prepare the morning meal. That's what my friend's mother did that night. There was a strong wind and the kerosene container was leaking. No one knows how it happened. Her mother had been suffering a lot with the kind of pain that saps all your attention. Perhaps her lack of attention was precisely what proved to be fatal. My friend was awakened by the crackling of the flames, by the smoke and the great heat, and roused her cousins by shaking them. They all rushed outside unharmed. The neighbors had run over with buckets of water and sand. They were hoping that her mother had escaped through the window, or that by chance she had gone out for a moment. Instead, she was trapped by the flames. She was the only one who did not escape, poor thing.

I had come to the end of my story and Maxamed X had fallen asleep. My colleague was looking at me. She hadn't understood one word of my story. However, she said she understood the tone of it. I was exhausted. Without realizing it, I had told him my own story.

Fragments of my story: everything is so mixed up. The reasons dictating our actions are tightly woven threads. I felt completely consumed by that fire that is fed by seawater, as they dragged me out of that hospital room. My colleague had listened to me telling my story until I had poured everything out. I must have had such dark circles under my eyes, my face must have been so drawn, for her to say: You look awful, why don't you at least get a bite to eat.

A break to get back my strength. I wasn't hungry, I just needed a change of scene. I was already feeling stronger as I sat with the others complaining about the same old things. About what? Ordinary things: the snack bar sandwiches that were no longer any good and how it was better to buy them at the deli across the street. And all the while, the small television set was broadcasting the news, banal political details or stories of gruesome atrocities. Until something caught my attention.

There's a chance you might remember it even though they didn't really feature it very much, something about two Egyptians arrested for suspected terrorism. They found a map of Rome in their pockets with all the most strategic spots circled in red ballpoint. There was much talk about this detail of the case in order to demonstrate the efficiency and the precision of the police force. But there was hardly any mention at all of the fact that these circles indicated where the Caritas food distribution centers for the hungry were located. Was I the only one who had noticed that? To be fair,

so had my colleagues. Perhaps it was my expression that
set them off, we began saying it was really ridiculous, that
there was paranoia everywhere, that everyone had it in for
the poor and that you could be sure that the big shots would
never get caught. And it was while I was listening to them,
half stunned by the force of their reaction, that a missing
part of the story came out.

A piece of the story that involved Maxamed X, of course.
What, didn't I know why he had been arrested? Hadn't they
told me anything about the car that was set on fire near
our Somali embassy? Nothing about Maxamed X, who was
wandering around the area covered in burns screaming as
if he were out of his mind and refusing to talk to the police? Nothing about how they had taken him by force while
he struggled with all the energy he had left, throwing him
to the ground, making him eat dirt? A suspected terrorist—
they said, taking him to the hospital—that's why there was
all that security.

Bismillaahi. You have no idea how my heart jumped
at hearing that story, as I sat grasping the table with both
hands. I bombarded my colleagues with questions as they
grew increasingly surprised that nobody had told me of the
matter. Not even that the car was an old Fiat 131 which had
not been used in years. But their answers quickly came to
an end. Perhaps there were details I could find out on my
own. Perhaps by going to the Somali embassy and finding
someone who could tell me more. Something that the police
might not know.

Can you imagine that? No, I didn't go at once. It was
evening by then, better to wait till the next day to go to
Porta Pia and approach from the left, from Via dei Villini. Do
you know that area? A part of town full of embassies and
villas. The silence of exclusive places. It was ages since I had
been to the embassy. The previous time was last July 1, you
know, the anniversary of our independence. Liberated from
whom? Liberated from the Italians.

Bariimo luuliyoo, chanted an old woman with glasses,
holding the sheet filled with dense writing slightly away

from her even if she was reciting the words from memory. *Bariimo luuliyoo,* she warbled, covered from head to toe in veils and jewels. That was her *buraambur* for July 1. That was her poetic song, the language of a woman contaminated by the vanquished colonizer. Women of all ages whirled around together, while one kept still, beating out the rhythm on an upside-down plastic bucket, dhak, dhak, dhak, dhak, dhak, dhak, dhak, dhak. The camera was rolling and the youngest women covered their faces, while the older ladies, taken by surprise, shouted at the reporter, who swore that he had only filmed them from the waist up.

Bariimo luuliyoo, men and women prepare and plan political speeches. Outside in the garden, there's a small, flattened-out bedroll near the wreck of an old Fiat 127. At certain moments, it felt like being back in Somalia again, with the sound of the generator going and the hanging electrical cables: like the Mogadishu of the final few years when the electricity was always out. That building, so prestigious, so inappropriately sumptuous, with its sofas made of crushed velvet and dark-colored foam rubber in the garden, with the chandeliers, was the seat of the former Somali embassy. The party, at least, masked more than a few details of that desolation.

However, on the day I went to get some information about Maxamed X, behind the gate all was silent. I had knocked out of politeness. I was waiting for someone to come and open the gate when a boy appeared, slouching along. We greeted each other.

"Do you need to come in?" he asked me and I replied saying, "Yes, I would like to, but what I'm really looking for is some information about a man, a certain Maxamed X; perhaps you know him, too."

The boy was standing on his right foot, one hand on his hip slightly tugging at the left leg of his pants, the other engaged in cleaning his teeth with an *istekiini.* He screwed up his mouth like someone who has drawn a blank. So I explained everything to him.

Maxamed X was the name written on the card, perhaps his real name was different. A tall fellow with *raamo raamo* hair, like that of fishermen who have extremely curly hair, stiff from the salt. Some people said he was involved in an incident with a car that was set on fire.

The boy's eyes: as if they had been turned on. Yes, of course, the Mute. All right, who knows if he's really mute or just someone who does not speak. They, however, had told the police the truth. That is, that it wasn't the Mute who had set fire to the car, what he wanted to do was save the girl. Hold on, hold on, I had said to the boy, I know nothing about this. I barely knew that it involved a car that was set on fire. Too much information all at once. *Tartiib*, slowly. A girl, you were saying? What girl?

The youth then spat on the ground and shifted his weight to the other foot, throwing the toothpick away. Perhaps I would like to go in? There was no need to stand talking at the gate.

You know, there's something I didn't tell you, something our ambassador should have spoken about at the funeral but didn't. He forgot to speak about Her Majesty the Embassy. He did not complain about his beautiful villa, about the pit in his garden, *godka*, about Saddam's hole. Do you know why they call it that? It's named for the well where the Americans found Saddam Hussein, after days of looking for him. *Godka*, the ditch, the cellar where at night all those people sleep, those who did not stay behind in the desert or who do not lie buried at the bottom of the sea or laid out in coffins all in a row. All those who wash up on these shores in the boats or who have escaped the shipwrecks, nicknamed Titanic by their fellow countrymen.

How was I feeling? Inside, pretty uncomfortable. I was the only woman there and the boys, who were sprawled around, had sat up out of politeness. They were wearing worn-out clothing picked up who knows where. They were quite young except for the old caretaker of the villa and some of his friends. They were listening to a small transistor set to the Somali station of the BBC. The young fellow had led me in and said to the caretaker: Tell her about the young woman.

The old man was irritated, he complained that they never left him in peace, that he had no desire to speak: Good morning, welcome, but if you have to ask questions, please ask someone else, I'm listening to the news. All right, uncle, I replied.

So, Luul's story was told by the others. Luul, the only woman who lived in that place where there were only men. Like them, she had come from the desert, from the sea. Someone to whom Maxamed X was very attached.

Luul? Where had she ended up? None of them knew. Maybe, as she had planned, she had been able to join her brother who lived in America. Or perhaps she had returned to the family that had taken care of her at the beginning, a couple, a man and his wife. That wasn't too long ago. Meanwhile the BBC news program came to an end, broadcasting the usual list of missing persons and of people looking for other people. But was it possible to get in touch with the family that had put her up? Certainly. They are people who have always lived in Rome. All you have to do is ask Qamar, the one who has the shop. Qamar who always knows everything. Qamar the conduit.

Maybe we need to pause a moment. Do you think this whole story is what you're after? When you told me that you wanted to write—and you would have certainly found a direction either with me or through the people you interviewed—I thought then that you were the right kind of person, with that disarming modesty that I expect to see in someone who is about to tell the story of such distant subjects. Yet I also realize that there are gaps in my memory, whole parts that escape me, that the improbable is taking shape. If something seems barely credible to you, the fruit of a mind fueled by too much imagining, don't keep it from me. Everything is so closely woven as to seem almost artificial.

Was there a mysterious force that was driving me, forcing me to endlessly seek out explanations? Explanations that can be revealed. Then, I don't really need to tell you that Qamar knew absolutely everything about Luul, that she even had the telephone number of the couple that had put her up. Diriiye Yuusuf and his wife, fairly close relatives of hers.

Me? I wrote down the number on a bus ticket. But I just couldn't bring myself to call, I was questioning myself too much. Why was I continuing the search? After all, it was almost certain that they would leave poor Maxamed X alone. And even if they didn't leave him alone, it was surely none of my business. How many relatives and friends have I saved with my meager income? How many people ask me for help every month, one for a serious operation, another for her daughter's university education, another because he just cannot stand being mistreated by the Kenyan police any longer, another because they stole his government subsidy at the market, another because with seven children it's hard to get to the end of the month, another because, I swear, Holland has become unbearable and I just can't stay here any longer. And, I'm telling you, sometimes the only thing you can do to survive is to cover up your ears and pray, pray that they can get by on their own because me, I'm at the end of my tether.

Instead, there I was worrying about Maxamed X, who was not even a relative. Worrying about someone that no one has asked me to help. Someone that I won't be able to add to the long list of good things that I have done for the family. That bus ticket kept going in and out of my pants pocket. Then I got home. How can I explain it? It might have been the silence. The impossibility of being alone with the silence. The attraction of that ticket as if it were a lottery ticket. I could call and they might not answer. That would have been lucky. Not really. Without a doubt I would have tried again. Unavoidable obsessions. I managed to hold off for a day. The more I procrastinated, the more the number multiplied, growing bigger and bigger in my mind. How ridiculous. Really, what harm was there? So I dialed the number.

A man's voice on the other end of the line: Diriiye Yuusuf, himself, of course. Pleasantries and introductions. Me: Barni Sharmaarke, profession midwife. All these years spent in Rome. Yes, they had heard of my name. Who still lived with them? Luul, their relative. Taageere, her brother who lived in America, was the one who had contacted them about her, when Luul had landed at Lampedusa off the coast of Sicily. Diriiye Yuusuf and his wife Safiya had done all they could to arrange for her to come to Rome as their guest. As everyone does when a family member arrives.

Taageere? Yes, I knew him. When I heard his name—heard his name again in the space of a few days—it was as if my heart leapt in surprise. I guessed there were connections. First, his ex-wife, Shukri. Then the relatives who had taken care of him during those few months when he lived in Rome. Why am I telling you this? Perhaps I can discern things in this story that don't just have to do with me? We live by making distinctions, don't we?

Taageere and I knew each other. Yes, perhaps I had already met Diriiye Yuusuf through Taageere—or had I only heard of him? Taageere. A long story. Perhaps another time. No, not in Rome. We met in Xamar, Mogadishu, many years ago. As luck would have it, I saw his wife with their child just a few days ago. God bless him, he's really grown. But what about Luul, is it true that she lived with you?

Sure she lived with them. She arrived six months ago. After having lived for years in a refugee camp on the coast of Kenya, after having tried her luck on a series of trucks, she got as far as Libya. It took months. But Luul did not talk much about it. Strange girl. One day, after an argument with Safiya, she went off. Diriiye Yuusuf had not seen Luul since then. Someone told him that she lived at the embassy. Had he heard her speak of Maxamed X? Yes, something. But nothing that I didn't know. Only that they are connected in some way, if you believe what people say. Perhaps they had met in Somalia. Or on their journey. God only knows.

I didn't want to end that telephone call without speaking to his wife. Diriiye Yuusuf hesitated, but Safiya must have told him that she wanted to speak to me. They must have discussed this between themselves because I waited almost five minutes, as if they had forgotten about me. I was tempted to hang up.

Then I heard Safiya, her voice transparent, like crystal. A voice that I like. Perhaps the pleasure was reciprocal because

Safiya invited me to her house for lunch. There were certain things she preferred to talk about face-to-face.

Do too many details bore you? They're worth listening to. When you come to write the piece, you can cut out the superfluous bits. At times, I really believe that you're enjoying my story and for this reason I am not leaving out the details. Too many? Or too many all at once? It is a tight weave.

Well, Safiya was a majestic and imposing beauty, with a strong gaze and very delicate features. Skin as dark as night, a moonlit night. She wore a fiery red *shaash* with a few *cillaan* curls peeping out.

We immediately felt comfortable with each other. Like you and me. Sometimes you don't need to know another person for long to feel close. She spoke about the children she couldn't have and about her life in exile. Did Safiya feel the harshness of her fate? Perhaps that was the reason why she was not able to bond with Luul, who was too young to absorb so much adversity. She was still traumatized, a victim of so much loss, probably she felt the need to be protected.

We were sitting in front of two cups of coffee with ginger as I watched Safiya struggling to find the right words to describe the last, most painful part.

To tell me that Luul was pregnant when she arrived. Nobody knew about it. Even Safiya had found out purely by chance, during a routine medical visit. The doctor was examining that bulge. There was no concealing it. Was she ashamed? Perhaps more than anything else she feared what people would say, the absence of the father. Safiya was right to be worried. It seemed to her that Luul was barely able to look after herself. How would she manage with a child?

So she had tried to find some solutions. Luul herself kept saying that her son deserved a better chance, not a miserable life. Safiya tried to find rational solutions. Send Luul to her brother Taageere? Impossible. She would not have been able to pass the checkpoints. They would have checked her fingerprints and sent her back.

So Safiya had thought about it and had sought other alternatives, in the long lists of people who wanted to adopt a baby. Did she want to give the baby up for adoption? No, that was out of the question. Luul cried and cried. Then Safiya suggested that they stay with them, she and the baby, as their daughter and grandchild.

But no, Luul seemed worried that the child would be considered illegitimate. So then, in the end, why had Safiya and Luul had a falling-out?

I asked the question directly. Safiya had got up to pour some more coffee. It seemed as though she wanted to put the subject aside because she began to speak about the goat meat, that she uses tamarind as her sister taught her, and asked if I liked it cooked that way.

Yes, even though right now I'm more interested in knowing how things ended up with Luul.

So then she told me that Luul was like an unexploded bomb. She was liable to go off from one moment to the next. One day she would be singing, she was happy, she polished the house without anyone asking her to do so, and the day after she would shut herself up in her darkened room refusing to see anybody and if you bothered her she would hurl unspeakable insults at you. Perhaps it had been a mistake to tell her what the possible solution might be all at once. All in one go, without spacing it out.

Because Safiya had casually mentioned it to a lawyer friend. It was he who had come up with the idea: Luul could have the child in comfort in a hospital, she could either recognize her son or not, it was up to her. At that point Diriiye, Safiya's husband, would step forward and he would legitimize Luul's son saying the baby was the result of an extramarital relationship. It seemed the best solution. The child could remain with Diriiye and Safiya, and with Luul, and no one would have ever have called him a bastard.

What do you think? While I was listening to Safiya, I felt that all these bureaucratic intrigues were odd. Luul could just say she was married, who could say that she wasn't? As I listened, Safiya's machinations seemed like madness to me. The madness of someone who believes she is rational.

Well, it was that crazy solution that caused the bomb to explode. Luul said nothing at first. She seemed to go along with the idea. Then bit by bit, inexorably, like water at high tide, an uncontrollable rage rose within her. A rage that rose higher and higher, springing from a foam of suffering that filled her lungs. Safiya became the object of her hate. She had become the sterile whore who wanted to steal her son from her, the old hag who had to dye her white hair, who wanted a concubine for her husband who rejects her. A terrifying flow of unrepeatable words. Then she had taken off.

Safiya knew that Luul often went to the embassy to meet Maxamed X, the Mute. She was worried because the baby might be born at any moment. Safiya had gone to look for her there but it was useless. Luul did not want to see her again.

Safiya talked while she stirred the stew. As if to keep herself occupied, her eyes lowered. You know, it was ready and she turned off the gas. I thought she was going to offer me some, but she covered the pot and sat down again next to me. There was something she hadn't told me. The invitation to lunch? There was a reason for it. A reason that was difficult to describe over the phone. There was a new guest in her house, someone who had arrived a few days ago, a girl who lives in America. She wanted us to meet since we were both looking for the same person. For different reasons, obviously. Even if she hadn't quite understood what mine were. Was I looking for Luul for a specific reason?

To tell the truth, not even I really knew what that was. Perhaps I just didn't have much to do. Perhaps I felt responsible for that man. Perhaps it was just out of curiosity. The key motive is that for me, any tale of an illegal landing makes my heart beat faster.

But who was this guest?

The guest was about to arrive. She was Taageere's new wife. Hadn't I said that I knew him, that I had even met Shukri recently? The reason why Taageere had spoken on the phone to Shukri, his ex-wife, was that he wanted to show off, to let her know that his new wife was about to arrive. Did she think she was the only one who could get married again? He wanted to let her know that his new wife was half European and that if Shukri settled the whole business of the divorce in the right way, as she should, maybe Taageere and his wife could come to Italy together. Instead, only his wife had been able to leave, with her European passport. Taageere had not been able to, because his papers were not in order yet. It was because of those stupid papers that Taageere had not been able to come and take care of his sister. He was going to come to meet her here because, according to the Dublin Convention, or whatever, Luul would never, repeat never, have been able to join him in America.

But who was this wife of Taageere's? Can you stay with me right to the end? Taageere's wife, a guest? Can you believe it?

I already knew when the bell rang. I jumped up from the sofa in shock, like when you're about to drop off to sleep, and boom, you think you're going to fall. Even Safiya was feeling the emotion. What an incredible meeting you have arranged, Safiya! Shall I go or will you?

But perhaps it wasn't a good idea to meet her on the doorstep. The impact would have been too overwhelming. Or perhaps not. How can I be sure that she will recognize me? Here she comes, up the stairs. Recognize each other? And how! We scream like two crazy women. We grab each other's hands. We jump up and down like children. We hug each other in silence. I'm still taller than you, Axad, I'm still your older *abbaayo*.

Domenica Axad still had *kafey*-colored ringlets and that luminescent skin, almost pearlized. Her eyes had pale violet circles around them and her lashes were wet. Did she have those weepy eyes even when she was a child? The tone of her voice was slightly dramatic and had that unmistakable Italo-Somali inflection. Sad, no, she was never sad. Melancholy, perhaps. Someone who thinks a lot, who turns things over in her mind and who in doing so can create problems. But Axad and I together balanced each other. She toned down my impulsiveness and I energized her quietness. She moderated my hyperboles, I filled her silence. I was the advance party, she was the rear guard. Both of us risked a lot. But whatever Axad and I had been was way back in the past. Twenty years perhaps? I arrived and she left. The telephone linked us for a while, we called each other faithfully, almost every week, only to eventually lose touch when, for the umpteenth time, Axad had moved, changing house, country, and telephone number. Right then? She was living in America. Who could have guessed? What's more, married to Taageere. Taageere, a delicate boy, a delicate show-off. Did she love him? How had they met? What had they become? So many questions. Too much time, too much distance. divided us.

We shall find time to fill in the gaps. We must begin slowly, very slowly, with the everyday things, only that way will the weight of the years disappear. Your fingernails are just the same as when you were small. Let's begin to search, together. Like that time—do you remember?—when we didn't want to leave the beach so we hid behind some rocks, and the others tricked us by pretending that they were really going home. That time when, while we were looking for the people we had hidden from, we found a little girl searching for her mother. That little girl, lost like us.

Imagine a similar reunion. So much going around, so much worry for no reason, now it all made sense. Axad, herself, was enough. Would she have sought me out anyway? She, I, would one of us have found out about the other? Or would we have lost each other without knowing how to find the other? I see messages that cannot be rationally decoded, disseminated somewhere. Because now Maxamed X made so much sense. Was there finally a reason that connected me to the Mute?

Axad and I had to find Luul, by spreading the word and desperately looking everywhere. You see? Luul had searched for Shukri. She knew her from when she was a child. Possibly the only face that she knew in this big city, from the time when she was small and her brother Taageere had brought his wife Shukri home. I think that they even got on well together: Shukri was as sweet as sugar. An older sister for her? I'm telling you all this because it was Shukri herself,

Taageere's ex-wife, who called us saying that Luul was with her and that we could all meet at Qamar's shop.

Shukri was standing next to Luul who was sitting on a stool, in a corner, almost transparent in that crowded shop. Shukri, who immediately recognized us, came forward to meet us. We embraced. I wondered what it must be like to embrace your man's new woman. But the two of them seemed almost comfortable with each other. Had Shukri brought her son? No, he was at a friend's house, it was already emotional enough with all these reunions.

Luul seemed shaky on her feet, like someone who could barely stand. Perhaps it was the journey that had sucked her dry, who knows. Luul with her little head wrapped in her salmon-colored *fasoleeti,* her dress that was too long, too big, a pair of *jabaati* so threadbare as to make you think that she had not bought a new pair since she stepped onto Italian soil. Luul, named for a pearl, seemed more like a poor shrimp snatched from the sea. So wrapped up in all that cloth that you hardly noticed that she had a baby tied to her breast. Luul, her eyes motionless, who smiled when Axad kissed her on both cheeks.

I, on the other hand, was worried about Axad. She was capable of shedding a tear at the slightest thing. In fact, she was crying again. It took nothing. An emotion, words uttered in a lower tone of voice. Axad was staring at the child unable to summon up the courage to touch him. He was tiny, he was hardly a week old.

I asked her if the delivery had gone well. It was the first time she had heard my voice. Luul looked up without saying a word. Then, Axad said what she had forgotten to tell her right off: Barni is my sister. *Abaayadey.*

How did I feel? In that very moment I felt like a person who has picked two extremely delicate flowers, who must immediately put them in a vase and find a thin reed to support the bloom which is too heavy for the stem. To support the bloom which is too heavy and to add half an aspirin to the water to give them strength. I felt like a person who is eating out of two porcelain dishes, too delicate for her habits, two dishes of that precious, delicate Chinese porcelain. I felt like someone walking on eggs—crack!

Luul was unable to answer me. So I asked her if she would let me hold the baby.

Qamar, seemingly busy with her telephone calls and her accounts, suddenly intervened, as if offering a certificate of guarantee: Barni is a midwife, she said in a loud voice so everyone could hear. Then Luul stood up and moved her forearms close to mine so that the baby could slip over to me without being jolted.

How was he? Very well: he had that doughy smell of milk, his body all huddled up and those long fingernails that all newborns have. And lots and lots of black hair. I rocked him to and fro and examined him, until at a certain point I had a kind of premonition, a sudden jolt, and I asked her the question that one usually immediately asks a new mother: What name have you given him?

Luul gave us an answer. I will tell you. Because it is here, now, that you will be compensated for all your patience. Being able to listen: don't they say that it is a divine virtue?

The child is called Maxamed. She gave him that name in honor of the person who helped her.

In order to deliver the baby, Luul had sought refuge in a derelict car, just like a cat. She felt the first labor pains but didn't tell anybody. Without saying anything to anybody, she went out for a walk to get some relief. All the women had always told her that when the labor pains begin you must walk so that the baby will be born more easily. Almost immediately she felt the urge to push. A gift from Allah, a quick labor. She had to find a quiet spot and the car seemed the ideal place. It hadn't been difficult, praise God. A natural birth. After, she rested with the umbilical cord still tied and her newborn at her breast. She hadn't had the strength to move right away so she lay there, protected by her clothing, admiring her baby's universe.

And that is how Maxamed found her just before nightfall. She had taken refuge in the wrecked car and was awash in her waters. He was happier than he had been in a very long time, and he ran off to find something with which to cut the cord and a container for warm water. He was the one who washed the baby, sluicing away the blood and amniotic liquid with bucketfuls of water.

Don't ask me for any details. I know nothing about the cord.

I only know that Maxamed prepared a place for Luul to sleep in that car and brought her some milk with ice. Next morning Luul woke up and since it was extremely hot and since she was so happy to be alive with her baby, she went off for a walk. It was then that the car caught fire.

Seeing all the smoke Luul turned back. She didn't have time to get up close but she clearly saw Maxamed X throw himself into the car, heedless of the fire. Perhaps he thought she was trapped inside and wanted to save her. Luul ran off because she saw the police arrive, she was frightened that they would arrest her and the baby.

She told her story without stopping. And since it seemed that her tongue had been loosened, as if she had suddenly let go, I decided to summon up my courage to ask: Maxamed X. What is he to you? He's only the person who washed away your blood. What connects the two of them? And as I am asking her these questions I regret having had the courage to ask them. Because I'm afraid that Axad will burst into tears again, which in fact is what she does. But instead of being scared, Luul continues her tale with greater force. Poor Luul, she's crying, too. She sheds tears of water, of salty water. She cries and the baby cries. Wailing, they fill the street with crying. Such desolate crying that nobody has the courage to interrupt them.

Forgive me, please. This is a story that almost defies telling. My mind is still soaking up that wailing. In my throat I can feel that water that isn't there and I can see the desert that goes on forever. I hear people screaming and screaming because they are afraid of dying. I am squashed in, tight, compressed, kicked into the SUV with desert tires. I hear the breath of that vehicle that spits and sweats, that puffs and grinds. Up and down, up and down. Nausea that fills my throat. The thick sand burns my eyes and the horizon seems all one and the same. I forget where the sun will rise, where it will set. I see the tracks on the dunes that are quickly covered up, and I am tempted, but I do not have the strength, to run, run, run because my healthy legs are faster than those wheels. The desert swells and bursts inside of me, screaming and bubbling from my breast in the middle of the night, like burning fire. And I feel in my arms the weight of those bodies swallowed up by the white sea. Those lifeless bodies, Maxamed's sons, and Luul's husband who carried them on his shoulders in vain.

Can you be saturated by so much pain? Me, Axad, Shukri, and Qamar all around Luul, in different ways. A shield to protect her, to raise her up. We all wanted—in countless ways—to take care of her and the baby. To begin with, she was to go to Shukri's house. She had wandered all over the place, all week to find that house. Shukri was going to have her stay. I was going to take her for her check-ups, after accompanying Axad to the ex-embassy to get the bag that Luul had left there. A bag that hardly weighed anything, a few memories, photos, a pair of shoes, two slips, a *diric*, a top, but above all two baby outfits, brand-new ones.

The boys had put it aside. We went to the ex-embassy with a bag of food for them—milk, pasta, rice, canned tomatoes, oil, sugar, coffee, biscuits, and apricot juice. Axad and me: thanks. They wanted to have news of Luul and Maxamed.

"Luul is fine. As for Maxamed, they are still trying to interrogate him about that car that was set on fire. If only we could find a way to show that it wasn't his doing."

The boys did have a way. But it would have meant putting some of them at risk. Because, that morning, nobody knew that Luul had given birth—what's more, in that very same car. That old Fiat 131 that they had been messing around with for days. That Fiat 131 they had dreamed of getting to start. When he was small, one of the boys had worked for a tire dealer and that's why he thought he also knew about cars. So, fiddling around with some wires and some gas, they had managed to set fire to that old Fiat 131!

I am very happy to tell you this story. From the bottom of my heart, I hope you will write about it. Because, you see, later on I tried consulting someone in the legal profession, but he pretended not to know anything about pro bono work. Then a lawyer, thinking he had found a clever solution, told me that if the car had been inside the embassy grounds we could have pleaded diplomatic immunity. That way we could have discredited the accusation of attempted terrorism. That makes you laugh, right? How could that happen when the territory of Somalia isn't even officially recognized?

Well, since my story has now taken this turn, all that's left is for me to tell you how the tale of the Mute ended. I hope you are satisfied. In truth, the tale doesn't come to an end, not that of Luul and Maxamed, nor mine or Axad's. We're all still in the picture. But what I can do is thread the last pearl onto your necklace because I know that this is the way you in the West have of telling stories. Telling stories by ending them.

I went to visit Maxamed X one last time before he was discharged. As usual, I went at the end of my workday. They were still keeping him in the hospital even though he was clearly much improved. His face was more relaxed and they told me that he had actually eaten something. There he was, dozing and occasionally glancing at the television screen of the patient in the bed next to his. As soon as I entered he looked at me hard from head to toe with an intensity I had never seen in his eyes. I took a stool and went to the foot of his bed. Speaking as I usually did, without expecting any reply. *Walaal,* my brother.

My story? It dates from a few years earlier when something miraculous had happened in that same hospital. Perhaps Maxamed had guessed that I worked there, but he certainly did not know that I was a *ummuliso,* a midwife. As I was saying, several years earlier, in that same hospital. A Somali friend who was about to give birth had come in. I hadn't seen her for several months, but God clearly had decided that I was the one who should be there when her baby was born.

You know, her belly was this big, about to burst. And she was so unhappy, poor thing, because this was her second child, and she had lost her first. And she was so unhappy because they had examined her insides with a machine and had seen that the baby was upside down, his head near his mother's heart and his feet at the bottom. They used to deliver babies in that position, but nowadays they prefer to operate because, in a natural birth, they run the risk of suffocating.

So, my friend Ardo was in labor and was crying for those two sad reasons. She had prayed to Allah asking that her baby be born alive and she had begged Him to allow her to force him out through her own efforts—she didn't want them to cut her open. Many women would have been happy to be in her place because under anesthesia you don't feel anything.

When I say that Allah does exist, it is for this very reason. The girl went to have an ultrasound and do you know what had happened? The baby had turned round, right at the last moment! Isn't that what you call a miracle?

As I was telling the story, I moved closer to Maxamed, so close as to feel his damp breath on my forehead. So close and damp with emotion I said to him, "*Walaal,* brother of mine, birth is such a wonderful; thing, isn't it?" and I noticed that the Mute was moved. And so, without missing a beat, I seized the moment and told him that the important thing was that Luul was fine and that the baby was so beautiful, healthy and strong. He already weighed nine pounds.

At that point, the Mute began to laugh. To laugh out loud, laughing and slapping his hand against his thigh. Then he sat up, bending toward me. He came closer to me, pointing his finger just like this. He looked me straight in the eye and he said, "Listen you, you must do something. Tell these people that I want to speak to the Somali ambassador. To the ambassador in Italy for Somalia!"

3

TAAGEERE

HALOW? HELLO? IS THAT YOU, SHU-KRI? It's me, Taageere, your
ex-husband.

You hardly recognize my voice anymore, do you? I never call? Sure I never call. Every time you start off the same
way: You never call, you never call. By the end of the phone
call, the only thing you have said is: You never call. A whole
phone card used up to hear you say that I never call.

No, don't worry. Today I'm at the phone center. I told
you the way it works here. The owner is Somali, there are
five booths. They even give you a discount if you're calling
Somalia. Yes, like Xassan's Phone Center. Look, I always tell
you: you mustn't go to that dirty old man, but you, my
beauty, always do what you want. That's your problem.

No, this phone center isn't near the station. It's completely different from Rome. This city is big and what's
more, it's divided into neighborhoods, I don't know how to

explain it. We don't have such a large city center. A center that goes on forever. I remember when I arrived in Italy, I was stunned, speechless. Who had ever seen anything like it? All the streets were paved with ancient stones. Stones with names. And the houses. The houses and the tall buildings. It's odd for a Somali to love tall buildings, isn't it? When you're on the road, you're always dreaming of a haven. I'm probably a crazy Somali, what can I say? I would have stayed, I swear. But you know what the problem was. A man must find a way to support himself. But those stones, those ancient stones. They tickled my restlessness.

Yes, here in America things are very different. The neighborhoods could have been laid out with a ruler they're so straight, block after block. In one of these blocks there's even a grocery store identical to Xamarweyn's.

And then, you'll never believe this: do you remember the Chinese man? The Chinese man with the restaurant behind the Christian church in Mogadishu? The place where I took you to lunch that day and you were all excited because you had those deep-fried spring rolls and you kept on wanting more and more? Remember? That Chinese man, he's here, too, and when he got here he told the people at Immigration that he was Somali whether they believed it or not, he was a Somali, nothing else. I swear! Well, you can imagine what happened. Nobody believed him. And the poor devil shouted and swore that he was born in Mogadishu, that he had never set foot in that country of the small-eyes. He said that not even his father was born in China, even though the old man used to say that he was, just to boast. Don't you believe it. He used to say so, meaning that when he'd had enough, he, an old Chinese man, would go back to China, his own country. He used to say that when he was angry, meaning that he didn't want to have anything more to do with that miserable bunch of Africans. He didn't have much to boast about. Now, the people in Immigration decided to call in one of the small-eyes, one of the real ones. He spoke to him in their language and the Chinese man kept on shaking his head, saying: No, no, I don't understand a word of this blasted language. Then the Chinese man put his thinking cap on. He went to his Somali friends, his old friends, and he said to them: Come with me to testify on my behalf. But that wasn't enough.

Those folks in Immigration don't believe just anybody. They want real interpreters, the certified ones. Ones they really trust. They called up these real interpreters but it was slow. Bureaucracy takes time. And you know what they told me? That the interpreters' jaws dropped when the Chinese man opened his mouth. They were dying of laughter. Yes, sure, you see so many strange things in this world. The language the Chinese man spoke was pure Somali, real Somali! They gave him permission to carry on with his life. The life he had had before. So he opened a Chinese fast-food place for everyone, but they're mostly Somalis who go there.

It makes me happy to hear you laugh. I was worried that you wouldn't ever speak to me again after all this time and after that phone call—the last time we spoke to each other.

I had bought a telephone card, a card for five dollars. I could speak for three hundred minutes. Three hundred minutes, said the voice on the card. The taped woman's voice. You can use the cards anywhere. All you need is the card and you can call from the phone center, from a public telephone, from anyone's house, even from the barbershop.

I was at the barbershop that day. Here, even the barber is Somali. Whoever can, continues to practice the trade he had before, and when you can count on a guaranteed clientele, what's better than opening a business? And this barber is a wily one. He had a portrait done of himself right on the front of the shop. Exactly the same picture he had before back home, a handsome black face, half shaved, half soaped up. Good idea, huh?

I called you from his telephone. The barber's very nice. I didn't have time to come to the call center. At the phone center they give you the same good rates as the card, but there are always lots of people passing through and every-one speaks to you as if you weren't on the phone: *Haye*, Taageere, how's it going? Ah, that's your wife who's talking to you, right, say hi to her for me; *haye,* sister, everything okay? Your little boy has got bigger, *mashallah,* long time, eh?

Sure, it's not much better at the barber's, but I had a card that time and so I thought of calling the two of you.

I was speaking to you and as I was speaking I was watching Cabdallah's little boy out of the corner of my eye. Do you remember my cousin Cabdallah? Cabdallah, the one who got me the papers to come here. The one who could have gotten them for the two of you, if you, Shukri, had only wanted them. As I was saying, Cabdallah asked me to look after his little boy as he had some errands to run. You know better than me what little kids are like—there he was, happily spinning around on the chair and looking at himself in the mirror. Spinning around and looking at himself in the mirror, spinning and looking, then he began to touch things, the shaving cream, the razors, metal combs, scissors, brushes, the taps, turning them on and off. It was dangerous, you see, it's dangerous to talk on the phone while you are taking care of a child, that's why I said to you: Bye, bye, I'll call you later. If that "later" then turned into a long time, that's another matter.

Why don't you say that you are proud of me instead of turning on me all the time? All right, I'm with other people's children, but what you say is not true. It's not true that it's easy when you don't have any responsibilities. It's not true that I boast about things I can't do. Look, parents are always asking my advice. I know a lot about children. It's a gift from Allah, don't laugh! You must remember when, just after we were married, I was playing with my nephews and nieces, when I was throwing the ball around with them. Hours and hours in the garden to pass them the ball and then yell goaaaaal! They laughed and laughed and wanted to be with me all the time. Fun and games that don't put bread on the table. Fun and games that don't raise kids. Remember how we all had to behave at Koranic school, in silence and in fear. Mistake, down came the whip. How many belt marks do you have on your body? All right, it was a misunderstanding. I know, I know. Raising children is just like spitting blood. Raising them in the West. That's why all the people I know seem to have gone crazy.

I was telling you about my cousin's son. I kept him entertained pretty well and after a few hours I returned him to his father. We had to go back to his house and, at that time, his house was my house. Always the same problem of finding a decent place to live, and so, as a result, I go from one house to another. A life without ties, without fixed places. About two weeks before, I had taken all my stuff to Cabdallah's house and in return I looked after his son.

I'm talking about that day, the last time I called you. So, that day a pipe had broken in the bathroom at Cabdallah's house. In these houses you never know who lived there before you and it's always that way, everything half broken. The pipe had broken and was gushing out, like a river, a river that inundates and soaks everything: the mattresses on the floor, the clothes. So there we were, me wringing out the clothes and he in the kitchen with the child.

After a while his wife arrived. I don't know what happened, but after exchanging a couple of words, they started to argue. It happens every day. And his wife, Sucdi, shouts so loudly she could crack the windows. So loudly that if you can't see her, you imagine that some maniac is slitting her throat.

She was yelling and I was telling the little one stories to keep him from listening. While this racket was going on, we heard someone knocking at the door. And boy, how they knocked, bang bang bang, just like someone who wanted to knock it down. Bang bang. No question about it, it was the police. You have no idea how many times it has happened. Sucdi yells as if a maniac is killing her and the police arrive. Well now, there's no time to tell you all the reasons why I acted this way, all you need to know is that I couldn't afford to be found in that house, not for any reason in the world. I hurriedly grabbed my wet clothes and slipped into the bathroom. There was an almighty racket going on, and

I was terrified that they would find me, so I jumped out of the window. And as I jumped, I realized that all my stuff was soaked through and that my bag was dripping. I know what you're going to say. That I'm always inventing things, that I get my stories from the movies, but believe me, it's the truth.

Well, there I am in the street with my bag that weighs a ton because of all the water it has soaked up and I don't know where to go. I really don't know where to go because, besides Cabdallah, the only other person from my family still in that city was my aunt. My aunt, the one you knew, too. But this aunt of mine has just moved to Illinois with all her children, after her husband sent for her to join him.

What? You remember that I had quarreled with Cabdallah? Yes, yes, that's an old story, it happened so many years ago. Sure, I remember what it was about. I flung the truth into his face. I told him that his crazy wife was incapable of doing anything at all. And I was right, he must have come to the same conclusion himself.

I'm not wrong, it's the truth. What I'm telling you is that when he came to Italy and stopped by to see you, when he saw how beautiful you were with the baby, he was seized with bitter envy, even though neither of you admit it. Why do you think he gave you all those gifts? Definitely not to make me happy!

He fancied you, you don't want to believe it, he liked both you and the baby. But he was very careful, that snake. He knew that if he didn't behave when he returned I would kill him! It's for this very reason that he immediately did what he did. He married that crazy woman, Sucdi. He married her out of blind envy. Out of envy when he saw that I had a son and he didn't. Not yet. Out of envy, he married the first woman he could find, the only one who would put up with a piece of rubbish like him. A crazy woman like Sucdi who grabs him round the neck in front of all his friends. A nut who is always dropping her son off at other people's houses. A woman who is incapable of looking after her own son, what kind of woman is that?

I took Cabdallah aside and I told him the whole truth. I said to him: The reason why you want a son is obvious to everybody. Cabdallah only wanted a son out of envy. I even said to him: Your wife is nothing but a crazy woman, you have to know how to choose women.

The trouble is, you never listen to me. I'd like to do all the talking but you keep interrupting me. You argue. I need to speak to you about important things. I'll get there, little by little. You say that I'm a father who doesn't take care of his own son. That I believe that everything is just as it was back home. Lots of women who busy themselves with household chores and men who are excused from them. Stop it, how can I talk to you, woman with a one-track mind? I was explaining why I couldn't call you. You keep on interrupting. Are you fed up with my chatter? Let me at least finish.

So, my aunt isn't around anymore and you know how things are at my cousin's. There I was in the middle of the road, late at night with my bag dripping all over the place. And while I'm there not knowing where the heck to go, sitting on the bench and deep in thought, I see this homeless man that I know.

We hadn't seen each other for a long time but we recognize each other all the same. You're looking very well these days, he says, you've changed, I almost didn't recognize you. Actually, it is I who realized it was you so don't try to pull a fast one on me, I'm thinking to myself.

When he met me years ago, I had just arrived. At that time, I was overwhelmed by sadness, by a deep and shabby sadness, a crazy sadness that sprang from the cold and the disillusionment. I couldn't shake it off. And with this sadness, I went around the city, dirty and unkempt, speaking to no one, and I slept wherever I happened to be, just like a hobo. I was so dirty and covered in hair that not even my mother would have recognized me if she'd seen me.

And it was during that time that I saw how much sadness there is in the West, that there are many more homeless people on the streets than we imagine, in fact we can't even imagine how many homeless people there are here when we're back home and hear of these countries that are doing so well.

So, seeing me with my leaky bag and my head in my hands, this person I know tells me to go along with him, because there's a place where at least we won't die of cold.

It's a real foul-smelling hole full of men, there's a fire going and people are passing around a container of alcohol, partly to keep warm, partly to forget. There are those who always sleep there but there are also other people. I can't tell you much about these other people or what they were doing there. In the middle of these men, though, there's one all dressed up like a respectable person who, seeing me sprawled in a corner with my bag soaked with water, comes up to me. We begin to talk and, realizing that I am Somali like him, he says to me: Brother, I can't stand seeing you so down and out and he invites me to go to his house for the night. I follow him as the cold freezes my bones, turns me to ice, and I become a man who cannot control his body, the body of someone else. I follow him, and as soon as I get into the warm house, I suddenly fall asleep.

In the morning I wake up and am about to lay out my clothes to dry. I want to dry them, wash up and think about the day. My host is freshly dressed and no longer kind. He has a way of speaking like a hysterical queen; in fact, he's a real *khaniis*, I'd bet. He says: You mustn't touch any of my things. Like telling a guest to keep his hands tied in your house. I'm so angry that I am determined to make him pay for it. First, I ask him if I can stay until my clothes are dry. Dream on, he says to me. So I pick up all my stuff and, while his back is turned, I slip his bunch of keys into my bag. I leave when he leaves and I stay around waiting, walking around the building. I make sure that he has gone off.

Then I go back into his house and put my clothes in his dryer—that bastard has one all for himself. Once my clothes are dry, I give a good, strong kick to his television set and

I go out, leaving the door open. I'm an ignorant bushboy? Then you haven't understood the story I've just told you! Someone says: Come along with me, brother, and then you discover that he is a *khaniis*. A *khaniis* who wants something else. He deserved it, believe me.

But now that I've finally called you back, things are going much better, I'm all settled. In what sense? I'm settled, more than settled. I so much want for you and the little one to be proud of me! The project. I wish I could take you to the warehouse and show you what I have thought up for the future. Some other guys and I have rented a warehouse. We'll have to live in it for a while until we recoup our money. But who cares, we have a small stove and a bathroom and we're fine. Do you know what snow boots are? We have a storage facility full of these snow boots. We're going to sell them in Nepal and with the first money I get I want to buy you a gold watch. A gold watch for you and a remote-control toy car for the little one.

No, this is a new story. It's not one of those I tell and then tell again. Look, that business with the Ghanaian has nothing to do with it. The whole thing ended badly, as you might have expected. Damn me and Saciid Saleebaan for having believed him. If I see that man, he'd better kiss his life goodbye. I don't care if he was a boxer. Now he's a loser, that's it. We went into business with him like two turkeys. We entrusted our money to him so he could go off with his pockets full. He hadn't been home for fifteen years. And Saciid Saleebaan right behind him, just couldn't stay put. After the war, two years in Australia, then Europe and then here in America. Here in America for two years, then back to Ghana with the Ghanaian to set up the business. They were going to set up the business and I was here waiting. And Saciid Saleebaan had even rented a motorbike, a Kawasaki road bike, to remind him of the one he had as a boy in Mogadishu. He wanted to take a ride around Accra, a

ride around an African city on his motorbike. Nice, huh?
Remember the time I got Saciid Saleebaan to lend me the
motorbike? The two of us on Saciid Saleebaan's motorbike
going to the Hamburger House which had just opened. How
good those hamburgers seemed to us then with the ground
beef and the mayonnaise. Shukri on Saciid Saleebaan's motorbike: when you wore pants, you were a knockout!

So, what happened?

The old boxer was seized with a kind of obsession, a kind
of crazy jealousy for a guy who was courting his wife. Courting the Ghanaian's wife, just imagine it. A sad wreck who
had given birth to seven children. A poor woman with ap-
palling hands, hands that had worked for years and years
loosening, dyeing, braiding, and straightening curly hair, *ja-
reer*, tough as wire.

According to Saciid Saleebaan it all began years ago, an
old, old story from when the Ghanaian and his wife were
young and still lived in Africa. The old man could have rested easy because his wife didn't want to have anything to
do with the suitor. So many years have gone by, she said,
what's left of my body, I've had so many children.

You know what really happened? The truth is that stupid man's brain was fried from all those punches he took on
the head. That's exactly why that blind-jealous fool called
on a friend to get him a gun. A friend who got fifty dollars
for getting him a gun. Without saying a word to anyone, the
Ghanaian woke up one morning and went out with the gun
in his pocket. And you know what he was riding? He was
riding the same backfiring motorbike that Saciid Saleebaan
had rented to go on a sightseeing trip round Accra.

What happened after? What happened was that he fired
his bullets into that sad, old loser who was courting his wife.
Just like that, in the middle of the road. In the middle of a
crowd, right in front of everybody.

The police carried out an investigation, and it came out
that the guy with the gun was on a motorbike, and after in-
tensive searching, they found the motorbike abandoned in a
corner, right near the shooting.

And what else did the police find out? They found out that the motorbike was a rented motorbike and that the person who had rented it was no less than that wretch Saciid Saleebaan, the Somali who wanted to set up a business right there in that stupid African country. How did it all end?

To cut a long story short, all because of the Ghanaian's jealousy, Saciid Saleebaan was sent to jail and the other poor wretch ended up in the hospital. Thank God the Ghanaian was useless at firing a gun.

But he caused a real problem because in order to free Saciid Saleebaan and get him back here, they used all the money we had put together. All our money went to pay his bail, and so goodbye, business. That's how all my money was wasted.

Get myself into trouble? Spoken like a mother. I do not get myself into trouble. Blame it on luck every time. Bad luck. You attract bad luck like a magnet: Spoken like a woman. I know what you're thinking. But it only happened once, the one time you choose to remember, just once.

It was the wrong way to go about things. A string of bad luck. The only thing I could do was pray. Pray to God for a once-in-a-lifetime solution. So, there I was, lost in thought, my head in my hands, all huddled up on the back stairs of the building. An empty stairwell reverberating with loneliness. Outside it was cold and the miserable hole where I used to sleep was even colder. And so I went up and down the stairs, praying, up and down. Right up to the top. After that, I was going to go to sleep.

It was there that I saw it. A large box, made of bluish cardboard and, on it, tall white mountains and a cloudless blue sky. A box of Swiss chocolates. What's a box of chocolates doing here? A temptation from the *shayddaan*, I think, but that can't be because I was praying to God. And with that thought I opened it, my thoughts pure.

Inside? Wrapped in tissue paper, like crystal, a pile of hashish and under it, further down, the gun, the revolver. I had never held one in my hand, not even during the war!

Confusion—what was I to think? That this was what I needed, that the finger pointing to that box was the finger of God. A chance. Doing good while doing wrong.

Now the contents of the box were mine. Alone in the park with all that stuff. Done for. The police was doing the rounds, going up and down, up and down, all along the length of the park. There I was, checking out hiding places. But they saw me all the same. I ran, ran fast.

I'm running through the park. I'm getting out of breath. I throw away the gun. I throw away the hashish. A cop comes at me from the front, I flip over, go through his legs, grab them, he's down, then I get the other one, spinning on my back, I'm about to slip off when other cops arrive on the scene.

I ended up in jail for three months. Then I was sure it hadn't been God who had shown me that box. But Allah must have been with me because if they had found the gun, I would have gotten five years.

Shukri, your relatives pop up everywhere and tell you all about it. I know they speak badly of me. You would deny it? It doesn't bother me in the least. If they have nothing better to do than call you from the other side of the world to say that the father of your son does such and such, poor girl, what you must have suffered, thank goodness you got rid of him. Mouthpieces of the devil. Riff-raff. Lazy good-for-nothings. Wretches. They're filth, that's what they are. Gossips. Inventors of lies. Empty days that they don't know how to fill. So they end up making life difficult for people like me. Why? Out of envy, that's why. Because I manage to get by. Because I'm not always there begging for favors. I'm someone who minds his own business, that's what I am. I keep to myself. I don't say very much. And minding your own business and speaking little for them means acting superior.

That whole business? Everyone gets into similar situations. At least I'm not ashamed of what I do. It rarely happens to me. And when that occasionally happens, I admit it.

I can admit without being ashamed that my friend received a consignment of hashish and I helped him sell it. Bad habit? I don't deny it, that day I was selling drugs.

Ruining my reputation? Think for yourself, Shukri. The truth—bitter as it—is that nobody has the guts to tell you to your face how things really are. Do they talk about you? You think you're deceiving everyone with your polite ways, but you know what they think, don't you? Everyone thinks, You live with a *gaal* and therefore you're a *sharmuuto*.

People still have that mentality; if you don't see it clearly it's because your self-deception blurs your vision. Who's more shameless: a woman who lives with a *gaal* or a man who trafficks in drugs? When you were married to me, you can bet you cut a better figure.

Listen, in all good conscience, everything I do, I do for our child. You know that. A son is not an excuse. But what I'm building inside my head is a project, a plan that works in order to put aside a little pot of money, pay for his education, and that way, as long as I'm alive, he won't ever need anyone's help.

I'm not interested in that guy you have married. Patient and generous? Keep those comments to yourself. You've turned into a *gaal* yourself—the next thing you'll tell me is that you love him! Me, your ex-husband! Who has given him the right to raise my own son? If he wants a son, let him have one. If he wants a son, I tell you, he can have one! Or tell him to buy a dog. Yes, give him a dog. White infidels, dog lovers. Dogs treated better than their own children.

Who do you think you can dupe with this story of an Islamic marriage? Let me tell you, no one will fall for it. A good farce, that of the *aroos*! But if you're going to marry a *gaal,* why don't you marry him according to the *gaal* custom? Oh, sorry, stupid me. As always, above everything else, the family's approval. How convenient for me, Islamic law says: If you have repudiated your wife three times in front of witnesses, you cannot remarry her unless she first has been married to another man.

You're worried about your family. You're afraid they will renounce you and so goodbye, interpreter's job. Don't tell me you can continue to do that job without their support.

I'll never stop going on about this family thing, and the fault is yours, you're the one who ruined my family, keep that in your thick head, my family, me, you and our son!

Being on one's own for a long time stings like a badly treated wound. I lack endurance. I feel the need for roots, now, today. A family. A family again. To feel like a man in a man's role. To take care of someone other than myself, to be a man worthy of trust.

You never trusted me? You never have. But just the child, even just him, would have been enough for me. With the child here with me it would be a different matter. Me, take care of him? I wasn't born crazy or stupid, you know. I would have learned. Everybody learns. If you had brought the child here, if you had come with the child, I would have known where to go back to at night. And then, to take care of someone other than myself, to take care of him. Out of fear of also getting him into trouble, I would have been more careful, always. The child would have helped me see the light of things, given me a sense of priority. Talk is cheap? You just don't understand: women have in their blood teachings that men can only drink from the source. I'm certain that the essence of things is learnable. We are not like you women, Shukri. We're not like you who feel the child rising and growing inside you. And then there is this new way of asserting yourself that you have learned. As if it weren't God who decides that we men will not experience menstruation, labor pains, the milk that flows from nipples. Sometimes I really think you don't use your head. And yet you seem so clever.

The child is like pure gold for you? I'm happy when I hear you speak like that. What you say is beautiful. And you also know what's good for our son? So why have you forgotten that usually children need a father? I have faith in you: I have let you raise him. It was me who decided to let you raise him. Do you think you are the only one who has this right? It's not true that I count for absolutely nothing. Take on my responsibilities? If only they would let me. But I'm going to say it again: It's thanks to me that you have been able to have him; I let you raise him. You know that you are both mine. You were mine and he continues to be mine. My child, my possession.

When I think that it all began with those stupid photos. Ridiculous things. I will repeat it as long as I have a voice: Saciid Saleebaan, who is my friend, would never have shown you any compromising photos. Photos of a young people's party—why did you concoct those stories? Idiotic things that men don't realize they're doing? Of the gravity of our dim-witted actions? Wow, how well you speak, my dear! A girl who can speak well, the girl of my passions, thanks for the lesson!

Rebuild my life, it's something I have to do, Shukri. At my age, how many children did my father already have? Eight maybe? And he supported us all by himself. God only knows how. I, on the other hand, am running after this one son. Does it seem right to you? You have to know that for me, my son comes before everything else. Don't forget it. For you and for him. Looking for you both, always looking for you. Walking around in circles. Never finding you. I call, the telephone rings, and no one answers. Where do you keep that child? I ask myself.

You mustn't cling to him. If you cling to him, he'll become a *ciyaal maamo*. Yes, yes, you have stopped nursing him. Sure I remember how old he is: six—sorry, nine years old. And yet he's still a child. A child who needs his mother.

Mama's boy. Mothers in these blasted countries have to work.

But do you really need to have him picked up from school by that man? He already has a father, darn it, he's still my son! Two parents? You've really bought into that *gaal* mentality, you're brainwashed. Where have you heard of a father and a mother being interchangeable? I say it now and I'll repeat it again: As long as you are a child, it's your mother that counts. Women are the most important thing.

All this talk: you make me feel like a dead man. Money? I can't just guess by myself when you need money. I've asked hundreds of times if you need anything, I have. I've asked and asked. What am I supposed to do, remember it in my every waking moment? If you need money to spend more time with him, if it means that you don't have to spend the entire day away from home, here, I'll send you all the money I have. Everyone eats lunch at school? I don't care. Even if all the children eat in the school cafeteria, I demand that my son eat clean food! They've even told me at the mosque—the one time that I went—that we must be careful to read labels. These *gaal* are crazy, they even put pork fat in shampoo! Place my trust in a *gaal* cook? What does a *gaal* cook care about removing unclean food from my son's plate? About what she does with those filthy hands that cut up the *khansiir! Bismillaahi!* Are we or are we not Muslims?

I have retained my right to decide for my own son, don't forget it! You and he, two distinct persons, but as long as he's a child I also have rights over you. You cannot hide behind your Muslim *gaal!* Nice performance, but nobody believes that he has converted. Anyway, a child knows how to recognize his own father. I am alive and I retain my paternal right!

Love, love that comes to an end, people who change: now you are the one speaking as if you were in a movie. If there's one thing I'm certain of it's that yes, there were problems, but together the two of us could have solved them. Money, that fixation of yours, you can always find money, money that's really needed. We are in Allah's hands. I would take care of the child and you—you make me so angry. You must, you should have come here with him.

Time—time is running out. My son's growing up and you can't make me feel like a man with no strength, without rights, without power. Only I can. The child can grow up with you even without his father there. Take your son away,

keep him with you. I have a son. It's not true that I don't
have a son anymore. One day I'll take care of him when you
let me do so.

* * *

Shukri, Shukri, don't hang up, I beg you. I haven't told
you the important things. The reason why I'm calling you.
Time is rushing by, sugar. Was I meant to wait for you forever? What's passed, is passed. Now I must rebuild. Minutes
that are slipping by. The telephone's just the same. You buy
a card for three hundred minutes and you think you have all
the time in the world. Then even those three hundred minutes are all used up. All the effort you put into remembering
to buy the card. You have to wait until you feel that same
energy, that new desire that makes you buy another card.
It's not about the cost. The excitement I feel when I take it
out of its wrapping and scratch it, revealing the secret number. I see that number shine, carved like gold letters. The
secret number is my treasure. A secret number that makes
everything right again. Then—the card that is running out,
time that is running out. Don't let the time run out without
saying what is important.

I have to speak to you about Luul, my younger sister.
How old was she the last time you saw her? Five? Or four?
My little sister. Who always wanted to be with you. And you
made sure that she didn't have lice. Luul who followed you
around and played at being a grown-up. And you treated
her seriously, like a grown-up. You went along with her
game: Help me wash the dishes, hold the soap, come on,
let's go and do the shopping. With her small shopping basket, the right-sized basket for her that you had bought for
her. Shukri, sugar, you made a part of her small life sweeter.
What happened after that? Luul won't tell me, my little sister. A sea of salty tears. And now, with no papers, I cannot
come to get her. You do understand, if only I had the papers.

But you with that charade, that meaningless charade.

It's necessary for the divorce to be recorded? In Italy
they don't recognize our divorces? I beg you, Shukri, don't

yell. The divorce should have been recorded, now you'll understand why. Every so often it's a good idea for things to be carried through to their conclusion.

And then, another thing. They tell me I can't do anything to get her over here. I've spoken to her, yes. She's in Sicily somewhere. I called my relatives, Diriiye Yuusuf and Safiya. I called them to ask them to go and get her. They'll go to get her, poor thing. But how happy she would be to see you. To see you again and remember that sweetness.

It's hard to dig things up again. But if you really want me to, I shall tell you what I've always said: It wasn't me who wanted this. Shukri, you hothead that imagines the unimaginable. I've never heard of a woman who abandons her home all because of some photos. Things of no importance. Saciid Saleebaan, who is my friend, would never have shown you compromising photos. Whether it was you who saw them and not he who showed them to you doesn't change anything.

Whatever. Sufficient reason for you to go back to your mother? To go to your mother's house in secret, without saying a word. You didn't even give me the chance to talk about it. Even the girls told me: Let her be, she's only tired. It's because of the pregnancy, you'll see, when it's all over she'll come back, she'll come back. And so I left you alone. I really cared about you, and how! I let you go for this reason, because of what the girls said.

How stupid. I should have spoken with my father. But I didn't want to, I didn't want to hear the same old words: Taageere, you're not worthy of that girl.

I should have spoken to him. Because he was the only one who knew. The only one who continued to see you. The only one in my family that you trusted.

Shukri, candy sugar, who ever saw a woman who spoke more to her husband's father than to the other women? You're odd, I've said so many times.

You didn't want to speak to me, I left you alone. I thought: She'll forgive me, sooner or later. You fooled me, you and my father. He never told me he came to see you every day in his taxi. That, as soon as he could, he came to see how you were. That he had seen my son, his grandchild. He didn't tell me that you wouldn't open the door to me but that you would to him, and how you welcomed him.

Do you know how many times I tried calling you? At your neighbor's: Please, auntie, would you be so kind as to call Shukri. And she replied: No, Taageere, she won't come, she says she doesn't want to speak to you. How many times I dialed that number: three six zero five one. So many times that I still remember it.

I left you alone out of respect for you. Could I imagine what it was like when the curfew began? Every day: stories of terrible cruelty. And then, I told you what it was like at the beginning. At the beginning there was still that fear. Unaccustomed fear. The smell of a dead person stuns you when you are not prepared for it.

Then, everything changed. But about Xirsi, no, I can't bring myself to speak of his bloodless gaze; no, I can't. I do know that he told me about my son, that he had been born. And so I, Taageere, having received this news, I started walking back across the divided city. I walked and came to the roadblock.

My head was shaved like that of a dead man. People were afraid of my shiny head, a head that reflected the colors of blood.

At the roadblock they said to me: Hey, you with that shiny head, are you a soldier or a madman?

I couldn't answer, I was so full of pain. The people at the roadblock wouldn't let me through. And I was so weak, empty, passive. A few days later I went back with my father. Together we convinced the people at the road block. But you were no longer there. It was fate. If I had gotten through, it would have been a completely different story.

My dear Shukri, I don't know what you told my father, what you and my father spoke about, the actual words. The old man did not change; day after day he repeated those words, words that crushed me, "You, my son, are not like her, she is better than all of you, Shukri is not like the other women." I was consumed with irritation and anger. How can a father love his daughter-in-law more than his own son? But wartime and grief make you think a lot. It is the war that made me understand. That, and all the years I've spent here. All these years spent asking myself the same questions again and again. Pondering questions about the old man and about love. Enough time to come to understand what the old man was mulling over in your presence: the stirrings of love. Love: at first, a white flower of hope, bathed in light. Love: bated breath, sleepless nights, the trembling of a leaf. The old man recalled his many years and his loves. Because—when he became fond of you—you were exactly the same age as my mother. As my mother was when he met her, loved her, and stole her away. He stole her to marry her secretly. Destiny keeps going back and forth along the same path. Only now, through the passing of time and through grief, is the truth clear to me. The old man felt he was unworthy of my mother. You, Shukri, were as young as she was when he stole her away. The old man wanted to redeem himself. And he thought he could save you from the same indignity. His unworthiness became mine.

Today, what I think is that neither you, Shukri, nor my father ever understood me. I do not act like other men, I am different. I do not subscribe to this sick tradition of keeping my woman for myself. Mine, inside and hidden, to the point of consuming her.

* * *

Take, for instance, a certain Domenica, an Italian-Somali young woman that I have been seeing recently. This young woman always tells me I'm different from the other men. What do you mean, how can I even think of talking to you about my girlfriends? This from a woman who is married to a *gaal*! Yes, I am reminding you. Did you forget? It's not a matter of being jealous. I don't want to talk to you about Domenica, anyway. At least not yet. I want to talk to you about one of her cousins that I happened to meet through her. Shamsa, a cousin on her father's side. Their fathers were brothers.

Domenica has been living around here for a little over six months. This city, for her, is like an empty map, with no emotional attachments. So, she said to me: Accompany me, and I answered, Yes, I will.

Shamsa, a cousin with whom she once lived. Not in Somalia, no. Because Domenica only lived in Mogadishu as a child, until she was nine. Not too long, and not too short a time. Enough to have the ebb and flow of life there well imprinted in her mind. The ebb and flow, the questions, no small feat.

And Shamsa was supposed to stay in America for a while—for tourism, they said—to get away and see other people from back home in this big city, because there are many Somalis here. Unlike Finland, where she lives. There you have to look for them here and there, they're scattered all around in icy villages. It seems that this looking here and there, with six children hanging from her skirt, filled her with an immense sadness. A terrible sadness, depression, says Domenica, who knows about these things, about that kind of sadness that makes Somalis say: He's crazy and he has no shame, poor thing. Living from day to day, a person forgets about what matters. Your mind is taken up with what should I eat today, how do I survive tonight, will I find a place to sleep in peace? Like an animal. Slipping away, time and years go by, without realizing it, far from you all.

But I was telling you about Shamsa and her trip to wash away her unhealthy thoughts. You know what? I saw her husband, and I understood. I understood everything.

Shamsa, as clear as the deep sea, as beautiful as a mermaid. Straight hair all the way down her back. I saw the before and after. The before? In the picture album she brought with her from Finland, to show to her acquaintances, she says. The after? A husband who was ugly, so ugly, really ugly. Short and half hunched over, poor soul. May Allah forgive me. A husband with the jealous heart of a snake. Every night he brought her a glass of milk and honey. This way I'll make her nice and fat, he used to say. And she won't ever run away from me.

I heard this with my own ears, he actually said this to me, I swear: So I'll make her nice and fat, and he was laughing. He thought he would make me laugh too. And I did, just to make him happy. The children she gave birth to? They were not enough, in and of themselves, to have such a profound effect. It was that milk and honey that made her so sad.

This is what I mean when I say "consume." Keep for oneself? It gets consumed, that's all. But who knows, I let you slip away. Free, I used to think, my sweetheart. Everything is, in its own way, wrong. Who knows how to tame destiny?

Man must accept Allah's will. He must accept that that's the way it went, and we can't know if it's worse or better. Anyway, who are we to know what's better or worse? But listen, I have another story.

Not far from here lived two identical men, not related, but like twins. Indistinguishable: same body, same temperament. They were even born on the same day.

It so happened that they both fell in love with the same woman. Ahh, this woman was absolutely beautiful, bright as the moon and still a virgin. Her father kept her locked up in the house like a treasure. He didn't want to show her, he didn't want to give her away in marriage to anyone. So neither of the two men could do anything but peek at her shadow behind the windows, the golden-brown shadow of a woman. The men did everything they could to win the girl. But the father, no, he would not hear of it.

It so happened that the truth came out. The girl was promised to a rich merchant from Sanca. The two men lost all hope. They could only give up.

One of the two forgot her quickly. Like a passing thunderstorm. He found a wife and had children.

But the other man lost his peace of mind, he neglected himself, dragging himself about, not eating. He let his work, his house, his relationships all go. Now he wanders around the city like a vagabond, you should see him, he can't even remember his own name. We are always at a crossroads. Two roads, two destinies.

My destiny? One random event after another. What I do know in all certainty is that my destiny is stamped with my son's name. Things just happen. I was at the mall the other day.

In Rome I don't think there are any malls. Here instead I am in a modern country. Different in its own way. Ancient stones are my passion, but I do not disdain modernity. I like Italy, that's true. But the Italians, the Italians seem to always want to show off, they are half Africans, half Africans like us, and yet they put on airs. They treat us like dirt, like trash, with a sense of entitlement.

For me it is the exact opposite. I remember when I joined the Italian Cultural Center in Mogadishu. My book bought with lots of shillings, a thick package of wastepaper. In order to learn Italian! Going around like a student, with my notebook and the pen in my pants pocket. What use was Italian to me? It was the idea that attracted me; the fact that it was spoken by proper gentlemen, with good jobs at the ministry, in a school, in the army. All classy men, fluent in Italian, so fluent that it pops up here and there when they speak Somali. Here and there, often. I want to speak like that as well, every third word an Italian one, I thought. It's elegant. Will it come so naturally to me too? Like a language learned as a child? I never found out, war made me give it up.

I was talking to you about the mall. I was walking around the mall the other day. I wanted to buy something for my son: clothes, toys, that kind of thing. Even if you think that what I send you sucks. I always like to go into children's stores. It's like pouring rosewater on my longing. You're saying you don't think the things suck? I always get the wrong size. There's no reason to get mad. Children grow very fast when you don't see them. Now, listen to the story I said I wanted to tell you.

I was with a friend of mine, a Jamaican. Jamaica is always by my side lately. Rough loyalty, a persevering friend. I don't know why. He was with me when a girl caught his eye. He started to follow her. He was walking funny and he kept half winking at her. She would go in a store and he would follow behind.

She was Portuguese or something like that, I'm not sure. That's what the language she spoke sounded like. There are lots of Portuguese here.

I was half disgusted to have to witness this scene because the Portuguese girl had a child hanging on to her leg, and he was looking at us with the eyes of a small, worried son. Small growling eyes. So I imagined what my child's eyes must be like when someone who's not his father looks at his mother, and I began to pull my friend by the shoulder to make him understand "That's enough, stop it." And since he wasn't taking any notice of me, I began to pull him away more, tugging him: I don't like what you're doing. The mother of a young child deserves respect. And since he kept persisting, I put my mouth near his ear and I said to him: Forget about the girl; she is with her child. But he couldn't care less. Well, you know me, I punched the Jamaican right on the nose. The people around us got scared and called security and those stupid bouncers grabbed me and pushed me out of the door although Jamaica, while he was covering his mouth and spitting blood, kept saying that it was nothing, that we're friends.

The Portuguese girl—or whatever she was—stood there with her child, staring at me intently, wondering if I was crazy or what. But she was also kind of happy because the child was bursting with laughter, hiding behind his Portuguese mother's rear end. And at that point I was very moved because I understood that the little child was just like my son. The way he looked in the pictures you sent me, I swear, exactly alike. The same eyes, the same mouth. And the mother came over to me and asked me: Where are you from, be-

cause her son's father is Ethiopian and she thought I was
Ethiopian too.

* * *

Women with children are like magnets for me.

This happened several months ago; these neighborhoods
are like this, partly Somali and partly Jamaican.

I was sharing a house with a couple, a young man and
a young woman from Jamaica and their child. Living with
them wasn't that bad, she was very nice and her child—ah,
her child, a perfect little gentleman. He liked birds and he
was always at the window looking at them, you know, looking at how they fly in the sky. One day he came back home
with a baby bird, one of those tiny ones that haven't learned
to fly yet.

Do you know what happens to me? When I see children
that do the same things that I used to do, I am transported
back to my childhood, to how I felt in that moment, and that
is why children usually love me so much.

So, this story of the baby bird was the first incident.
Then the child, seeing that the father did not feel like saving
little birds with him, seeing that perhaps he didn't feel like
doing anything with him, began to talk to me all the time,
in a strange way, I don't know how to explain it. As if I were
the father instead of the other. Did the father notice it? Not
really, he was hardly ever home.

The one who noticed was the mother. A mother in love
with how a father who spends time with his son can be,
with how he might play with him. A mother happy at how it
must be to have a man who helps you carry the grocery bags
upstairs, a man who keeps you company while you cook, a
man who can wash his own dirty clothes.

I know how to be a good husband when I'm not the husband? Mean, poisonous remarks, Shukri. Everything came
so naturally to me. Perhaps it was because of my affection
for that child. But a situation of excessive closeness can become dangerous. A story of closeness, cohabitation, a shared
story. Was I blind perhaps? When she said to me, You're
different from the others. All the women who are not my

sweetheart tell me that. Bitter destiny? Because one night I woke up all of a sudden. With my eyes staring into the darkness. Imagine my fright when I found the Jamaican woman all naked next to me. You want to get me killed! I shouted. But I shouted in a mixture of languages, I don't know if she understood. A woman who feels rejected, her body scorned, becomes very mean. She wants revenge. Pouring bleach on my clothes, telling tall tales to her husband.

I couldn't explain clearly how I felt. That she and the child were like one thing for me. Something sacred that should not be profaned. I decide to leave in a hurry. Not out of fear, no, I could have killed the Jamaican man if I had wanted to, but it was because of the child. His eyes, eyes that love birds.

Loneliness, you were saying, keeps you glued to us. Mistaken impressions. Man is constantly turning over and over in his own past, trapped in his imprisonment. But giving up—at this point I have given up. You and the child are two separate things. The time has come to follow other paths. I've crossed so many barren lands. Lands so dry one could not even stick a sharpened piece of wood into them. So much of that time doesn't allow me to forget. Destiny is beyond our reach.

My friends thought I should have given up right away. Male voices that hide a heartfelt truth: Forget about that one, take another one!

For me, Shukri is honey syrup.

Everything began in those years when we were young. Our hearts were innocently pure and all of these things hadn't happened yet. In love with love, rushing to start our life in those uncertain times, we ran away from the city, far away, as far as the ninetieth kilometer, where we could get married without our families' consent.

We didn't feel like trying to convince them, and above all, we had to hurry. A quick marriage. When I took you back home: This girl is clean, my father said, and I was just happy to watch how you washed my clothes with the other girls.

My father used to say: This girl is clean and as tough as a rock, and you washed everything, bent over the round tin washtub, and everyone knew you were with child, but you beat the clothes with all your strength and then stretched them out to dry in the sun.

And my mother scolded me: You good for nothing, move! And you half smiled, generously you washed other women's children with the big jug, and you peeled the garlic for the cooking. With lemon, with lemon, the smell goes away. Then, at night, on one side of the room, you were the only one my father loved to talk to, because of your restraint and your dreams, he preferred to receive food from your hands. She will be the mother of my first heir, he said.

Give up—my friends thought I should have given up right away. Male voices that hide a heartfelt truth. That woman bewitched you.

Women have certain powers.

At the phone center there is a young man who always sits outside. He told me a story.

He told me that he had fallen in love when he was twelve with a girl of his age who lived across the street. Whenever he saw her his heart started beating faster. She would sit there, on the doorstep with her girlfriends, her hair fashioned beautifully, always elegant with ribbons in it. He realized that she loved him too; she would whisper in her friends' ears and keep looking at him. The boy always played soccer with his friends in front of his house and when the ball fell in his beloved's courtyard, he was always the one who went to get it. And she would be there, next to her aunt, looking a bit embarrassed.

And so it happens that in due course the two meet and swear eternal love to each other. The relatives don't say anything because the love between these two young people is of the marrying kind, they speak with restraint, choosing their words, respecting their limits. The years go by and he continues not to kiss her. He thinks he loves her, and he doesn't want to take advantage of her. But the young woman meets another young man. She begins to see the other one for two, three, four weeks, until this newfound relationship is on everyone's lips. The first young man? With teary eyes, he listens to her cutting words, she has had enough, you cannot always behave like child-fiancés. His virility is offended, the young man is desperate and begins to go with many women. But the unexpected happens. A year goes by, and his beloved returns. Does he welcome her back? Does he leap for joy? No, he doesn't want her anymore. He doesn't have another girlfriend, he doesn't want her, period. She had been with another young man who had taken advantage of her.

I am telling you about this young man because he's still there obsessing over this love. Over that beloved, that purity he did not possess. He cannot get her out of his head.

You see, this is what women do. I told him he has the evil eye and needs to get rid of it.

I also gave him that talk about resentment, about becoming a slave to resentment. The same speech that Saciid Saleebaan always gave us, saying that we need to free ourselves from resentment, from resentment against the person who looks at you sideways simply because you are black, and you don't understand why he does that. Everyone is black in your country, why the heck are they staring? I told Saciid Saleebaan that I hated those people, that I wanted to burn their houses down. And he said: No, we who have a land shouldn't poison our lives with resentment, we must help each other to overcome the pain. Saciid Saleebaan, madness of the highest heights, speaks well. He speaks so well that when I listen to him I say to myself I will become a perfect man; but then he goes away and I feel that bitterness again in my throat, so hateful that it makes me spit.

But you know, when I hear from you, it's as if a piece of resentment is broken off.

Treacherous flattery? Shukri, you are obsessed with betrayal. Saciid Saleebaan always reminds you of those photos? But how—tell me—how will I ever be able to dispel your suspicions? Those photos mean nothing. Saciid Saleebaan, who is my friend, would not have shown you compromising photos. The fact that it was you who happened to see them and not he who actually showed them to you doesn't change anything.

But Saciid Saleebaan's photo machine was beautiful, wasn't it? A fully automatic picture-developing machine right there in the center of town, Shebelli, near the Azan Bakery, which was owned by the Italians, yes, I remember: bread, pasta, egg lasagna.

But I was talking about that automatic machine. It did everything by itself, the pictures went around the belt and came out, one at a time, and piled up. Saciid Saleebaan was keeper of the city's secrets: do you remember when we used to go in through the back door and found all the pictures of rich folks' parties? We would recognize the people in the street after seeing them in the pictures! Ah, Saciid Saleebaan and his passion for cameras! He's still obsessed with them: even here he's always filming, and people think he has lost his mind. He speaks to himself and goes around the streets with his video camera. Moving images. And he started out by just developing photos. Entering from the back door to see those photos of the important parties: so many surprises!

Let me say it yet again—Saciid Saleebaan, who is my friend, would not have shown you compromising photos.

Betrayal is far from my mind, believe me, I didn't betray you, not even after I had been looking for you for days. They would tell me: She left without knowing where she was going. I would think of you and our child and I would be overcome with the profound anxiety of my impotence. Thank God you both made it.

Those months when I was barely able to stay alive, when I knew nothing about the two of you, waking up every morning was terrible. My father had taken all the women away from the city. Those who stayed there with the women spent their nights guarding the watermelon field, to defend it from the greedy warthog. The watermelons were precious.

And then there were Saciid Saleebaan and my father. They found a large garden, just the right place. One of them knew about electricity and the other about video cameras. So, with a video recorder and a generator they built a cinema that was good enough for wartime. People came, and cassettes were available. Indian and Chinese films that made us understand their ways of doing battle. Melodrama and revenge. A profitable business in wartime.

The city was worse. In the morning when you woke up there was only that dirty water and a bit of coal. We would sit there all day drinking the dark brown tea, glossy as varnish. The only thing that grew—work of the devil—was hashish, a thought-sedative, a painkiller for body spasms and an antidote against ghosts. One day a woman came to see us; she was tall and very light-skinned with the bony frame of a strong woman. She was looking for food. Fearful, defeated. *Shayddaan* fakes shyness. I understood too late that she was a spirit-woman. A woman who wrapped herself around me. That was the only time. But that betrayal is the work of the *shayddaan*.

Faithless woman, you only remember religion when it serves your purpose.

Yes, like that day at dawn: I was woken by the voice of the *wadaad*.

You say: Where I am it's lunchtime, I've been looking for you for days. The heck with your tricks! When you want to find a person, I'm telling you, you can certainly do so.

That morning, in the shadow of deep sleep, I was still in the other world and the three of you there, at the phone center, I can just imagine you crammed into that booth. And then, those booths at the phone centers stink, they reek of saliva and melancholy, the exact same smell everywhere, right?

How did all three of you manage to fit in? You, the *wadaad*, and the witness, I mean, Xassan, that dirty old man, of all people—I don't want to know. Only you could do such a thing. I was there sleeping peacefully and this voice from the other end of the world wakes me up, "*Salaam calaykum,* peace be with you brother, is this Taageere?"

I swear, it sounded like the voice of the archangel; I thought I had died.

Instead it was a venerable religious minister calling me at dawn, "Good morning, *Allahu Akbar.* I have your wife here next to me. She came to me because you're not passing her any money to support herself and your son. She's asking to be repudiated."

What does one say to a *wadaad* who wakes you up when in his part of the world everyone is fully awake and functioning? I was asleep, praise God, I was asleep.

I said to him: Wait, I want to talk to her first. Then I said: No, I don't want to, in a broken voice.

And what did you do, honey voice? You who can never find me, who never knows where to find me, you call me again, at night. You couldn't care less about the fact that I was sleeping: work of the *shayddaan*!

Your words, I can recite them to you by heart: You know how difficult it is for a woman on her own, with a child. It's not that I want a separation, no. But every time I need to give him a pill, every time I give the school permission for a field trip, every time I have to sign my name so that he can breathe, they ask about you, about his father, about your seal of approval.

I, I just can't go on living in this hell of your unjustifiable absence, at least allow me to sign his papers without having to ask for permission from four judges. If—may Allah forgive me—something serious were to happen one day, we would run the risk of being crushed by time.

I believed you, woman, you malevolent spirit. But you, you only said that to trick me. Did you tell this to your *wadaad*? That poor man did what he could, he tried to get you to change your mind. He tried his best, if what you tell me is true. He took you aside and talked to you about my love, about my broken voice that didn't know how to express itself.

What could he do in the end except tell me with the voice of authority, "Repeat the formula of the *fasakh* three times, repeat it three times."

And while I, tricked by you, was repeating the dissolution formula three times and heard the *wadaad* pass the phone receiver around so that everyone could hear that I was repeating it three times, I can imagine what you were doing. You were there laughing with satisfaction.

You were laughing, work of the *shayddaan,* because you could go off free and happy to do whatever you wanted. Remarry, even marry a *gaal*!

But have you perhaps forgotten that a repudiated woman doesn't have the same value?

It's futile for you to tell me that it was all a waste of time. I don't believe you. Who would believe it? That in Italy they do not recognize decisions based upon laws different from theirs or by judges that are not their own? Making life difficult for me is your favorite pastime. If something is valid before God, it's valid in the face of any other law. It has to be that way. Repudiate you, I did repudiate you, how can you say that there is no way to communicate this to the Italians? What I want is my marital status in writing. Next thing you'll say is that I am dead. Dead!

Give me a few more minutes.

You speak about freedom. But thinking only about oneself is not freedom. People always judge you. They judge you and they reject you. You want the freedom of not having to talk to me again. Freedom to erase me from all the official papers, from my son's blood. Our son, as long as he is a child, will always have to go through you and you alone.

When I reached the neighborhood in Mogadishu where you were living with our child and I couldn't find you, I was stuck there, just thinking, for all the thirteen months or so that went by. Then I found out you were alive. I was sitting drinking the dark, glossy tea. My father arrived, I wasn't expecting him. I thought he was bringing bad news. Instead, he had been to the airport where that acquaintance of his works. He had been telling everyone your names for months in order to find out if you were someplace, in the camps in Kenya, who knows where.

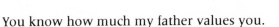

You know how much my father values you.

He arrived and he had that dirty envelope in his hand, dirty from so much traveling, the photo of you and our child against a background of shiny fabric. It looked like one of those photos that Saciid Saleebaan used to take of his clients. You with the baby in your arms looking like he was about to jump out, toward me, with his little feet planted against your arm. With those sad eyes of yours and your head covered in the *bluug* scarf.

You were skinny and your eyes had a very old color, like varnish. Instead, the child was all light, with fat, chubby cheeks. I thought then, my father was right, you are as hard as a rock. Only rocks have children like that. The picture was a bit stained and on the back were your words: You were in Mombasa, you were both well and how were we doing?

So my father said to me: The first one to leave must be you, because he didn't want you to be alone with the child. Again and again he went to the airport to cut a deal. I already told you how he made me get on a small plane full of *jaat*. I had some presents for my wife and child and they threw down my bag shouting: Did I think I was a tourist? They were right, I did not need those gifts after all.

But how could I have known that day that my wife and child were no longer where they had told me they would be and that you, exhausted and in silent desperation, had joined your relatives in Ethiopia? Paths chasing other paths. Italy, a stop on my route. You had come wanting to join me there, but I had just left. Retracing our wanderings I find paths that you did not follow. You already know what I think. When you arrived in Italy, everyone was already running away from there, everyone left as soon as they could. Everyone but you, you, my wife. Everyone goes where he or she can. I didn't want to stay in that country, you were the one who was supposed to come with me.

After a few years I settled in America while you two were still in Italy. You learned Italian along with our child, you could have done that here, even your brother said that this is a better place than the one where you settled. All right, children must be respected. Respecting them does not mean keeping them—implanted seeds—far from their fathers. A child has only one father and our child is only nine years old, even if he has never seen me in his life, nine years can be made up! You say that you are no longer eighteen like you were when we met. You never really wanted to join me, never, even if I was waiting for you, Shukri, I really was. He has never seen my face, but you have forgotten it too, you have erased it too.

I feel I can talk to you, from here, with renewed energy. That's why I asked you for some documents I might need. I never told you how I found myself again. About the time when, in my pointless wanderings, I was so full of rage that I couldn't understand that it wasn't rage but disgust. I was disgusted with myself for not being able to connect again.

Until one day, by mere chance, I happened to be at a wedding, a party for women who want to be filmed in order to find suitors. Outside, by mere chance. As time goes by, you let yourself just live, no defense, no reaction. So, as I was telling you, there I am, and the girls are going by, dressed to the nines, but I, with my cigarette, don't notice them at all.

I am there with my cigarette and I see a light-skinned girl coming out of the door leading to the party, she has a video camera around her neck, khaki pants with side pockets and a cap, yes, an American-style cap. She shakes her head, then from her pants pocket she pulls out her cigarettes, do you have a light?

You already know, don't you? For me, with my mentality, a girl like that doesn't have a chance. Instead, there I am, I want to listen, to drink in her voice, hear her talk about what's right and what isn't. Because she has thought about a lot of things, a lot.

Domenica, a girl I barely mentioned earlier. An Italian-Somali, *iska-dhal*, born-together, born-mixed. That's why she has seen so much of that world of ours: we are like pilgrims on this planet, she says.

Why am I talking to you about her? Suddenly I felt the dream again, the desire for a home. You threw me out, I finally accepted it. Was I meant to wait for you my whole life? I felt the need, Shukri, the need for that woman. Of that world of hers, that world of ours poured into her eyes. Yes, like water from a spring. I married her, I remarried.

This is the only way I could tell you. I don't beat around the bush. And then, as soon as I remarried—the hand of destiny—Luul arrived in Italy.

Luul, my sister who had landed in Italy by boat. I wanted to join her. Domenica and I tried to register our marriage. It seemed like the easiest way to get a visa to come to Italy. Married to an Italian, an Italian after her own fashion.

This man appears to still be married, they told us.

So Domenica left on her own. Now she's in Italy, staying with my aunt and uncle, Diriiye Yuusuf and his wife, Safiya.

We should meet? I would like that. To see my son again, to return to the land of the woman destined to be my love. But how?

You have one minute.

Oh no, did you hear the message? We're out of time. Only one minute. I beg you, call me back, call me back. We still have to tell each other . . .

4

AXAD

MY DEAR BARNI, THERE'S NOTHING left of the person I was when you knew me. You must have heard something about me from someone. News about these past years, about what happened to me. Even the way I express myself, the way I speak, has changed considerably. As they say, those of us of mixed blood are like sponges. Mixed travelers. There were so many languages I had to learn, that I wanted to learn, in one place or another, to get inside people. Because, you know, after all, it's the same old story everywhere. Inside our Somali homes, completely wrapped up in ourselves, you could even ignore what was around you. Ignore the temperature of the air, take no notice of other voices, live only among ourselves and learn only the very bare minimum.

In the beginning, like a soap bubble carried by the wind, I tried to find my direction again, leaving it to chance.

What I should do is tell you when everything started. In this airport, in this city of Rome, with Libeen by my side. The trauma of war, interconnected paths. If only I had met up with you before. But no, this is the right moment.

The beginning: the insanity of feeling lost. My story that I had put aside, a story of so many separations. I left you, my sister, I left and I erased everything with a single stroke. Nine years old, we were nine and ten when we last saw each other. Do you remember? Did we ever imagine that we would find each other again today, more than twenty years later? But strong ties of affection are made of deeper stuff. They endure.

Twenty years, I was saying, cut in half.

The first half: a life here in Italy shaped by forgotten things. I quickly erased the Somali language. That's what our mind does: it removes things, it locks things up in closets. With my mother, far from my father. I needed to quickly disengage myself from my old world, I needed to erase one territory from my mind to build a new one. Missing points of reference. I patched together things here and there. My father's absence. Patches that, sooner or later, would come unstitched. Glimmers of light, Barni, when I dreamed about you. Always the same dream: I would arrive, but I never managed to see you. But that person wasn't really you. A face changing shape. Then, even my dreams left me. I lived by camouflaging myself.

The second half of the last twenty years? The usual life of the diaspora, aimless peregrinations. How did this come about? I was telling you about my last trip. I arrived in a city that was on the verge of evacuation, my native Mogadishu. It was Libeen who saved me. From panic, from desperation. We left for Rome together, on the last scheduled flight. To stay over just for a short time. At that point, my destiny was his destiny. I languished, a persistent pain that made me dizzy. With no respite. At night, my eyes were wide open. The hours ticked by like a small scalpel chiseling away at my flesh, bit by bit. I searched within myself trying to find the roots of my existence. I wanted to reclaim it, in a disorderly fashion. My life has always lacked order. Now, perhaps, some peace. By telling you about all of my different adopted identities.

* * *

Taageere: Is he the one you are most curious about? As the story progresses, you might find some answers. Maybe we both will? I was falling apart in Rome in this delirious state. Rome, a completely new city for me that I have now come back to again. So different from the small provincial town where I had lived before, an Italian provincial town full of certainties. Instead, this city ignored me. No schedule, no familiar places. I wandered around and the street names meant nothing to me. I looked at the people and I felt ashamed. I, who was so miserably out of place, could not find the root of so much pain. Me, in my insignificance. You know, I was disgusted with myself, how can I put it? That sadness that has no name, with no way out. The truth is that inside of me, deep down, I felt empty to the very core. What had become of me? What meaning did my life have now?

A blinding flash of light, a pause: for me, Domenica, living one day of war in Mogadishu meant being reborn, changing skin, being reincarnated. Could I go back to living as I had done before? Living in a provincial town with my fiancé, having Sunday dinners? Getting married, having children, finding peace in monotony? Life sometimes means asking oneself too many questions.

My eyes are stinging, tears are on the way, I'm choking up, a dry sob: can this be the effect of asking too many questions? But no, I didn't want to cry; rather I wanted to raise my skin. Any sharp object would do. To cut myself, to see the color of blood. A spider's web of marks on the surface of my skin. Many people asked me what I had done to myself. I shuddered: the revelation of secrets. But you know, I felt so detached. I could not speak. My arms were covered in long sleeves, only my hands were visible, my carved hands.

Libeen kept me close to him, as much as he could. He felt responsible for me. What surprised me is that he never wondered about my ties to Italy. For Libeen all that mattered was that I had left Mogadishu with him and that was that. Same destiny. This is probably why it all began. At the Termini train station, I started out from zero along with everybody else. From that crossroads, coagulation of grief, the threshold of oblivion.

I hardly remember anything about that journey. The thing was, Libeen was traveling with fake documents and I wasn't supposed to think about it. My documents, Italian documents, were accepted anytime, anywhere. They are rock-solid documents. Libeen? Different picture, different face. I kept thinking, they will notice. But to Customs officials black faces are all the same. But I still thought they would notice. Libeen was changing his name, forever.

I continued to call him by his own name, his real name. Try to imagine each border crossing. I was afraid as well. I was afraid of being searched, and yet afraid that no one would search for me. Did anyone wonder where I had ended up? For sure, they did. Call my mother? Cell phones were not in use yet, very few people had one. I could disappear, and perhaps risk being reported missing. But that would take some time. My mother was still at the airport waiting for me. Many, so many years have gone by. Write, yes, I do write to her: I invent things, because she already lives a life of desperation. Speak to her, rarely. Interrupted calls, unintelligible voices. Perhaps I am the one who has given up communicating. Because I still hear that demanding voice. The one that keeps asking only things what she can relate to: Are you studying? Who do you live with? What about work? Over the years, she stopped asking me questions. Questions that have no context. The trouble is, this put a barrier between us. No one, it was no one's fault. Because, even though she might not have known how to ask, I didn't know how to answer. At some point she gave up. She calls only now and then, just to make sure I'm alive. Because to her I have become a dead daughter. A daughter who died without a funeral. And Taariikh, my father? It makes me so angry. Angry at defeat, at giving up without a fight. Because too many times I dreamed that he was going to join me. To unite those two worlds. But he didn't want to, or perhaps I didn't allow him to, I am not sure. I remember her face, the gracefulness of my mother. Here's her picture. But it was taken almost ten years ago. What she looked like, what I looked like. Would you still recognize me? Our paths diverged so much from one another, I wish they could finally meet, in the middle. Now I am back here, but she doesn't know.

But I was talking about Libeen. Libeen and I in a car heading north. An old, beat-up car, a Lancia Y-10 repainted light blue. A leaden sky and that dry winter air that he was experiencing for the first time. The white north speeding toward us. Crisp whiteness and I, snuggled up in the car, wrapped in a light blue blanket, a gift from the airline. The softness of travel, no word spoken, I was emptying my mind. In my bag, within reach, a small tube of medication, scar cream to heal my cobwebs. There were so many things I wanted to hear; Libeen would tell me all about it later. About our projects, about our future. About how everything would always be unforeseeable. In the meantime the landscape changed. Piedmont and the Swiss lakes. Germany and fast, straight thruways. The oaks in the forests. I thought of how impenetrable it must once have been. And I thought of man dominating nature out of his fear of death. Contain and survive? But controlling and looking ahead, doesn't this perhaps mean killing oneself? And I could have stopped off anywhere, it would have made no difference. What has been: passing by one sees so much of life and, a little here, a little there, everything seems so very attractive. As long as you avoid the risk of everything becoming commonplace, a prison of immobility. The Netherlands, our final destination. Fields, the monotony of fields, and an unmistakable density. That's where we would settle down, Libeen and I.

* * *

Libeen and I: nine years of shared childhood. There are ties, established in the cradle, that can never be weakened. Libeen, the son of my father's brother, my own brother, almost.

Libeen who sips his Fanta orange drink when everyone else is already done. Meticulously, objects used parsimoniously, while the rest of us rush to consume them. The first one to finish his homework, even just to have the pleasure of mocking us.

Libeen caught up in the fashionable hobby of the moment of raising homing pigeons. A little wooden house with many little doors. That's where the pigeons come back to, to the food that awaits them. And the eggs they lay, we cannot touch the eggs so we don't alter their smell. That nauseating smell of excrement that doesn't bother him.

Libeen who talked us all into pooling our resources to buy a leather ball. The sandy streets of the Bondheere neighborhood: our soccer field. We, the little children, watch, our backs up against the walls of the houses, squatting down in the shade, we watch the children who are just a little older playing soccer.

I think: Taageere grew up in Bondheere too. Who knows, perhaps he was among those children, asking to play with the same ball.

Who knows? Perhaps he too was among the children who used to split their sides laughing when my mother went by, yelling at the top of their lungs: *Gaal-gaal, gaal-gaal, gaal-gaal.* Almost lying flat down on the ground, mixing the sand with their hands. *Gaal-gaal, gaal-gaal, gaal-gaal.* Were they really having that much fun?

Libeen. Memories mixed with gratitude. Toward the one who had saved me. The one I wanted to learn everything from, hanging on to his every word. The forgotten Somali language. Every day I jotted down words in my notebook, verbs I needed to memorize. A Western habit, Libeen said. In his opinion you can only learn from the spoken word. Was he mocking me? You know, for him I was like clay, something to be molded. I was something that belonged to him. He cared little about my past experiences. This is something I understood much later. In the early days, he was my wellspring. I drank from it, without a thought.

I remember that party.

It was a beautiful wedding celebration, one of those where we're all together. Not like the usual party with women on one side and men on the other. There were even some Westerners present. Every time I tried to remark how absurd these celebrations were, all the women lashed out at me!

"It's obvious your mother is a *gaal.*"

That was the long and the short of it: Clearly your mother is a *gaal.* You're a half-white who doesn't know how a woman should behave.

Enough to shut anyone up. Can you believe it! But dance, they dance fabulously. Just women, their hips tightly wrapped in their *garbasaar.* The ass seems to be something separate. Unbelievably sexy if it weren't for the size. Size is the prejudice of a half-Western woman, you say? That's not what Somali men like. Somali men like undulating flesh, young and firm. *Sida, sida, sida,* and they keep on going, damp with sweat, almost touching the ground. Dancing among women is fine. But video-recording the dance to find a husband somewhere in the world, is that fine too? The video camera focused on those undulating hips, the men who will watch them, feeling up the screen. The amateur cameramen excited by seeing so much. But they can, actually they have to be able to go in. Otherwise, who would shoot the video?

But women-only parties are not my thing. If I have to dance for someone, I do it, freely. That evening at that mixed party we were all on the dance floor, and I was having a grand time. I danced, I danced a lot. I love dancing.

Until, at a certain point, a woman came up behind me, tapping my sweaty skin, as if she were knocking, on my shoulder.

"Sister, do you know that you're naked?" she whispered.

My friend, Ayaan the wild one, was in front of me, she immediately came up to us: Sure she knows! She sure remembers which dress she put on! This is a new dress that cost her a hundred and fifty dollars. That neckline that you see is worth one hundred and fifty dollars.

She took my side. But my desire to dance had suddenly vanished. With my dress the color of a ripe plum. A long dress, a sheath covering my body. I looked for Libeen with my eyes. He was there, not far away, chuckling. Alone at a table, a cigarette in his hand, and a mocking expression on his face. He had been watching me, never taking his eyes off me, from the very beginning. As if my body belonged to him. So I went over to him and asked. Why? Smoke blown in my face.

"You behave like a *gaal*," he told me. "A *gaal* shows you a leg, like this, her back. Her body has no value. But dreaming about a woman is different. A man dreams of her whole beautiful body, all for himself. You can't see, but you can dream."

I was listening to everything, to all of his words. I was hanging from his eyes. I sat near him and he ran his finger down my back, "Cover it. Put on a *garbasaar,*" he told me.

Was he getting fresh with me?

You have to understand, I admired him. A man who knew what he wanted, who had adjusted quickly. Libeen, a worldly man, *ilbax,* his eye on the future. He worked with computers and spoke English very well, much better than I ever did. And he joked, he joked with the *gaal.* He understood what made them laugh, their sense of humor, he got it.

"As long as you're with me, you mustn't work," he told me. And I stayed on with him, we were inseparable.

But the tie that bound us, the nature of that tie, left us free. We had no obligations to each other. Consistent, Libeen certainly wasn't.

Barni, how can I explain it? Desire like that is like a burning flame. I felt I was living for him, I was alive because he had wanted me to be. Pleasing him: my audacity. I had left my suitcase at the airport in Rome. I kept going, adapting myself along the way.

Ayaan the wild one, for instance, sought out my friendship. Perhaps because she didn't feel judged by me. Libeen didn't like Ayaan. An emancipated woman who provoked him. Ayaan who smoked in public, dyed her hair auburn red and used blood-red lipstick, her lips petals of flesh. Hanging around with her, I too had started to smoke, dye my hair auburn red, and wear flesh-colored lipstick.

Libeen shook his head, without saying a word, just like this. Until that night, the day of the party. Disapproval? Everyone disapproved of Ayaan and me, of both of us. But I only cared about Libeen's opinion.

One morning I woke up early. My hair needs a lot of care. Combing through the conditioner, a softness that runs through it, a weekly treatment. Once it was dry, I gathered it into a single braid and slipped it all under a veil. The first one I found, almost cream-colored.

When Libeen woke up, I was already in the kitchen waiting for him. A toasty smell in the air, he sat next to me with his cup of coffee in his hands. Searching for my feet hidden under my dress, he didn't seem to have noticed my veil.

But from then on I kept wearing it, every day, and I stopped wearing such provocative lipstick. Ayaan thought Libeen had talked me into it. She couldn't fully understand our relationship. Neither could I.

Smoking, I kept on smoking. One day I was at the bus stop. I had a lighted cigarette hidden in the palm of my hand. Libeen saw me from way off. So I threw it away, instinctively, I don't know why. Libeen never used to scold me. With my hand I looked in my purse for the little bottle of *catar* Ayaan had given me to perfume my fingers. And as he was getting closer, I pulled out a stick of mint gum.

"Would you like one?" I asked without even greeting him. He smiled that confident smile of his.

"Are you a believer now, Axad?" I lowered my eyes, ashamed. He dominated me. I still had those scars on my arms.

"Think about it, Axad. You can become a believer if you want to. But remember. Two months ago you used to dye your hair red. You were a redhead. You wore revealing clothes. Not to mention your lips."

Then he started. He had a story to tell me to make me laugh.

He said he was waiting for the subway on the way home when he saw a woman a few feet away. She was completely covered in gray, from head to toe, with a *tusbax* in her hand. Nothing strange so far. Then she started up in a loud voice, *Allahu Akbar!* Every two seconds, *Allahu Akbar!* He wanted to laugh.

He said that people are convinced they are doing their duty, with their *salli* under their arms, "it's time, it's time" everywhere, as they unroll their mats to pray. Libeen continues to tell me this story to make me laugh, "And then, I shouldn't say so, but with their rear ends up in the air, in front of everyone. That's really crass."

"So then what?" I asked. And he, trying to keep up with all my questions.

"How do you say 'trend' in Italian? Trendy? That's it, religion is now trendy."

Then suddenly he got serious, "Do you follow trends too?"

I was like a small creature caught in the act.

"Come home with me," he said, his hand tight around my wrist.

I always acquiesced. I always followed him.

Sitting in front of the mirror I looked at him behind my shoulders while he untied the knot of my veil—a pink veil, a delicate color—and loosened my braid. He ran his fingers through my hair.

I spent more than two years depending on him. On the brink: intermittent worries. Until something happened. Our unhealthy relationship had to come to an end. One night we were in the car together. It was our nightly ritual. Every evening Libeen took me for a car ride. We would roam around aimlessly, we would go downtown to have something to drink, without even getting out of the car to go for a stroll. The air was too cold. I felt cradled by this habit. But that evening Libeen was nervous, I can't quite explain it. Usually he was the one who spoke. This time, instead, he kept quiet.

"Libeen, where are you taking me?"

"You must be patient," he answered.

Then, while we were getting closer to the neighborhood, he told me he was going to see a woman friend, a divorcée. Divorcée: that was the exact word he used. I was supposed to wait for him in the car for ten minutes. Only ten minutes, he would make that do. Just ten minutes to set up a date.

I, my dear Barni, didn't say anything, not a word. And he didn't ask me if I had anything to say either. So many things. The meaning of those ten minutes. You see: everything was falling apart. Perhaps this was Libeen's way of trying to separate himself from me. Because, had he wanted to, he could have easily found those ten minutes at any other time. Libeen knew perfectly well that I would get out of that car, that he would not find me waiting for him.

What happened next: I went alone to the one place waiting for me. Ayaan, the wild one, was my only friend. Libeen knew that, that's why he felt safe. He waited and then he tried to call me again. But even this halfheartedly. If only he had wanted it—but I feel inside of me that he did not want this—if only he had wanted it, I would have returned to our house immediately. It was for the best that I didn't go back.

Our phone calls? Libeen and I from the Netherlands: do you remember? We called you all the time. I thought it would be that way forever, Libeen and I together. Living cut off from him meant returning to my other life. You, Barni, didn't see me during the month I spent with him in Rome. I didn't even have the strength to mourn the death of Aunt Xaliima with you all. Other mourning? I have my regrets. I was sick from too much loneliness. Libeen, from the first moment, protected me. We were both too complicit. Today I think it was supposed to be that way, out of necessity. I and my own path. With Libeen I felt I was constantly convalescing. I had to heal, I had to lick my wounds alone.

Ayaan, the wild one, lived in an empty apartment when I went to stay with her. She had just left her husband. So much intensity, so many lives.

Ayaan loved her husband. They had gotten married with everyone's blessing, the relatives were happy. It seemed unbelievable that the wild one had settled down. Ayaan was redeeming herself. She had been astute enough to fall in love with a young man with the same genealogy. Had it happened purely by chance? You know, Ayaan had had many boyfriends, but he was the only one she wanted to marry. Even the wedding was organized in the proper way. But she had paid for everything. With drops of sweat, hard work at the fast-food restaurant. Did the husband work? Only one week a month. The rest of the time he pretended to be studying. He chewed *jaat* all night long and, in the end, all day long as well. That was his life. But Ayaan didn't care, she was so infatuated with him. What mattered was that from that point on she would be a woman in strict accordance with the rules, married to an approved young man, no small feat. Her husband was a simple, open guy. They had met in a disco, Ayaan was wearing a nice evening gown, low-cut and with a train at the bottom. Just imagine. After they got married he began to act like a traditional man. He had expectations. Ayaan, an independent woman who supported herself, was supposed to wear a veil and have children. Who was going to support them? That was the least of her worries. Even her mother and sister-in-law had started pressuring her in a heavy-handed way.

You know about Ayaan? The wild one, an armored leopard. What I saw: sparks flying. We were twenty-three years old at the time, with a passion for life. Ayaan was not the submissive type. She was tough on the outside, looked hostile, but she was a softy inside.

Her husband? *Berri,* tomorrow, was his favorite word. Why can't you find a job? *Berri.* Why don't you get a driver's license? *Berri.* Why don't you ask your father if he can get us some furniture apart from this mattress on the floor? *Berri.* And from one tomorrow to the next, what he never tired of telling her was what his priorities were. Ayaan was not the type to put up with that.

Her husband had already been kicked out a long time before I moved in with her. Having been kicked out a long time before didn't prevent him from blaming me for the failure of his marriage. I, according to Ayaan's husband, was the *iska-dhal*, mixed-blood, the *missioni* who had led his wife astray, when, in fact, it was Ayaan who certainly was better able to lead. To a Somali man it's always another woman who leads his wife to perdition. But for me, at that point, everything was still very new. Ayaan's husband and his ambushes, a daily challenge.

I tell you, the scenes he created in front of cafés, the commotion and the punches he gave his imaginary rivals. I've never met anyone so insanely jealous. And I was only a pretext; never once did he dare insult me to my face.

Who did we used to see? For a certain period of time, a group of Italian-Somalis who lived in the city center. I was curious to find out how they had solved their dilemma. They were full of contradictions.

There were three of us who went around together, Ayaan, a certain Marina, and me. We were continually buzzing around Luca, a fearless young Italian-Somali man. I was not part of the game, I was so mixed up with my detachments, constantly thinking of Libeen and his disapproving ways.

That was the way Ayaan was when she was consumed by a new passion; when she set her mind on something, there was no dissuading her. Her lifestyle? She was a liberated woman; she enjoyed pleasure and her own body without any taboos. There was no vulgarity in her carefree lifestyle. She was the one who used men. I don't know if you follow me. She found attracting young men exciting, she liked making out under the stairs, but nothing more. Luca? A target for both her and Marina. But Ayaan was much more experienced in the art of seduction. What can I say? Luca was bound to fall for her, and consequently Marina left the threesome, joining a group of other Italian-Somali women. The aftermath? Marina and the Italian-Somali women confronted Ayaan and demanded that she keep her hands off their men. Their men, the Italian-Somali men! I know, I know, it seems hard to believe. My dear Barni, the truth of the matter, though sad, is that when the going gets tough, we all claim to belong to a group.

But Ayaan was not easily frightened. That girl: a mixture of lightness and heaviness.

Lightness. Ayaan had run into Marina again after a few months. She had not immediately recognized her, because Marina had gotten really fat. Marina, on the other hand, seeing Ayaan from afar had immediately run toward her with a broad smile on her face. What had happened to her? Had she forgotten how they had parted? Marina, Marina, Marina, she had married Luca right away. Had she been able to keep her man? Sure, at that point she was even pregnant. About to pop any second. And Luca? He was in Italy for work. Ayaan, no, she's not mean-spirited; she's not one to criticize a pregnant woman for being slovenly. But there was one thing that made her feel completely vindicated: the smell of *suugo* on Marina's clothes, on her hair, her skin. Hey, she had to say goodbye to her quickly in order not to suffocate! Ayaan who knows the names of all the expensive perfumes by heart, who taught me how to scent my house and my clothes with incense and myrrh, Ayaan who never left the house without a small bottle of *catar* in her purse.

Heaviness. When I went to live with Ayaan I began to work. A series of jobs, whatever I could find: teaching Italian, waitressing in a pizza parlor. I easily found jobs with a connection to Italy, to that part of me that didn't have anything to do with the way I looked: in those places they didn't ask many questions. All I needed to do was state where I came from. Of course, Libeen had offered me money. But I couldn't accept it. Was he trying to keep me dependent on him?

After a year of canoodling, Ayaan met a young man with whom she wanted to settle down. An unbalanced story of hiding places. Ayaan was abandoning our world without having the courage to talk about it. The young man lived far away and dreamed, like everybody else, of moving to London.

All I had left was our empty apartment.

Did I at last have a good excuse to go back to Libeen? I felt tempted, yet ambivalent.

But indirectly Libeen himself dissuaded me, "Go to my sister's in London. Shamsa is in London with her children and she would be happy to see you."

He was still manipulating me.

Do you know about those years? What I can't do is describe those places. It was a continuous internal movement from one apartment to the next. Exist, one could exist anywhere. For me, for all of us, it didn't matter where. You simply had to get used to a different set of store signs, different prices, and draw up a new map: a map of your links to the others, and of the junction places where we could meet, where we could call, where we could shop, as if we were constantly carried along in an air bubble, and inside that bubble was our sound, our smell. Sounds and smells so strong that they masked all others. By alienating ourselves, we continued to live.

Libeen had sent me to take some classes. I attended diligently; it was my daily point of reference. I attended those classes, but I could just have easily prayed or brushed my teeth or eaten at that same time. It helped to impart a rhythm to my days. But I couldn't care less about those classes.

"What would you like to be?" Libeen used to ask me. A clear-cut question but a confused answer. Libeen decided for me. He imagined me as a reporter, capturing images. I have always been good at making myself invisible. That's probably why his idea was insightful.

Well, these are the places. Telling you about them is so difficult. But with a video camera perhaps it becomes possible to tame those overwhelming smells and sounds. So, far from Libeen, I started to use the video camera, a present from him that I had left on top of the closet in its original packaging. I was now leaving the Netherlands; I was saying goodbye to that place. Libeen's territory, so dominated by his presence, his protection, his opinion. A place I was leaving to go to Shamsa's.

Barni, you, Shamsa, and Libeen grew up together, the three of you are like siblings. Telling this story is very, very limiting. Living it is so much more. It's what I felt I saw. Because far from Libeen, I challenged myself. And Shamsa, my cousin, needed help. She was in London temporarily, like me. How many people did I meet over the years who were only temporarily in a country, but who stayed far too long to define it as temporary? What Shamsa wanted to do was run away from her husband. She could go where everyone else went, to London. But had Shamsa thought things through? I said to her, "Shamsa, your children. You have been living in Finland for many years. Think about what they have learned, what you have achieved." And she made a face. When I think of her I see a smear of badly applied lipstick and windows perpetually covered in steam. Could this be as a result of the cold weather she used to tell me about? The thing was, without knowing those places, I imagined them so differently, I imagined spectacular views.

Shamsa was running away from her husband, from so much desperation, so much loneliness. Just imagine it, Barni, with all those children. I don't know much about children, but I do know one thing for sure and that is that I love them, with a love fueled by infinite patience. A life with many children was fine for me. But, I say this—I say it for myself, I say it on behalf of all of us women—just being one thing and nothing else all the time, and being all alone in this world, is a situation no one can bear. And this is what I came to understand being with Shamsa, because I knew nothing about that kind of life, but it was with her that I saw children living independently, like adults, but with hearts as soft as butter. The problem was that Shamsa had so many children and no one to help her. To help her, I'm saying, but just for lack of a better word.

Just imagine, even just ten minutes in the bathroom: you wash up in a hurry because you're afraid the children might get hurt and the two younger ones are peeking at you in the tub while you sing a song to keep them there near you. The song continues and you keep your eyes on the boiling pot: careful—so many children get scalded by boiling water—don't trip on the little one who is walking in between your legs. And when you need to go out, even just to buy milk, in that cold and all the milk this brood drinks, your husband disappears without telling you and you haven't yet resigned yourself to planning a life without him, without him and without a single person from home.

Run away. Shamsa had found the courage to run away. I, sent by Libeen, was going to rescue her. As you know, I stayed until she went back to Finland. Her husband talked her into it. I couldn't meddle. During the course of those months, being around the children, their joy taught me a lot. I saw Shamsa regain her strength.

She constantly sought my presence. As if she could no longer live without me. Was she once again afraid of her past loneliness? I asked myself, how did she do it before? How did she do it after? Friends? A mother's schedule does not allow for new friendships, and there are more than enough old ones to nurture as it is. In London Shamsa felt better; she found faces from home, so many Somalis in that city. London was where everyone was going.

I don't think she wanted to get rid of her husband. What she wanted to do was for him to change, that was it, and he wanted her back, too. Shamsa had given him many children, and he wanted to take care of their education. I was overcome with disgust, but God forbid I say anything. Because when he talked about education, he meant taking the boys to the mosque. Now that they were older he was the only one who could take care of that, right?

Shamsa believed him, I could see that. All he had to do was mention religion. When he called in the evening, the two of us were awake enjoying that one hour of freedom, of peace and quiet. I painted her toenails. And Shamsa told her husband that with me there she had even found the time to put on lipstick again before going out. After all, Shamsa was amazing, not one of those mothers who in the morning scream like madwomen to hurry their children along. I've seen a lot of those. She, instead, used to sing. She sang and spoke softly. No scolding: the children knew very well that they should not make her life difficult. They moved around quietly. I only saw them acting wild when their father was with them. A wise balance.

What I know for sure is that Shamsa was not convinced when she left for London. It took very little, too little, time for her to be persuaded to change her mind. Her husband used to call at midnight and she became restless. What she needed was to have something to do, a reason to prefer one place over another. But without roots—without a prevailing reason to be there—a place loses its importance. Having me there wasn't enough. That's why I helped her move again, move back to the place where her children were born. How many times did I see her again over the following years? Three, perhaps four. The last time I saw her was in America during her trip there. She didn't look well; she looked haggard and her nail polish was chipped. Was she unhappy? The first thing I noticed was her laughter, it sounded hollow. She had lost her zest for life. I was with Taageere that day; you know him and his silly theories. As if a glass of milk and honey a day were enough to ruin Shamsa. Taageere spoke as if he had uncovered a diabolical plot. As if her husband, in order to isolate Shamsa and keep her all to himself, had fattened her up with milk and honey. The modern version of a metropolitan ogre? *Dadqalato,* I suddenly remembered this word. *Dadqalato,* cutthroat, bogeyman, concocted to make sure we did not stray too far from home. Shamsa, who must have been eleven or twelve at the time—five years older than me—telling me a scary story. She tells me of how they have released all the madmen from the asylum in Mogadishu and of how three *dadqalato,* roaming freely around the city, had disguised themselves as taxi drivers in order to kidnap beautiful, plump girls and cook them on a spit after cutting them up with sharp knives. *Dadqalato,* cab drivers with bloodshot eyes, or the poor drifter Cali Dhareerow, drooling Ali, that we terrified children trailed singing: *Cali Dhareerow, xaggee u jeeddaa;* Drooling Ali, where are you going—and then my memory fails me.

But—by demystifying it—I think I uncovered the root of Shamsa's sickness. You, Barni, will help me see clearly. My way of reasoning is convoluted and it alienates me from other people. I articulate and develop my thinking by becoming rigid and isolating myself. It's my fear of being a burden. Time—the time spent traveling—has helped me. Little by little my thoughts become clear and I find again, here and there, my own way, without having to pretend to be someone else. What was weighing heavily on me during those months—when I took Shamsa's children to school, when I went to buy her medications, when I helped her clean the house—was a suspicion that was subtly insinuating itself into my thoughts. I couldn't figure out why my people that I considered so supportive were leaving Shamsa to her own devices. You see, then the whole story of our solidarity was shaking under my feet like Jello. It shook and it made the foundation of my beliefs shake, the reason why I had come running to help Shamsa, without questioning anything. I had mistaken solidarity for a cultural trait. But what culture does not strive for solidarity?

Today, after seeing so many people scattered in so many places, I finally have the courage to ask you, Barni, without fear of being a burden, without fear of having misunderstood. I recognize in part the harshness that was shown toward Shamsa. Why did no one ever go to help her? She was depressed so many times, too many times. Libeen wasn't the kind of man who couldn't understand that. That's why he sent me: he was aware of it, but he didn't want to take care of it himself. Was it a matter of man to man, woman to woman?

I believe the underlying problem was a question of disobedience. Hadn't Shamsa left Mogadishu against the will of her father, Uncle Foodcadde?

She talked to me at length about her determination, about how, long before the war broke out, she realized that there was no future there for young people. To dream: did she also have to give up the right to dream? In Mogadishu even dreaming had become impossible. Nothing, a life of nothing.

I listened to her story: how she waited for a visa outside the Italian consulate, about the rumors of visas for sale. But Shamsa had no contacts, or perhaps she just hadn't been lucky. She told me about her dreams and of how you, being practical, tried to dissuade her. Any place was fine for her,

Italy, even Russia. One country was as good as another, as long as it was far from that prison.

You know, don't you? Someone got her a visa for Moscow, where she flew on Aeroflot. Uncle Foodcadde was against it, Shamsa was still too young for the world. But even in weakness, unexpectedly, we find a way to survive. To survive unhappily perhaps, because I don't think she was happy when she, along with a small group of people who were in the same situation, put herself in the hands of two penniless Somali ex-students. Students who spoke Russian and who, in order to supplement their meager scholarships, had turned themselves into improvised guides for Somali refugees. These expensive ferrymen had only accompanied them as far as Leningrad, so that each one of them could then follow his or her planned route.

Shamsa felt very lonely in Helsinki in the temporary immigration facility for 170 people. She was too lonely and too young not to put her faith in the young man who kept coming back and forth from Norway for her in a brand-new silver-gray car. As for that cold, with no one to warm you, who could stand it?

I try to forget Libeen and his contempt. His air of superiority crushing all illusions. To Libeen, his sister was just a woman without an ounce of courage who had accepted the courtship of the first penniless buster, agreeing to marry him without the mediation of an elder male family member. Could she complain about her five children—the first three exactly a year apart and the last two sixteen months apart— and about her abandonment? No, she had no right to do so.

Disobedience: I began, little by little, to grasp my own fleeting understanding. Libeen was losing his substance. About Shamsa? I could sense her naïveté, the earnest feeling that made her believe in her husband, following him back home.

*   *   *

Nine months? I lived with her for less than a year, then I returned with her to Finland, where I spent a few months— six perhaps?—to make her move back easier. I let her ease in gently. How did we live? On meager subsidies and through my job, whenever I had one. There was always a house for us on the outskirts of some town. But I couldn't go on living her life.

By then, Ayaan, my wild friend, was living in London. Her fiancé had talked her into moving there and she was urging me to leave that godforsaken place where I had ended up living with my cousin. In her opinion, we needed to go back to London, the city where everyone lives.

I remember when Ayaan joined us the first time: she, Shamsa, and I in the same house in England, even if shortly after, Shamsa and her children would go back to Finland. So much commotion and such close intimacy. At no other time was Shamsa so comforted. Can you imagine it? In almost nine months we never even thought of going sightseeing. Ayaan had asked me about which places to visit. I was being transformed. Little by little I was regaining my knowledge. I had visited the British Museum years earlier, on a school trip. One thing in particular had stuck in my mind, it was my picture taken kneeling with Atena in front of the Metope of the Parthenon Marbles. Atena, my high school friend. We had originally posed for that photograph to send to her grandmother who had helped us with our Latin and Greek homework and who, on the eve of our trip, had said, "You're so lucky to be able to visit the British Museum. I had always planned on going. Were I ever to stand in front of that Metope, I would drop to my knees!"

You can surely imagine how different this second visit was. Ayaan, Shamsa, and I with the five children on the bus. Ayaan loved to stir things up, so, getting on the bus, she had stopped to chat with the driver—a young man of Caribbean descent—asking him if he knew where the British Museum was. When he answered: No, in all my twenty-three years I've never been there, Ayaan, with one of the five children hanging from her neck, replied: Oh, really? That's a pity, you really should go, it's a place filled with culture . . . *a lot of culture*, she had said.

As for me? I, who had been known to spend an entire hour staring mesmerized at one single painting, after looking for the African Collection, and walking straight through that hodgepodge, I surprised myself and announced: OK, that's enough, let's get the children out of here.

Those months were fun. Ayaan and her angelic boyfriend who took us around, fascinated by our temperaments that were so different and yet so much in harmony. The boyfriend? Ayaan used to tease him because he was so generous.

He offers advice to everyone, she used to tell us. A guy with a crippled hand, a friend of Ayaan's boyfriend, had a Somali restaurant that, according to everyone, was pitiful: very bare, cold food, and no clients. Ayaan's boyfriend had talked at length with Crippled Hand, giving him all sorts of advice: arrange your tables this way, the walls are too bare, the food mustn't look as though it was cooked the day before, I think that if you put in hookahs lots of people would come because they're the latest fad. Unbelievable. They had gone back to that same restaurant and they had found it completely transformed and packed with customers! Why on earth didn't her boyfriend open a consulting agency?

* * *

After London: a complex web of different places. Letting things go, I lived. I think it was fate that introduced me to Saciid Saleebaan. Saciid Saleebaan whom you know well, Deeqa's brother, Taageere's go-between. Everyone knows how exuberant he is. But his story—a story of women, a story of weakness—few deem it important.

I met Saciid Saleebaan in Germany. He was fixated on his video camera and an interesting project. The crazy idea of filming the Somali diaspora. A video, a documentary or a movie, he hadn't yet decided. The one sure thing was the subject. A subject as unclear as the story of unsubstantial places could be.

Barni—how can I explain it?—his project became my project. I, who was getting on in years and desperately try-

ing to reinvent myself, had finally found a goal in life with
him.

First of all, though, I need to untangle his story. Saciid
Saleebaan, madly clicking away. He and his girlfriend were
passionately in love. Tender love, completely free. What was
wrong? I just cannot accept it, Barni. What I cannot fathom
is the rejection by his family—Saciid Saleebaan's mother
who has nothing better to do with her time than to cling to
prejudice. Something that had to do with origins, bloodlines.

They ask me how I can possibly be surprised by their
refusal, even though they had massacred us? I—*iska-dhal*,
half-mix—I who know nothing of my origins, poor girl, it's
not my fault, but I have to trust them, the reason for such
resentment has a foundation, watch out, they hate us and
they're just waiting for us to turn our backs to stick a knife
into us, they cannot be trusted. Poor Taariikh, what a legacy
he left us. History without memory?

Who were those people? The ones they say Saciid Saleebaan's girlfriend belonged to. Facing opposition on both
sides, the two lovers seemed ready to resist their assaults.
Resist Sacid Saleebaan's mother, who in a panic screamed
over the intercontinental telephone lines demanding that
they immediately send a brand-new wife from Somalia. Resist daily insults that every day poured like a storm on his
girlfriend: shameless, with no sense of honor, she was going
out with one of them.

I saw her arrive, Saciid Saleebaan's brand-new promised
bride from Somalia. A virgin, not even eighteen years old,
from the same genealogical divide. Can you imagine all the
expectations? Because, come to think of it, if the problem
was simply to find a way to make everyone happy, Saciid
Saleebaan could also pretend in another way. Saciid Saleebaan's wife—at first—felt lucky to have arrived in the West.

The years went by, and I had stopped feeling ashamed
for the way I thought. Was he swallowing the family blackmail? Saciid Saleebaan disgusted me. Marry her? Yes, he
would marry her.

What can I do, he stuttered, and I had a suggestion ready. A dual idea—the immaculate girl dragged from her village to the bed of a stranger who loves another, and the other girl, compromised purity. Dual idea born of my torments: He could get married, fine. But did he really have to consummate the marriage?

No, I don't—Saciid Saleebaan answered—you know, that's a really good idea!

Saciid Saleebaan, and his brand of truth. The immaculate young woman? What would happen to a young bride repudiated by her arranged husband? Many people were at fault. The first girlfriend had believed the story of the family blackmail, of the man that she loves against her better judgment, the man who doesn't care about genealogical nuances and is strong enough to hold on to both of them. Yes, there were reasons for both women to feel misled. Blame them? I cannot blame them. How many things do we dream up to avoid facing painful truths?

The years went by and, while Saciid Saleebaan continued living his lie, his wife not only remained in the apartment they were assigned by the government, but she also gave birth to several children one after the other. One, two, three.

That's Saciid Saleebaan's mentality, they kept telling me. What you can't understand is his mentality. I settled for that. He had given me his dream and I was thankful for that gift.

I know that in the course of my transformation I was slowly beginning to see the light. I was no longer blindly dependent on Libeen, fumbling along. Whatever I could retrieve from my story, I could only get from what my story had actually been. Was I supposed to feel out of place always and everywhere? I had lived camouflaged. Now those bitter knots of my sleepless nights—constellations of rejections—had to become my linchpin. Barni, do you know what loneliness is? What I have been fighting all along is this sense of abandonment. Do I belong? Because measuring, calibrating, the ingredients that make us who we are, is very, very dangerous.

What I am telling you about Saciid Saleebaan was, for me, the source of a blinding truth.

I have learned to recognize how much the mind distorts things. The problem arises when we are unaware that the lie we live is surfacing on our lips. Taageere, for instance, his words are fairy-tale ramblings. How astonished I was to hear about his little sister arriving on one of the boats. He had never talked to me about Luul, you know? Only, reluctantly, about an older sister, Caasha, a heroine and a champion of coherence.

Caasha who never lost sight of her goal. Who walked from Mogadishu all the way to Kismaayo to flee from the killers. Who arrived in Nairobi by car, and who, thanks to funds from her relatives, left for Syria a few months later. Caasha who, with a fake passport, flew to Germany with her four children, ages one, four, five, and six. Who was locked up in a German refugee camp and was able to escape thanks to a ruse. Who once in the Netherlands managed to survive for years saving pennies from her small subsidy and from the money she made preparing sweets and *sambuusi* for parties.

Caasha who, adrift in the world, never forgot her husband and dedicated her life to rescuing him. Her husband received all of the money she had saved, penny by penny, and once in Istanbul, he slipped onto a plane bound for Bangkok. He then got off in Paris during a layover to turn himself over to the authorities. Caasha's husband who was put back on the plane to Bangkok, where he waited for another two thousand dollars of the money his wife saved penny by penny. He flew back to Paris and was, at that point, tossed out onto the streets by the exasperated police. Free at long last, he was able to get on a high-speed train to Amsterdam and rushed to be reunited with his wife and children after eight years of separation. Eight years of being coherent for what? The woman who knows she has no value without a man is always the best of heroines. Caasha.

* * *

And still, what my intuition grasped, my mind tried to blur.

I was living in Germany and—bouncing from one country to the next—I was trying to find financial backing for my project on the Somali diaspora. The years went by, and I continued to film here and there, at times with little enthusiasm, at times with renewed enthusiasm. Until one day—a lot of time had gone by and I hadn't seen Saciid Saleebaan for over two years—I received an unexpected phone call. Saciid Saleebaan's girlfriend had something to ask me.

"I'm sorry I never called you before and now, well, I'm calling to ask you for a favor. But first of all I want to thank you. Grief and confusion make people forget important things. This is overdue, but I'm doing it anyway. I know that you tried to persuade Saciid Saleebaan. A lot of time has gone by and I'm still caught up in this web. Today, what I feel most of all is pity for that poor woman and her children."

Barni, do you know what love means? By then, for me, love was total dependence. What people call love, I mean. Mental dependence, physical dependence, whatever you want to call it. Because I had seen so many similar situations. But renouncing—putting aside something that belongs to us, something we really care about—that I saw very rarely. Finding a balance and accepting beauty and shadows.

So—I don't know how to explain this to you—with this in mind I had even convinced myself to accept the idea of marriage as a contract: such a difficult balancing act that even when it's fake, it makes little difference. I kept thinking—just imagine it—that love is not a fundamental ingredient of marriage. How many people who are madly in love with each other, after coping with children and the challenges of everyday life, end up getting on each other's nerves? Perhaps—I really believed this—in order to make a family work, couples need to find a balance that has nothing to do with love. Otherwise, how could you explain the length of time Saciid Saleebaan and his wife had survived together?

But I'm jumping ahead, forgive me.

Saciid Saleebaan's girlfriend was asking me a question no one had ever asked me before. She wanted to break up with Saciid Saleebaan for good, and she could only do so by going as far away as possible. But—I was aware of it too—it's not easy to cross borders with Somali papers. She and Saciid had even tried it, before the chosen bride arrived. Run away, flee from destiny. They had been able to cross the Eastern European countries. People were so unaccustomed to seeing blacks on those routes that they peeked into their compartment to look at them. They were planning on getting on a plane in Sofia, where it was rumored that immigration controls were less rigorous. Instead, they were caught anyway and sent back. Now Saciid Saleebaan's girlfriend wanted to try again, and I, Domenica Axad, with my Italian passport could help her.

Do you know, Barni, what it means to possess something you take for granted? The idea that no one can refuse you entry to any country, that at most it's a matter of paying for a visa? A passport, a pass-borders. Without this thing that you take for granted, a journey over a desert or over the sea, a long and dangerous journey, is much more expensive than a full-fare airline ticket. What's missing is the visa.

I agreed to surrender my passport into the hands of Saciid Saleebaan's girlfriend. This was before fingerprinting. I helped Saciid Saleebaan's girlfriend leave for the United States, thinking I was saving her from that dependency. How did I manage after that? The usual way: I reported a lost passport to the Italian embassy after she had crossed the border.

That was the first time. Then—with the idea of saving lives—I lent my identity to other women. My double identity, my ineffable essence, was proving to be useful.

I was telling you about Saciid Saleebaan's wife. It's just that I was so consumed with my new notion of love and marriage when it happened.

Barni, something terrible.

Was Saciid Saleebaan upset by his ex-girlfriend's departure? Maybe. But I'm guessing—and I am not the only one to do so—that he soon found substitutes. What happened to his wife, ex–immaculate maiden who, everyone said, by then was resigned to grinning and bearing it? Did she perhaps realize that Saciid Saleebaan's girlfriend was not the only reason for her unhappiness? I am well aware of what a terrible thing repressed feelings are. So many rules telling you how to behave, and yet, no compassion. How old was she? Twenty-two when they buried her. They say she slipped off a ledge. The truth is so very weak.

But that death—a voluntary death—was a bolt from the blue. The children, one right after the other, the youngest barely able to stand up by himself. Poor things looking down at a grave into which they are lowering their mother's body wrapped in a white sheet.

The only thing I filmed was Saciid Saleebaan's face, drenched in such madness.

The rest of the story is nothing new. The children went to their paternal grandmother's house. She must have been pleased; at least she had two heirs and a spare, of pure genealogical bloodlines. Saciid Saleebaan, overcome with grief, right at that very time received substantial financial backing for his documentary and left for the United States, saying he was going to shoot footage, while what he was really going for was to look for his ex-girlfriend. His ex-girlfriend who would reject him.

He asked me to join him there. At first I was so nauseated by the whole story that I refused. Then he made me an offer. We could work in different cities and only at the end would we assemble the material together. The filming lasted much longer than expected. Saciid Saleebaan, mad with grief, was looking for respite everywhere, while I continued to float on that primordial matter. I was in no hurry. Slowly, the repulsion that I felt for him diminished and I joined him. After a long time. And now that you have all the relevant information, I will finally reveal Taageere's story to you.

For years I have been called Axad. I was ashamed of the name Domenica. I reclaimed Axad, the name that you, Barni, had picked for me, and every time someone pronounced it, I thought of you. I didn't choose it deliberately. When asked our name, we learn to respond immediately. And me?

A double answer: Domenica or Axad, the choice is yours. And the choice of the double option has always been un-equivocally the same. For the last ten years, for everyone I have been Axad. Sometimes I missed the name my mother had chosen for me. Axad! It irritated me, I pretended not to hear it. This girl is hard of hearing. Did they suspect it was because of my name? I doubt it. You think Domenica doesn't suit me? It's cumbersome, sometimes I find it cum-bersome. Alternatively, either one or the other. Depending on my mood, on whether I feel I belong or I feel like an out-sider. I want to stress that difference? Then I use the name that the other person does not. Sometimes I would have liked to have a sip of beer without offending anyone. That's when I missed Domenica. Perhaps it was because I was tired of Axad that I got entangled with Taageere. No Somali be-fore him had ever chosen to call me Domenica.

How did I meet him? I met him through Saciid Salee-baan. At that point, I used to follow Saciid Saleebaan every-where, we took turns using the video camera. More than anything, to finish a job that seemed to be going nowhere. After the tragedy, Saciid Saleebaan had undergone a radical transformation. I couldn't keep up with him; he dashed here and there and I tried to contain him, to bring him back onto the normal, everyday path. Defining limits was a completely new role for me.

Taageere: the first time I saw him was outside a wed-ding party. During a break while shooting the video. The young women scowled at me because they knew I did not belong to the team hired to film the party, that I was work-ing independently. They trusted me, a woman, less than they trusted those Peeping Toms. They felt the outsider's eye was more intense, that's probably why they felt so reluctant. Taageere had realized this. I was smoking and fuming, feel-ing defensive. On guard for young men who come on to me just because they see me sitting on a wall wearing pants and smoking a cigarette. Taageere was relaxed. He was not disapproving, but he wasn't pretending to approve either.

That first day outside the wedding party we chatted. He's a good-looking young man, he had a guarded way of addressing you, as if he wanted to draw an invisible circle between you and him. I was telling you about Saciid Saleebaan because it's through him that we formed a stronger bond. It was the day of the big pandemonium. We had gone to film in a neighborhood on the outskirts of town where a large number of Somalis live. An interesting opportunity. During the hot summer months, people gather outside in their backyards to spend the evening together. That evening there were more people than usual, or perhaps something happened that I missed, because the police arrived in riot gear, as if they were dealing with a demonstration. At the beginning I was torn between disbelief and alarm. Saciid Saleebaan was arrested immediately. At that point he was holding the video camera while I had started talking to Taageere, whom I hadn't seen since the evening of the wedding party. Saciid Saleebaan was not the kind of person you could leave on his own. Taageere, who's known him almost since birth, says that when he saw him again in the States he seemed like a completely different person. Ranting and raving. It took him some time to realize he had changed. At the beginning he thought that Saciid Saleebaan was the old friend with whom he could share dreams and plans. Instead, I think Saciid Saleebaan made him lose money in a business venture they wanted to start up in Ghana. But I don't know the details.

Taageere is not the type of person who bears a grudge against a close friend, so we spent the whole night at the police station trying to figure out a way to get Saciid Saleebaan out.

I've lived these past ten years one day at a time, so I've lost the ability to formulate long-range plans. With people, things last as long as they are meant to, an unpredictable amount of time. What about Taageere and me? With him I was at ease, going with the flow. Serenely, no ambushes, no blackmail. The way I was was fine with him. And then, a tenderness, I don't know how to explain it. A person I wasn't entrusting myself to, but that I felt was all mine.

Taageere is one of those men-children who light up faces. He was constantly looking to please people. Even the grumpy waitress at the café, "Your tea's so good, miss." And she was all smiles. He seemed to always be thinking of others. But not as a form of control. He was aware of others. He moved me, you know? Even if he was not the kind of man to take on responsibilities, he was there, constantly reassuring. What he was up to when I wasn't there, or what would have become of him, was something I didn't have a chance to discover. Was it about six months? The time we got to know each other.

We got married almost right away, yes. It amused me. A party in which we two would be the protagonists. No desire to make our relationship legal. I've given up looking for approval. How was Taageere different from the others? Simply put, with him, I have always been able to identify my essence. An unbridled wind. I was fine the way I was, without having to invent parts of myself. I'm saying this, Barni, not because he had any exceptional qualities. Taageere is like an honest feeling, with no complications. A man of uncertain paths, a weak will.

That's a negative comment?

It's just that this is the only way I can explain myself. Could I have guessed that he already had a wife and a son? Not in the slightest. Can I stop believing in so much frankness? Isn't it easier to believe him when he says that he didn't want me to suffer, to be jealous of his past relationships? But an ex-wife and a son are not small details to keep hidden. And you know, even if on the surface—while criticizing him—I said I was happy at the news, I felt a subtle flicker of suspicion taking hold of me.

Were there any other reasons why he was hiding a part of his story? Deep down I cannot exempt him from his responsibilities.

Taageere talked about Shukri and their son shortly after the wedding. We were still eating the leftovers from the party when his sister Luul landed in Lampedusa. After years of peregrination, do you realize? Taageere was very agitated at not being able to talk to her, he thought of joining her immediately. The visa for Italy? The embassy employee told us that the simplest way was to register our marriage. One shock after another. This is when the whole business about Shukri came out. The story of his ex-wife who lives in Rome with their nine-year-old son. I don't want to be unfair, I really don't. I even think that wanting to see your son is a good enough reason to trick a woman. But Taageere doesn't have enough energy to come up with such a plan. This complication of my life is at the center of too many of my thoughts. A torment of connections, of intricate paths.

So, even Taageere, who has always called me Domenica, has become an overly meaningful detail. A sudden glimmer. Because favoring one of the two names meant above all choosing an essence. What Taageere saw in me was my Western side. His wife Shukri, remarried to an Italian, is the Somali. I was something completely different. Did he want to settle the score and get himself an Italian wife, too? We move unconsciously, trying to regain what we have lost.

A friend of mine, for instance, was jilted by her fiancé for an American woman after having been engaged for many years. After months of anguish, she got over it, and she too found a new fiancé, an American. Sheer coincidence!

Or else Taageere had indeed some secret plan I hadn't discovered, plans tied to documents, to the dream of not being a prisoner forever. I know this is getting far-fetched. What I fear most is a premeditated scheme.

Let's drop the subject. That same bureaucracy showed a paralyzing clause. In the West, Taageere is still officially married to Shukri even if they have both remarried. Relationships frozen in time? I think there's something that's still unresolved between him and his ex-wife. He must have created some illusions.

I left torn with suspicion. Derailed by silence, the silence of hidden places. I left with a lump in my throat. At the airport, I went past the checkpoint walking backward. And I could see Taageere frozen in that position, he who wanted so much to come with me. I and my pass for the fortress were going to meet Luul, who had arrived as an illegal immigrant. Did this make any sense? I only remember a feeling of nausea coming from my stomach, and an inescapable anguish. As if that brief goodbye were a final farewell. A farewell is never pompous. It's just flat, it doesn't dazzle.

As soon as I arrived in Rome, I looked for Shukri instead of looking for Luul. Perhaps out of curiosity, but above all because I was sure Luul would be happier to meet someone she already knew. Diriiye Yuusuf and Safiya welcomed me warmly. You know, ever since I came back, every morning I feel like throwing up. As if my body rejected this land of mine. Sure, Safiya helped me find Shukri. And Shukri helped us find Luul.

Shukri is so sweet. She revealed to me details I was unaware of. Because Taageere hadn't even had the courage to tell me that he had never seen his son. She spoke easily, without resentment. Shukri is not the type to store up anger. She told me about Taageere, of how young they were. Of how she fled the war with her child and how lucky it was that she had to take care of the baby, otherwise she could not have lived with her sense of guilt. Shukri felt anxious for Taageere even when she was in the refugee camp. She says that at last she found the strength to stop waiting for him by thinking she couldn't have her son live the life that people live in the camps. She says that one night she dreamed of Taageere coming toward her in tears, his body covered with talcum powder, saying to her: Shukri, why did you abandon me? His body covered in talcum powder, like that of her baby.

My dear Barni, do you understand all this tenderness? Later Taageere didn't do anything to join her and now he keeps blaming her, as if the choice was entirely hers, and he even has the gall to insult her because she married a *gaal*.

You say it's gutsy to look for the ex-wife of one's husband. I think it was a good thing for everyone. Even for Luul.

What are my plans? My dear sister, now that I have found you again, the plot is beginning to make sense. I had been wanting to come back for some time now. My absence had lasted for too long. What about my mother? My love damaged her greatly. And now, after ten years, I run the risk of doing the same thing all over again, and with a man on top of it. It just shows how we imprison ourselves without realizing it.

But today I saw a ray of light. I woke up just before dawn. The pharmacies were closed and I looked for one that was open. I was in a hurry, in too much of a hurry to wait. The lines, you know the lines in the test? I did it twice. And I saw two pink lines, forming clearly. Straight and strong, like the two of us, Barni. I have never felt such force in a desire. The same force I feel today. If everything goes well, I'm going to have a child, the child of my future.

My dear Barni, I want this child to be born here, in my motherland, whose facets of memory and deepest secrets of language I know so well. I will have to take care of my child. Without risking to love too much. But will you give up your space? Will you reveal the secrets of birth to me? Will you accept me, once and for all?

5

INTERLUDE—TAAGEERE

XAMAR, SHROUDED IN SILENCE.

You think that the most terrifying thing is to hear noise. Shots, mortar fire, dha, dha, agonizing screams. Instead, you look straight ahead into that hole down there in the corner of your room and you hear nothing. Crumbling walls. Even if there's someone around you. You feel like a naked body that's burning in that noise that is not there. The noise that is not there is about to materialize and perhaps it will get you, first. There I am all huddled up praying to Allah for the noise to begin again. Shots, mortar fire, dha dha, agonizing screams. At least you can work out the direction of those taking flight. Huddled in the corner of the room, not sleeping. I think of how wide my body is: will it still be wide enough to protect the children? How many can I hide in the middle of my chest?

Cursed silence.

One night we hear slithering. The thieves are terrible. Not like in peacetime.

In peacetime we laugh at Madoowe, black as coal, famous throughout the neighborhood. Madoowe who, in order to steal a radio, takes off all his clothes and covers himself in oil. In the dark of the night nobody can see anything except the whites of his eyes. And if someone tries to grab him, squish, he escapes by slipping away. But Madoowe doesn't take into account that there's also electricity in the house where he's stealing the radio. So then, black and naked as he is, they find him doubled over the stereo! What a fool, that Madoowe!

In peacetime we laugh at Mr. Cumar Shariif when the neighborhood is full of small-time thieves. Everyone is pissed off and Cumar Shariif says: If I find one in my house, I'll strangle him with my own bare hands! One night he wakes up to go to the bathroom. He goes down the stairs and hears some noise. That's him, that's the thief! And the thief says: Cumar Shariif, what are you doing here, awake? And he replies: I was going to the bathroom. And the thief: Go right back to your room! And Cumar Shariif goes right back to bed to sleep. And the thief steals everything he wants.

At night we hear slithering. The thieves are terrible. Not like in peacetime.

Cossoble hears the slithering and everyone's eyes are wide open. The thieves are armed and they kill you for no reason. He hears slithering. He can't take the risk so the thief is shot to death. Then Cossoble has a fever all night. A fever that lasts for days. It's true that in wartime you get used to death, but killing, no, killing is another matter. These are not things you can get used to. Instead, you get used to death, to bodies that you must piece together again and gather up, here and there.

The first to die by my side is my dearest friend, Xirsi. The thing is that in the beginning it's different, you're not used to it. It hits you just like that, suddenly.

So, Xirsi and I go out, quite unconcerned, just like in peacetime. Just to calm Maryam down. There's a moment of truce and we must go and get the photo of her little girl. At that point everyone comes out to escape, everyone like a river, and above the river, things floating: mattresses, children, pots and pans, clothes all bundled up. And Xirsi is so calm that he even lights a cigarette. We're just going to go and come right back. But after a bit, we begin to see the streets of Xamar. The bodies and the dried blood covered in sand. The wind blows strong in Xamar. And within the perforated walls and the bombed-out houses people gather the things left behind by the armed bandits. Everything is worth something if it's free, even an old sheet. Somebody who's enraged at not having found anything pushes a tattered armchair off a balcony. You hear the thud and then the laugh of the person who pushed it off. Further on, in another house that's been taken over, they've broken the pipes; it's odd that there's still running water in the neighborhood.

It spurts out hard, shooting into the air in an uninterrupted flow. Slime everywhere.

Then I remember. From around the corner farther down the street comes a loud noise, a truck. Five boys standing up in the uncovered part at the back. A leaf of *jaat* sticks out of the mouth of one of them. They see the people and then they begin to laugh. Then, dhhhhhhhh dhah. Whoever can, throws himself to the ground. Those boys just keep on going, laughing.

I see Xirsi with his hand on his belly and I see Xirsi's eyes, like this, wide open. I understand very little in that moment.

I know that I'm carrying his body and that I am covered in his blood. It covers my eyes, my mouth. Then I see a Toyota in the middle of the road. I'm desperate, my only concern is for Xirsi. I'm so desperate that I am not aware of the danger. The people in the Toyota ask me some questions: Who are you, who's your father, what are you doing here. They could kill me. A desperate man running down the middle of the road with a body on his shoulders.

They take me to the hospital. It's beginning to fill up. Xirsi has lost too much blood.

The doctor comes up to me and says, "My boy, you were very brave to bring in your friend but he has lost too much blood, it's too late now."

The doctor doesn't have time to add anything else. My friend did not make it, *amiin*. He rushes off to take care of those less seriously wounded. I try to follow him, he says, Taageere, help that man lie down, I pass him the gauze, I hold the scalpel for him. I'm standing there and I see all that blood and people's bodies, how they are made inside. I don't think of Xirsi anymore or of Maryam who's waiting for us, or of Shukri and my newborn son. I don't think of what I have to do.

The doctor doesn't have time to stop. They call him Gaandi because of the country where he studied medicine. Since he came back he always dresses like an Indian, his shirt the same as his pants, khaki-colored.

Now he's wearing a long shirt all stained with red. He goes from one place to the next. Gaandi doesn't eat, doesn't sleep. This is the way we spend our days. Five, maybe six, I can't remember.

At the end of those days I see him talking to a man, older than him, with a tuft of white hair on the top of his head.

"Foodcadde, go and get your brother, don't worry about me. He's in greater danger. I can't follow you now, there's too much work to do. How can I, there's nobody to take my place. When I find the courage to leave, I will leave. For the moment, I don't have that kind of courage."

Then the doctor turns to me and says, "Foodcadde, take this boy with you. He's been here for more than a week. Since his friend died he hasn't been able to leave."

So I leave. Foodcadde takes hold of my hands after Gaandi has hugged me. In peacetime, Gaandi takes care of children, now he's taking care of dying men. Is it more painful to see a grown body covered in red, in the trembling grip of death, or more painful to see a slender body that still smells of milk? I didn't ask Gaandi. My brain has stopped and my eyes do not see. It's tough at the beginning, when you don't yet know what death is like.

I move on, following the old man, but my eyes do not see. And together with the old man we pass the checkpoints, we pay bribes, we collect other people. I sit in the back seat with my knees against my chin.

Then we reach a gray gate and I ask him, "Where are we?"

Foodcadde opens the car door and knocks on the gate. Then he looks at me and says, "My boy, you don't tell me where I must drop you off so I take you with me."

Two men open the door with Kalashnikovs strapped over their shoulders. A drop of sweat runs down Foodcadde's forehead framed by a cloud of white curls.

"I've come to look for my brother. The neighbors tell me that he left his house to seek refuge with you."

The man with a *rummay* stick in his mouth says, "Wait."

Then a thin man with glasses comes up and hugs Foodcadde. It's his brother Taariikh. They go inside and after a few minutes, come back.

"I'm taking you inside, my boy," says Foodcadde and starts up the car. Inside there are offices and there are some Italians. Foodcadde's brother says he doesn't want to leave. So they go in and I stay out there sitting on one side. And while I'm waiting for the two brothers to come to an agreement, they open the gates and some men arrive, with Kalashnikovs, too, and they make a young girl get out. The girl walks straight in front of them, holding herself tall. She says she wants to speak to their leaders. I think that she has all that courage because she hasn't seen death yet. I don't hear anything, I only notice that she comes out of the house and sits right in front of me. So I look at her with my eyes that are beginning to see a little and she says to me, "Why are you staring at me?" And I reply, "This is the first time that I am able to actually see somebody since my friend died." The girl has a firm gaze and a sharp profile, her nose curved like a knife and a dark mark in the middle of her forehead.

Then the girl introduces herself: Barni, that's her name, and she apologizes for having spoken rudely. Then she starts telling me things.

She says that the leaders are inside, and that by some strange coincidence she ran into her father's brothers, and that even though at the beginning they didn't want to let her see them, they did manage to talk and they're trying to come to a decision. The Italians have some very powerful radios, so if the leaders protect them and help them leave, in exchange they can keep the radios that belong to the Italians.

She says she saw Foodcadde trying to drag his brother to one side, but that his brother doesn't want to leave, because he believes that the regime has fallen and that it's time to rebuild the country.

She says that they must decide quickly what to do with her. She must hurry to her friend who is about to give birth. Deeqa. That's her name.

We are sitting there waiting. I see an Italian, short, with a red face, he's smoking a cigarette and he has curly, yellow hair like fishermen's hair, hair made of sun and salt. Next to him there's a woman, she looks as if she's his woman. His woman speaks to the boys with the guns and he holds his cigarette like this, in the hollow of his hand. The *gaal* nods in assent when his woman speaks to him.

At that time nobody knows him yet; later everybody will find out who he is, the Tunisian.

The war goes on and this *gaal* holds the city in his hand. He arranges deals with everyone, and he has, as his armed guards, his wife Fay's cousins, Fay the very beautiful ex-widow. Through the deals he makes money, a lot of money. And with that money he builds a hotel, a big luxury hotel where he puts up all the important people. In the hotel there's a restaurant where he employs those who in peacetime were the cooks at the legendary Croce del Sud, the old Italian restaurant in the center of Xamar.

They say that during the first days of the war, the owner, an Italian from the years of colonization, is devastated by the loss. People go in to ransack the place and he is desperate. He wants to defend his restaurant with his own hands. And people throw everything at him. The *gaal* speaks on a small two-way radio and wants to call in the Italian army to stop

these invaders of his property. But his chefs are so important that they find work, even in wartime. All these chefs
cook for the Tunisian, famous throughout the city because
he only eats fish. No one has ever heard of a man who only
eats fish. Who knows if even his skin has begun to stink like
those slippery creatures. The Tunisian says that fish is good
for the blood and makes you think up lots, lots of intelligent
ideas. That day I saw the Tunisian for the first time.

After a while Foodcadde comes out and says that we are
leaving. He hasn't been able to convince his brother Taariikh
to leave. Perhaps he'll go back to get him later. Meanwhile,
I go looking for Shukri and our baby, but they are no longer
around. So I go back to my house and my family is happy
because many days have gone by. They know nothing about
me or Xirsi.

Then months go by. Your stomach gets used to not eating.
It gets smaller and smaller and you learn to put up with it. Sitting around with the friends who are left, you drink the dirty
tea that has no taste. And you feel a little bit of warmth in
your stomach which helps to deaden the pain. Days are endless. Then, bit by bit, even the fear goes away because you are
so weak that you don't even have the strength to be afraid.
Days go by and your legs, your arms, get thinner and thinner.

Before the war, many people died of cholera. One of my
neighbors caught it and she was doubled up, diarrhea and
vomiting emptied her out. They got a car to take her to the
doctor, and in one hour you could almost see the woman's
skeleton, her skin clinging to her bones. This makes you realize how much we are made up of water, how quickly a
person can be emptied out.

We only drink tea and yet we become like that woman,
so dried out that our skin seems to cling to the bones of our
faces.

Xamar became like that. Like a woman whose skin
clings to her bones. The roads so full of holes that there's no
asphalt left. All around, the smell of death.

Xamar waa lagu xumeeyay. Xamar, they have ruined you. Who will pay for the sins committed? City of mine, city where they buried my umbilical cord. City where everyone lived in peace and harmony, in safety and in freedom. Magnificent city on the African coast. My brothers, parents, and cousins all lived there. But because of the blood and strife these same brothers are fighting among themselves.

Xamar waa lagu xumeeyay. Xamar, they have defiled you. Filled you with bullets, destroyed and burned you, devastated your neighborhoods, sacked your treasures. The respected families fled across the borders. The just and the honest people liberated the country from criminals and from foreigners. Today all of them lie buried. Nobody cares anymore about the wisdom of the elders.

6

BARNI

AXAD, *ABBAAYO*, IT'S SO wonderful to have you here, to experience this magical moment of revelation with you. I feel as though I myself were experiencing this metamorphosis in my own body. And to think that I have assisted with so many pregnancies. Today, on my way home from work, I thought back over all those things that I teach my patients. I listed them quietly to myself. How to wash the stitches with marigold extract dissolved in water, how to sponge yourself down with hot water to make your milk flow, how to treat the umbilical cord with alcohol and Mercurochrome, how to rub almond oil over the baby's body, how to immerse him in warm water, how to wash the sex of the baby girls with a cotton ball soaked in diluted bicarbonate of soda. I felt a tremor, something so different. I have seen my fair share of mothers in that moment, at the mercy of their bodies, torn by agonizing pain; you get to see what they're really made of. No small privilege. Does instinct prevail? Not for all women. The veil falls away, each one of them digs down into the recesses of her very soul. Sometimes what they find there is unmentionable. I am by their side, but I am with them only for the first few days. I only know the very beginning of the lives of the newborn. So, what am I missing?

To see the infants growing, to see them when they are weaned, the first strained vegetables that they eat, their passive mouths, the eyes that gradually distinguish the shape of things and the hands that suddenly latch on to you. Their backs get stronger, lengthening, a live tree supporting the bark that is expanding. For me, these are stages of growth that I have only heard about.

Only once was it different: with Ardo and her baby. Today, after work, I found myself thinking about that again and again. I kept on stopping in front of shop windows. But you said that we mustn't buy anything for him before he is born, that's why I didn't even go in. However, passing in front of the shop, I remembered, I thought back to the time that I bought a little dress for Ardo's daughter. A little red dress with a white border and two pockets in the shape of birds that, when you press them, go "peep peep," crazy gimmicks that the Chinese invent to make children laugh. Around Termini station all the shops belong to them, the Chinese. Ardo's daughter. Yes, that was the only time that it was different. Remember, I told you about it. So many years have gone by. They don't live here in Rome anymore, even they have gone to England. You don't recall Ardo? I met her when I lived along the Casilina Way. A strange business, one of those decreed by destiny.

Every morning I used to catch the little train that goes along the Casilina Way; I don't know if you ever took it. It's like being suspended in time. You experience what it must have been like in the early days, a way of getting out into the countryside. Every day I traveled the same route. And in order to live so far out, I had to wake up early. But I didn't mind, it felt like my own space, an in-between time that I needed to get back in touch with the world. All those faces. And then, that's when I used to read the newspaper or a magazine, my way of getting information.

It happened one day, at the train stop. That morning it was bitterly cold, unusually so for this city. A northerly wind was blowing, a wind that penetrates even the smallest opening. My hands were dry and my mouth, wrapped in my scarf, was blowing out hot air. I was shifting my feet, trying to find a way to get warm when I saw her. She was coming down the steps, wrapped from head to toe in an enormous, dark gray down coat. Her small head peeped out, covered in a canary yellow *fasoleeti*. A color so bright that I couldn't help noticing it. How thin that girl was, I tell you, shockingly thin. Very dark and very thin, so worn out as to make you feel sorry for her. I wanted to acknowledge her with my eyes, but no, she didn't look at me. And from that very moment, I felt annoyed, I can't explain it, as if she had deliberately not greeted me, as if she had pretended not to see me. Because with that canary yellow *fasoleeti*, there was no doubt that she was Somali.

And as I was standing there, absorbed in my irritation, I remembered what a colleague of mine always says, that we Africans always greet each other even if we don't know one another. According to him, we greet each other because in our country everyone knows everyone else. I was thinking about this colleague, about the fact that I had not been able to contradict what he had said and that instead of contradicting, I had told myself that it was true, that when I see a Somali, I always greet him, and while I was thinking, I retrieved a fact that turned that reasoning on its head, as it were. A little while ago I was standing in line at the greengrocer's and the lady who was serving said to me: What would you like? Pretending that the other people in line didn't exist. I nodded at those around me, in case she hadn't realized that there were a lot of people in front of me. What did she do? She came up close to me, giving me a wink: Let the owner take care of them, she whispered. And before I left, do you know what she added? I'm a foreigner, too, I'm Ukrainian, she said to me. As if Ukraine and Somalia were adjacent countries. Does this mean that all foreigners identify with each other? What do you think?

But that day, in that icy weather, there at the train stop was a skinny Somali who was pretending not to see me. The train arrived; the sudden difference in temperature from outside to inside and the humidity were enough to make you feel ill. Early in the morning, you know, when your sense of smell is so acute? I could make out the smell of fried food and mustiness on people's coats. Nauseating. The girl got on right in front of me. Stubbornly, she continued not to look at me, and I fixed my gaze on her to pulverize her with my eyes. Perhaps that's what it was. Or perhaps more than anything it was something in particular that I could not stop looking at, something that would not let me look away. A pair of drop earrings that were dangling to and fro, to and fro. Enough to make you dizzy. Two earrings in the finest pure gold filigree. Embedded in the center was a tiger's eye. Were they the same ones? Because, Axad, you won't believe it, but inside myself I was ready to bet, I was sure that those earrings had belonged to me.

This is not just some absurd thought that popped into my mind. The fact is, you were still small. Who knows if you remember the goldsmiths' market. You were only nine when you left. The tamarind market with that beautiful portico and, beneath the arches, the goldsmiths' shops. All of them did superb work in gold filigree. But there was one whose style was unmistakable, for the way he wove the filigree, in a curving and unpredictable fashion, almost crazily, a touch that made each piece of his one of a kind. No one piece was the same as another. It almost seemed contrived; instead it was entirely authentic. You could say to that goldsmith—part Arab, part Pakistani, part Somali—make me some earrings, I'd like this stone, this shape, and he would make them for you, but he made them in such a strange way, in such a distinctive way that you could not mistake one of his earrings for any other. He took a long time, but whoever was willing to wait received in return a unique pair of earrings.

Jewels, had I saved any in the chaos? When I left, I thought I was going to go back. I left with those earrings tossed into a bag together with gauze, cotton balls, suturing thread, scalpel, enema, ethyl alcohol, hydrogen peroxide, Mercurochrome, a surgical sheet. Oh, Axad, so much time . . . You're bringing back memories. It's been ten years since I left home. The world had changed so much in those last few years. Everything was so different from the way I knew it.

Uncle Foodcadde had called the blacksmith to come and reinforce our front door. He did not want to hear of buying a firearm. He who has a gun thinks he will use it, he used to say, and I have no intention of shooting anybody.

Then there was our custodian, Yuusuf, the same one who had been with us for fifteen years. Yuusuf who no longer possessed the courage of his earlier days. Do you remember when we were small how he liked to frighten us with his terrifying stories? He was from the Ogaden and he used to tell us about the cruelty of the soldiers during the war between Somalia and Ethiopia. He had been a glorious warrior and he still had a menacingly large knife that he pulled out to terrify us. But time and malarial fevers had worn down his strong constitution. In the end, Yuusuf's presence was like that of an old nanny when the children have all grown up. The last time the robbers had come, they had stolen our car and even the clothes that were hung out to dry. So Uncle Foodcadde had taken Yuusuf aside and told him he could not carry on sleeping under the stars, that he had to come inside with us. It was too risky to stay outside, these were no longer small-time thieves who would run off at the sight of a scarecrow. These were real criminals.

Was Shamsa still with us? She was, and her presence was so pervasive. She used to get agitated, she found the limitations oppressive. Not being able to leave the house, on foot, with the constant fear of being knifed or raped. And then the curfew, the child soldiers who were more dangerous than the bandits themselves. Weapons circulated everywhere. You felt a perennial prisoner, but with a certain resignation—do you understand what I'm talking about? That was the way our life had become; what were we to do, flee and let everything fall apart? Or—what the old men, Uncle

Foodcadde and your father, Taariikh, wanted—witness the downfall, wait patiently in order to be there when the right time came? Did we believe that too? I don't know. Sometimes all you want to do is wake up in the morning and live your everyday life, putting off all decisions, perhaps because your loved ones are still there close to you and that faint warm feeling of hope is sufficient. Change my life, the cold, the uncertainty: it didn't attract me, you know?

But for Shamsa it was completely different. Leaving became her reason for living, her sole, fixed obsession. She was so consumed with the idea of leaving that she was unable to do anything else, almost a year of not going to school and she was letting herself go. Even I, like everyone else, had no patience for her hysteria, her stubbornness. Where do you want to go? I used to say to her; where your best friend went, to Italy, to wash the floors of a *gaal* family? Didn't she have any shame? And Shamsa would throw whatever was at hand at me, violently, and say no, she wasn't ashamed, that we were all good at playing the role of spoiled brats, that in any case we girls washed the floors every day at home and that we had never thought of rebelling, but if one of us should start thinking for herself, if she wanted to free herself from the collective family plan, everyone went against her. Understand her? I just couldn't. It only made me angry. She invented nonexistent conspiracies that she believed were initiated by Libeen. Because he, Libeen, had always had that habit of not talking, of expressing his opinion by keeping quiet. An irritating habit, I agree, but he wasn't wrong. That energy, that righteousness, in Shamsa could be so destructive that it was liable to rebound on her. I know that you think differently, you think she was abandoned. But it's because you project yourself, you were looking for someone whom you could finally identify with. Each family has its own rules and she wasn't able to respect those rules. Otherwise, Uncle Foodcadde would not have abandoned her, do you understand?

I'm not sensitive enough? Always having to read between the lines is so exhausting, Axad. There are even things about you that I don't understand. Your mother, for example, what's keeping you even now from letting her know? She doesn't know that you are here, and pregnant to boot. What did that poor woman do to merit such hostile treatment? Do you understand what being a mother means now that you are about to become one yourself? I have my doubts. We are all so imperfect. A mother is what she is. Even what you believe you understand is only what you didn't have. How can you know what your son will want? Will you be capable of giving him what he wants? Life is so repetitive.

Do you know that story of the heartless son? No, I can't tell you the story, you would get angry. But it's only to explain to you about respect, about how the Somalis view the relationship between parents and children.

The heartless son abandons his old blind father under a tree next to a termite hill. He says to him: Wait here, I'll be back right away, but he has no intention of ever going back. He abandons him because he finds it burdensome to look after him and so the old man is left there. In turn, once the heartless son gets old, he is taken by his son to the tree next to the termite hill. But when the heartless son realizes that his fate will be the same as his father's, he calls his son back. He calls him back to tell him that he knows what the son is about to do because it is what he did to his own father. But he doesn't try to convince his son not to abandon him. That would be too simple. No, the former heartless son absolves his own son and sends him on his way with his blessing. The former heartless son takes upon himself the sin and frees his son from the guilt. Do you understand? This is the meaning of the story. Not what everyone perceives it to be, namely that old people should be respected if you in turn want to be respected in old age, but that the circle must be broken, that you have to have the courage to forgive and break the circle.

I am digressing; we were speaking about Shamsa. She had had her own intuitions, she was always repeating that expression used by the president, "After me, no one." That's it. A typical dictator's expression. It reminded me of the bubbles in comic strips.

So I continued to scorn her and everybody snubbed that poor Shamsa while she stood in line outside the Italian consulate. I was presumptuous, I was reasoning like an invulnerable person, someone so strong as to be immune to the very bullets themselves. As for Shamsa, you know her story better than me, right?

When Shamsa left, the air became heavy at home. We were people waiting for something to happen. Aunt Xaliima was hysterical and I was constantly on pins and needles. I roamed around the city at all hours, regardless of the curfew, challenging fate. I used to think: Soon the liberation army will arrive, an army that will march on the capital, that will destroy the seat of power, that will distribute the wealth to the beggars. I used to dream: The radio will blare out that the dictatorship has fallen, my parents' names will be among those of the heroes of the past decades. I was reasoning like an adolescent. Then everything happened so rapidly. Libeen got hold of a gun to defend the house. Our relatives who lived in isolated places came to us in search of protection. People feared being on their own. And when the liberation army marched into the city, the president didn't just sit and watch. He pulled out all his most terrifying weapons: Kalashnikovs, hand grenades, tanks, machine guns, rifles, cannons. "After me, no one."

In the chaos, criminals spread like the plague. They broke into homes. They stole, they raped, they destroyed. Broken walls and silence all around. We were so very afraid and we didn't even have the courage to go out and light a fire. Huddled together in silence. What happened next is something I've have never told anyone. During a period of calm, I thought to myself: I'm going out, I'm going to take advantage of this lull to light a fire, cook some rice. Then I heard a voice from outside the gate that was calling me, urgently. Who was calling me?

It was Saciid Saleebaan. See how we all know each other? Our generation and those who lived in Mogadishu. Sooner or later we all ended up meeting. Saciid Saleebaan, I was saying. Saciid Saleebaan had a sister, Deeqa, that was her name. A very close friend of mine. The reason for Saciid Saleebaan's urgency was he had come to tell me that Deeqa needed me because her contractions had begun. Deeqa, his sister, my friend. I had made her a promise. But at the time could I ever have imagined that I was the only indispensable one, me who was still so inexperienced? In order to reassure her I had said to her: I'll be there with you too, Deeqa. What I meant was, together with a doctor or with an experienced midwife. Deeqa was so scared, poor thing. She had asked me: Promise me that you will be with me in that moment, you must be careful with the baby's head, his little head. It had gone badly for her sister, that was why she was afraid.

I didn't think twice about it when I saw Saciid Saleebaan urgently calling me for Deeqa, his sister, my friend.

I put on a clean dress and into my bag I quickly put gauze, cotton balls, suturing thread, scalpel, enema, alcohol, hydrogen peroxide, Mercurchrome, a surgical sheet, a photo of my mother, and a pair of gold earrings that had belonged to her and that Aunt Xaliima had put aside for me.

So, when I was ready to leave, I went to Aunt Xaliima, almost hurriedly, without looking at her in the eye, kissing her hands that were pushing me away. Aunt Xaliima was shouting and begging and cursing: Cursed be the day that I let you go to that hospital to see those wretches who are frightened of bringing children into the world! Then, seeing that she couldn't dissuade me from going, she hugged me hard and whispered into my ear: Remember the earrings.

I had already taken the earrings. I knew that she would remind me to take them, Aunt Xaliima never wanted me to be parted from them. Each time I left, that I went away from home, even just for a few days, she made me take them. She believed they protected me. Two pure gold earrings of the finest filigree. Embedded in the center, my mother's eyes?

But let's go back to the train along the Casilina Way and to the girl who pretended not to see me. I think pain reflects back the gaze of people. A hypothesis that I have only begun to develop, little by little, ever since I met that girl.

Her earrings captured my eyes. Mixed emotions. Back and forth, back and forth, I have a strange taste in my mouth, of decomposition, like organic matter that has gone bad. Back and forth, back and forth. The boat rocks and the deep hold, buried among hundreds, thousands of fish, goes back and forth, back and forth. The sea grows, it gets bigger, until it fills my entire throat. I'm drowning. Down, down, down. I can't breathe, I gradually breathe less, less, less, my heart beats slower and slower, the whites of my eyes fill everything and the hands slip down damply, grasping on to the panes of the train window. Can you imagine that? Falling down like that, passing out among all those people squeezed next to me.

I don't know. The girl—the one who pretended not to see me with the dark gray down coat and the canary yellow *fasoleeti*—took me into her skinny arms, pulling me off the train, getting help to pull me off, of her own initiative. I was coming round and she was there in front of me holding my legs against her shoulders. Seeing me come round, she handed me a packet of sugar: Take this, it will make you feel better. And, fearing that I was going to faint again, she put my legs down and said: I'll be right back, and ran across the road. Without prompting, she went to a café across the street to buy us *kabushiini* and croissants, the breakfast we had not had.

Then?

You're Somali, right? I didn't see you on the train, I said, pretending, and she gave a brief smile without even answering. So I asked her if she was new to the area, because I hadn't ever happened to notice her before.

Yes, I came here recently, my husband was already living here, but I wasn't, I don't know this area well, even though by now, to tell the truth, we have been here for almost a year, heavens how time flies, but you know I hardly ever go out, and you, what are you doing, are you going to work?

Yes, I'm going to work, I said to her, I'm a midwife, and you, what do you do, do you work for a family?

No, today is my first day in a *farmashiiyo*. I have to take care of the storeroom, but it's still unclear to me, they will explain everything.

Then, moving back a little, she picked up the plastic cups which we had used, to throw them away. She smiled: Do you feel better?

I nodded, saying: Don't worry about me, today's your first day at work.

Who cares, she replied, I'll explain what happened, if they don't want to understand, tough for them, I can find a job like that anywhere.

Somali, just like the rest of us, with this pride even when you can't afford to have it. I used to think it was dignity, but at times it is only rage that can't explode. We got back onto the train, exchanging names: Barni and Ardo.

Ardo, that was my mother's name. Dark, solid earth.

And do you know what I couldn't stop doing? I couldn't stop looking at those tiger eyes that were dangling from her ears.

We can see each other again, perhaps we can have breakfast together, said Ardo, winking.

All right, when I'm on the morning shift.

And she: You're lucky to have that job; I want to study so much, but till now I haven't been able to.

It takes willpower, I said to her.

But I do have willpower, only that the jobs we find are full-time jobs in families. Is there any time left for us?

I used to work full-time, too.

In a family?

Yes, even though I had studied to be a midwife. They took me on as a nurse to look after old people.

My stop, we parted. I saw Ardo go off. She was waving and waving to me as if she were afraid she would never see me again.

Ardo, my mother's name. Do you remember her, *ab-baayo?* Distant memories, the same consistency as recurring dreams, buried in time. My mother who every night pre-pares me a cup of warm milk and who hugs me tight to get me to fall asleep. Who tiptoes out of the room and leaves the mosquito coil burning. I am reassured because I hear her speaking softly to my aunt, on the veranda.

Living alongside my Aunt Xaliima and Uncle Foodcadde's family was my salvation. I never felt the burden of not having any brothers and sisters. Even my father Sharmaarke's absence, which dragged on for years, was something that I was used to living with. It was the presence of numerous family members that kept me whole. It was so wonderful to grow up together. The times when, in the evening, Uncle Foodcadde piled us all into his green Fiat 124 and dropped us off at the cinema to watch a syrupy Indian movie and then came to pick us up at the exit, a group of loud, chattering children. Or when, more often than not, he took us to the Lido and we sat on the veranda facing the sea, sipping our Fanta orange drinks. The only one who made us mad was Libeen, with his perverse habit of saving his drink untouched till the end so as to make all of us who had finished ours green with envy. And the special days, the holidays, with gifts for everyone: a toy car each or a patent leather belt for the feast of *Iid*, at the end of Ramadan. Your belt was red, wasn't it? Then the everyday things, the older cousins who washed us with a hose, lining us all up, our fear of the Koran teacher, the Italian lessons with the Sacred Heart nun, and the lighted incense at sunset to keep the envious *jinni* at bay. We had a good life and we lacked for nothing.

And I never thought about my father until I saw him for the first time. You never saw him, did you? Aunt Xaliima, perhaps in order to tell me something to sweeten my memories, Aunt Xaliima used to say that my parents had lived together very happily during those early years, when I was very small. Perhaps she only told me that in order to make me happy. I must have been five the first time I saw him. The time stored in my memory. That half day that Sharmaarke had managed to carve out of his life as a fugitive.

My father: a row of teeth like ivory and that birthmark on his forehead exactly like mine, the reason why I immediately liked him. I had always hated that mark. I used to look at myself in the mirror and try to scrub it away with the sponge. So when I met that man with that heart-shaped birthmark exactly like mine, I thought that at long last I could be proud of it. This was what our childhood was all about.

You know, with the war getting closer and Shamsa wanting to leave, for me it was as if someone was trying to destroy the golden memory of our childhood. All those things we used to do and the smell of them, the walks along the beach, the sun, the wind that whips sand at you, and you, Axad, digging, digging, digging bottomless holes, searching, searching, searching. Do you remember? All those small things that you gathered: sponges, sand lizards, seaweed, cuttlefish, flowers, seashells. Did you gather them in order to fill them with meaning? Our childhood, the tea boiling on the stove, the smell of cinnamon and cardamom and Aunt Xaliima grumbling at us while she chatted with the other women. Aunt Xaliima who had swollen legs and wouldn't hear of going on a diet: I'm not some starving wretch, look at my children, she used to say.

But she still wanted to be massaged—by me and only by me—when I was small and I had tiny hands, soft little girl hands that had never worked, as her friends used to say. So I would spread sesame seed oil on her calves and press hard with my little fingers and maybe I gave her some relief.

Sometimes, though, she would irritate me, when she stretched out on the straw mat and shouted orders to everyone: Cook the rice! But who taught you how to shop for food? Today of all days, when we have guests! Didn't you learn anything from your mother? Go and buy the meat!

She behaved like that but I knew that in her own way she really loved me as if I were her own daughter. I used to hear her when I eavesdropped outside the drawing room— a room with Persian carpets and Italian sofas, a room just for guests—and heard the way she spoke. She was proud and spoke of me almost more highly than of Libeen, Saciida, Shamsa, Maxamed, and Xusseen, who were all her children.

This girl is a marvel, she studies the entire afternoon! I should hate her to end up like her mother! If she hadn't studied all those years—mark my words—she would still be with us. But it was Allah's will.

I would listen to her and then go back to rinsing the dishes and my pain was deep in spite of everything.

I thought of my mother, who used to tease me: She'd put her finger right in the middle of my forehead and pretend that it was a switch. She would say that it was a magic tap, my father's magic tap and mine, from which flowed an infinite number of ideas.

* * *

Axadey, this tap is the source of all my sufferings! It dissipates my energy. But with the passing of the years, with experience, I'm changing. Can I already say that we're getting old? The maturing of passions, that's what it is. In those days, they were turbulent pools that I barely controlled. These days I approach Termini station with a light step, once it was so different. Streets to be avoided. But all the same I had to go by there twice a day, going and coming from work, crossing it along the length of all the platforms, from the terminal of the Casilina train in Via Giolitti, right along to the Metro B stop in the direction of the Polyclinic. It was one afternoon, around five o'clock, I had just taken off my white midwife's coat and I was wandering around the underground area at Termini station in a daze. I was lost in thought, in a sealed tunnel, my gaze fixed on my moving feet.

And suddenly, as if to waken me, I heard a voice calling me from behind, inundating me, furtively: Barni!

Barni. A damp voice, almost like a splash of cold water when you wake up.

It was Ardo, the yellow canary, how could I avoid her? She was laughing, happy at having run into me.

What was she doing all alone at Termini station? She had come to meet a friend who was arriving from Switzerland, but the train was running late so Ardo had time on her hands, actually right at that moment she had felt like talking to her sister and was going to Xassan's Phone Center, why didn't I go along with her?

I wanted, or rather I would have preferred, to tell her that I had things to do, invent any kind of excuse—I'm going to work, someone's waiting for me at home—instead, out of my mouth came a sentence just like that, spontaneously: Xassan? I won't go to that dirty old man's place, I replied.

Ardo seemed to have dropped out of a clear blue sky. Didn't she know anything about him? Perhaps she was pretending. I thought: Perhaps she's linked to him in some way, that's why she's going there. That's it, I thought, family ties, something of that nature. Because it happens a lot now, did you see in London? Now nobody seems ashamed to admit it. Two Somali restaurants in the same district, on the same street, with the same flag, with almost the same name. The only difference lies in the people who go there. One restaurant for us, one for them. Bloodlines. One shop for us, one for them. Family ties, I thought. That's why when Ardo asked me: Why do you say he's a dirty old man?, I replied: Nothing, it's doesn't mean anything.

She's not saying anything bad about him because he's a relative of hers, I said to myself. Otherwise, how could she not notice the way he looks at you with those eyes when you go into his shop and the way he says: This dress would look great on you, in a slimy kind of way, as if he were looking at the most embarrassing part of you, that pig.

What's more, he's an old man who buys young girls to be his wives, that pervert. Do you remember the story you told me about Taageere being interrogated by the police? When they questioned him about that girl who had disappeared? Well, that girl—Maryam, I think she was called—was married to him, that dirty old Xassan.

I remember when Taageere arrived in Rome, his easygoing nature, his calmness. And yet, there were things that made him lose his mind. And he had to work off those months he went in fear of his life, when you live day to day and you think that your life, like those of the people you have seen die, no longer has any value. But you must have spoken of these things together. He must have told you about when he arrived as a guest of Diriiye and his wife Safiya and how they welcomed him with that attentiveness of people who do not have children of their own.

And when Taageere appeared unexpectedly before my eyes at Termini station, I jumped, because I would never have guessed who he was if he hadn't called out my name.

He stood in front of me in all his thinness, I only recognized his eyes, but that was enough, his eyes and that tenderness of a defenseless being. *Haye*, doctor, don't you remember me? he said to me with a smile. Then all those images came rushing back to me—not too many years had gone by, perhaps two, three at the very most—images of when we had met and he had said to me that his eyes could not see, so filled were they with his dying friend. Now, Taageere loomed in front of me, with his long bones, and he was so dried up that he seemed a darker shade of black, like a burnt ember.

But as I was saying to you, when Taageere arrived, old Xassan was so full of resentment against him that he could not refrain from speaking badly about him. He knew how much Taageere meant to Maryam. And out of mean-spiritedness, that dirty old man began to spread strange rumors, treacherous insinuations, he wanted to discredit your Taageere, and he went around saying he would teach him a good lesson, so he would learn not to get between a husband and his wife. He reacted like a street hooligan.

Taageere had his good reasons: in his heart Maryam was indissolubly tied to the memory of his friend Xirsi. It seems that Taageere was deliberately walking around the phone center at a late hour. Was he lying in wait? I think that was probable. Because he waited for the dirty old man in a dark alley and he beat him up with all the strength he had in his body. Or perhaps with only some of his strength out of respect for his age. But the most humiliating thing for Xassan was something else. The most humiliating thing was that crazy Taageere took hold of his legs and forced him down on all fours. And all the time the old man was shouting, shouting to let him go, that he should respect old people, while he was spitting blood and crying, sniffling out of humiliation. Taageere shouted at him to make him remember: Old man, remember that I can do you in the ass whenever I want to! Then he let him go and the old man ran off as fast as he could.

You're shaken up by this story? I'm not surprised that he never told you about it. I only found out about it by asking around. And he laughed when he admitted to it. But is it really a manly thing to threaten to do a man in the ass? You go figure.

There are many things about men that I have given up trying to understand. Or are we the ones who stubbornly pretend not to see?

I'm thinking back to when my husband left me. I, my dear Axad, couldn't understand why. I was always solicitous of him, as if I were handling a delicate object, and I used to work all day, without letting it weigh on him. Looking after an older lady calls for a lot of patience. But everything beautiful that was inside me, all my desires, my enthusiasm, my joys, I kept them all for him, for when I returned home on the weekend, when I couldn't wait to cook for him, spend the day making love and in the evening go to the cinema with him. What I didn't want to see was his frustration, the fact that he didn't have a job of his own, that he was dependent on the salary of a wife who spent five days a week in a house that smelled of mothballs. But I believed that together we could make it, that he would get his degree in medicine, and that in the end we would hug each other, saying that it had all been worth it. So I would spend those five workdays imagining the house we would have, our children and my husband with his long white coat. I lived for those honeymoon weekends when he greeted me all freshly dressed and with a basket of sweet-smelling mangoes that he had bought for me.

When he departed from Termini station, his bag filled with just a few things, after he had told me of the pressures his family was putting on him for all the murders we—my genealogy—had committed, and that he couldn't sleep in my bed any longer, I believed him, I believed his words instead of acknowledging the truth, that the real reason was his long humiliation, his guilt at not being able to support his own wife, his revulsion at being dependent on a woman. But what sweet revenge, if you only knew how it ended.

Axad, my sister, after my husband left, I nurtured a profound hatred for Termini station. I had tried to free myself from those buzzing voices, that poison that filled the air after the shipwreck. Libeen used to say that his mother, his sisters, and his nieces and nephews died on that ship because of those people who had forced us to flee. But which people, if the man I love is one of them? I had ignored the buzzing and I had got married by holding my nose so as not to breathe that unhealthy air. I had married, quietly, a barebones wedding as befitted a time of mourning. And now, after having fought those voices, how much greater a condemnation it was to hear those identical words from the lips of the man I loved most in the world. Us and you, murderers and victims, victims and murderers, who is who, if all you have to do is switch perspective?

Termini station, where I had to bury everything. A place that exhales pestilence, a crossroads to be avoided.

And now at Termini station it was my fate to bump into that yellow canary of nauseating sweetness. What did she want from me, didn't she sense the churning of that wall of water between us, like a layer that deadens sound? Ardo was affectionate. I, on the other hand, sensed something strange as she came near me, like the smell of consumed love. And then, I immediately noticed it, she still had those tiger eyes dangling from her ears, eyes that I couldn't stop looking at. I was looking at her eyes and she was looking at the birthmark in the middle of my forehead. This swinging back and forth of gazes made my head spin.

Ardo stood there without moving, waiting for me to suggest something, anything. I didn't know what to say to her, can you imagine that? So I decided to ask her some questions, because I knew nothing about her. I couldn't care less about her answers.

Did you used to live in Mogadishu? Yes, until 1993. Then I managed to leave. You're from Mogadishu, too, aren't you? she asked me. Was she repeating the same question I had put to her? You're from Mogadishu, you live in Mogadishu—are they one and the same thing? For me, in that moment they were not the same thing. They stood for that buzzing and that unfortunate place. So I answered: I used to live there but I'm not from there. I had to leave right away, at the beginning of 1991. You know what it was like for people like us. Those who stayed behind in Mogadishu were all killed! Only the families that controlled the city were able to stay behind.

Ardo registered the accusation. She turned toward a café and asked if we could stop to have a *kabushiini*. Right there and then I probably felt guilty. For that reason, while we were standing waiting at the counter, I began to chatter animatedly. I came up with different topics, bits of this and that, to engage her in conversation. I talked to her about a patient, I showed her the gloves I had bought at the Metro stop. Ardo barely answered, nodding, drinking the ice water, stirring the sugar in her cup, taking small bites out of her croissant. It seemed like ages to me before she opened her mouth again. And do you know what she said to me?

The worst thing about this war is the hate it has created between us. Mogadishu was a great city: there were *gaal* and Indians, Yemenis and Chinese. Everyone lived there.

I seemed to hear her voice amplified, I heard her and I remained to one side, silent. To one side, while I slowly drank my boiling *kabushiini*. Wisps of white foam around my lips.

Can white foam at the corner of my mouth be due to repressed rage? A foaming mouth, Axad, can it be the same mouth that I gazed at fixedly, that mouth that kept chewing *jaat* leaves with bloodshot eyes? What our memory retains are images, in sequence. Not even all of them. When you have to talk about them, you make modifications here and there, you fill in gaps, you recover forgotten things. But it takes a mere detail to bring it all back.

Foam, I was saying. The rice starch that makes the boiling pot foam while Saciid Saleebaan is calling for me as loud as he can from outside the gate. I followed him with my bag. I feared nothing, I was almost flying: Deeqa, Deeqa, Deeqa, we're coming.

Then those four boys, playing with guns, chuckling while trying to keep their balance in the back of the Toyota.

Saciid Saleebaan stopped in his tracks, and put himself in front of me. Can arms—flung wide—protect you from bullets? And one of the boys, almost reluctantly, you know, with his mouth full of *jaat*, foaming with such bitterness, one of the boys grabbed his gun and pointed it at us.

Where do you think you are going?

Look, we have already snagged many others who were trying to be smart like you! Like this, see . . . dha, dha, dha, dha, dhah, shooting in the sand.

The bullet almost touched Saciid Saleebaan, and I could see the sweat pouring down, salty sweat, and it wasn't fear, that I do know. But the boy who had fired, the one who was showering himself with tears and blood, seeing that cold sweat, do you know what he said to him?

You, idiot, begin weeping otherwise I will shoot you in the forehead.

It didn't take much for Saciid Saleebaan to start sobbing. I watched him, hands on stomach, and I could read his eyes, because he wasn't afraid of dying, he was not afraid of that bullet, that I do know. What he was afraid of was not knowing the outcome of his sister Deeqa's delivery.

The boy with the gun, aroused by those sobs, grew bolder, provoking him.

I bet you're one of those stinking pigs who all deserve to be massacred.

He said this because they had already started with that business of who was who, and this because men, always and everywhere, need to decide who is the enemy and who is not. Saciid Saleebaan was not reacting and I was not thinking about anything: because when you think you're about to die, it's not true that you see your entire life pass before your eyes, you only seek out some distant object to hold on to, all the time controlling every muscle of your body.

We were impotent in front of those weapons, simple pieces of metal in the hands of four ignorant bushboys who, up to the day before I would have put in their place with a reprimand and who now dared to play around with our lives.

Axadey, when I say that certain things are written . . .

I had inadvertently opened my bag and I was clutching some gauze. That's probably what did it. One of the boys, more calm than the one who had fired, got down angrily from the Toyota with his gun pointed at me.

What did I have in my bag? Was I trying to be smart?

No, I don't have any weapons, I said to them, emptying everything onto the ground. And they, rummaging among my things, seeing the gauze, the disinfectant, and the scalpel, looked at each other, then looked at me, saying: You're not a doctor, are you?

Yes, I am, and I'm going to a woman who is about to give birth!

But they couldn't have cared less about that woman. It was already something if they thought that a nurse could be of some value.

They rummaged through my bag. They also found my earrings, my mother's tiger eyes.

It was as if they were splitting me open in the middle of my forehead. This is for the road toll! said the calm one.

Then they left Saciid Saleebaan and they took me, firing some shots at his feet, to force him to flee.

Dha, dha, dha dha dhah.

Don't worry, I said to him, each of us has his own destiny.

And as I said this, I was thinking of the *nabsi* that brings balance, that reorganizes things, and this thought calmed me, the fatalism of destiny.

Would you believe that they didn't touch me? It was my feeling of invulnerability that was protecting me.

The boys had even stopped their bravado. And I dared, dared so much, yelling that they were kidnapping me, that when the war was over I would go after them to have them put into jail, one by one, that my friend's life was at risk because of their irresponsibility. Them? Fortunately those boys had not yet turned into practiced killers. They still had some sense of life. And I think they found my complaining amusing.

You know? In my recklessness, I didn't realize that it would have only taken a grain of sand, a mere nothing to rile them, to dha dha dha dha dhah.

But fate decreed that I should reach their general command post safe and sound, the former headquarters of an Italian firm now occupied by the rebels.

The firm? It mainly built roads, at least that's what I think. No, not in the vicinity of Mogadishu—a road going north that is fully operational now, completely legal. It seems that, digging deep down in the sand, they ended up filling the holes with toxic materials. But these are just rumors, gossip.

The headquarters of the firm was a large villa with a beautiful garden full of sweet-smelling papaya plants and periwinkle flowerbeds, lots of cars coming and going, armed men, men deep in discussion, women with children seeking some shade, looted possessions lined up in a corner of the garden to be divided among the militants. Several leaders had set themselves up there; they were drinking tea and talking euphorically. They were happy because there were sophisticated radio transmitters in the firm's headquarters that allowed them to communicate with the entire world.

The leaders seemed sane, educated men. Their shirts were clean, their look reassuring.

Fated coincidence, Axad, my dear. I was there complaining to a leader, complaining that his three bushboys had made me lose time, precious time, when I was meant to be assisting a pregnant woman who was seriously at risk if they did not release me immediately. I was there complaining, as I was saying, when in the nearby room I heard the voices of Taariikh and Foodcadde. I told you, my *abbaayo*, how your father was: he was in very good spirits. He said to me: My daughter, your cousin Domenica, is in Mogadishu, you must meet.

A great time to come back! I replied. But uncle was confused. I think he had a deeply rooted faith in the change. Foodcadde had come there because he had found out where his brother had ended up. You know what Foodcadde is like, he would never have abandoned his brother. But Uncle Taariikh didn't want to hear about it: I'm not moving from here, he said; he trusted those leaders, he trusted their words. And seeing me Foodcadde was quite shocked: Barni, what are you doing here? And I told him everything, about how Saciid Saleebaan had come looking for me and that Deeqa was about to give birth. Uncle Foodcadde was very worried because now there were two people he had to take care of.

So, seeing his eyes so full of apprehension, I felt sorry for him and I said I was going outside to get a breath of fresh air; that way he would have the chance to discuss the matter more calmly. Because, although I still underestimated the situation, I was beginning to realize that it was becoming more complicated and there was no guarantee that they would let me go, or that the leaders were as serene as they had first seemed to me.

I sat down in the garden, at the edge of a flowerbed, and I kept thinking and thinking about Deeqa, about how little time was left and about that phrase that broke my heart, that I had to be careful with the baby's little head. I almost began to cry. I was drying the first tear when I noticed the boy who was staring at me.

I thought he was one of those bushboys and that really annoyed me. He looked at me fixedly, in a crazed way, which made me feel frightened and sorry for him at the same time, so, in order not to let him see my discomfort, I spoke to him like a snarling dog, on the defensive. Why didn't he stop staring at me?

It was he, *abbaayo* mia, your Taageere. I had never seen him before and I didn't even know he was a friend of Saciid Saleebaan. There he was, with his reflective eyes, poor Taageere. I think I may have helped him a little. To release his burden, the burden of his pain. Because it was to me, after days of silence, that he began to speak. Does speaking release the pain? Taageere began telling me everything. But it's a well-known story, you could even write a song about it.

What happened next? Foodcadde came out. He gave me a big hug, he knew it was the only way to make me under-

stand. It wasn't something that could be discussed. He said:
We have reached an agreement, Barni. They need someone
to act as a liaison with abroad, who can speak different languages and who can speak on the radio. They would prefer
a woman, it makes it seem more civilized, they say, so that
the international community will be convinced that they are
not murderers. I think it also serves their purpose to have a
nurse around, in case of an emergency. Two days, they told
me, maximum three. Then, they will have you leave with
the foreigners they are protecting here, they will help you
get out. Taariikh does not want to leave this place. He will
be your guarantor.

I could not even express my opinion. Wanting to get to
Deeqa in that situation seemed almost frivolous. You can do
nothing against destiny.

The leaders kept their promise. I stayed on for three
days, protected, well-fed, well-treated, until they took me
off in a Land Cruiser together with a small group of foreigners they were protecting.

Your father, that was the last time I saw him. He said
to me: Go, and his last words were for you, Domenica, his
beloved daughter.

What about Deeqa? Those words have always stuck in
my mind: the head, the baby's little head. How often we
blame ourselves for tragedies that are beyond our control.
Did Saciid Saleebaan ever talk to you about it? Walls that
cannot be scaled.

I think that was what it was. Because, digging down,
I discovered what was distancing me from Ardo, an un-
confessed fear. What I feared was the recurrence of that
barrier, of that abandonment, of the shipwreck. Distorted
imaginings that I was creating. How could she possibly have
my tiger eyes, my mother's very eyes, eyes that had been
snatched from me?

Had Ardo received them from one of the bushboys as a
love token? You're laughing, but this was what I was thinking: If Ardo had those earrings then she surely had to be one
of them, one of those bushboys who called us filthy pigs.

She had to be one of them, the one who had taken possession of my tiger eyes, eyes that were mine by right.

Was what disgusted me a part of me? Was I reasoning in an unhealthy way?

It was that oppression, the fact that everybody continued to know who was who, and that resentment: the idea that something was implied, unspeakable intrigues. Everybody knew who was who, even though they pretended not to care, and they made a mental note of the names in the book of good and evil. They construed plots and threads, dispatching sentences from the most godforsaken places in the world, and you were the only one left alone with that fear of being just a loose thread, with nothing to hold on to, no safety net. Perhaps it was Ardo who had to help me understand how everything is connected in our lives. For this reason she did not give up, following me while I tried to flee her.

Ardo asked me for my telephone number and I could not refuse.

She called me and there I was with the cell phone in my hand, looking at it and praying to God that it would stop ringing, but I did not have the courage not to answer. I answered and Ardo from the other end, *Abbaayo*, you have to help me, I beg you, we have to meet.

Ardo was at the train stop, the one where we had first met, still wrapped in her down coat that was too large for her, and with the same sickening earrings. She was waiting for me and her eyes were the eyes of someone who can see beyond things. The same eyes that Taageere had when I saw him for the first time. So I sat down next to her, because I could see that what she had to tell me, she had to tell me right now, she couldn't make it as far as the café.

She said she'd been wanting to ask me this for a long time. She wanted the name of a good doctor so she could be examined by him. A woman's medical examination. In fact, it would be a good idea to have her husband checked out, too. Since I worked at the hospital, I could probably give her the name of someone good.

Axad, I didn't ask her anything. It was she who started telling me the whole story. I realize that this is not the best time for you to hear it, but I also know that you are strong and, after all, these things have been written, it's useless for us to feel frightened and try to fight destiny.

She told me about her pregnancy. About her attentive husband and all the careful checkups. A pregnancy in the West respecting all the rules of the game. Prenatal exercises, morphological ultrasound, and monitoring. There are just a few weeks left and Ardo goes for that checkup. The doctor checks the baby's heart rate, as they do in all routine checkups.

Ardo trembles at the recollection. She isn't able to shrug off that worry, the expression of the worried doctor, who hurries off without saying anything and who calls another doctor, still without saying a word.

Ardo remembers that she waited a long time, that the minutes weighed like lead, then a third doctor arrived, a complete stranger to her.

"He said to me: Ma'am, your baby is dead."

Ardo has already cried so much over this event that all she has left is a silent sob. And she wants to give me all the details: of the pointless labor pains, of the refrigerated morgue, of the white coffin. She continues her story because her husband said that by telling her story she will free herself. But what does she have to free herself from?

It can happen, they told her. No scientific explanation. So she thinks there's something wrong. Perhaps at the hospital, perhaps in herself. This is what I have to help her find out. She says that she goes to the cemetery every day, and she sees that it happens again and again. But even if the earth continues to fill up with small coffins, she just cannot free herself. She is still here with that knot.

I, a midwife, someone who works in a hospital, must help her.

Because she has finally figured out her problem, and her problem is that she did not trust this country, she did not trust her future, because inside herself, inside her body, she continues to feel the pain of not being in her own country. And I have to help her find out in the *nabsi* what she is guilty of, because she will only be free of this knot if she expiates it.

You know, Ardo hadn't been sleeping for a long time. She suffered from insomnia.

Axadey, the power of the *nabsi* is terrible. It is the *nabsi* that makes rich men poor, those men who have cruelly treated the poor, that turns the betrayers into the betrayed, the murderers into the murdered. Everything is connected, everything has its own balance. Ardo wanted to find out what her sin was. And while I looked at her I almost felt impervious to her pain, my body could not absorb it. And I felt a bit abnormal because of this, because such deep pain cannot possibly leave you cold. You know what my problem was? It was that I continued to stare at those earrings, the tiger eyes that the bandits had taken from me. There was no doubt that they were one and the same.

My mother always wore those earrings, two tiger eyes framing her face. At the most my mother allowed herself a yellow amber necklace, the color of egg yolks. She wasn't one for jewelry, she didn't like to show off; the only exception was those filigree earrings, the work of a creative artist commissioned by her beloved. My father, Sharmaarke, had put money aside each month for that gift. He who loves must show his intentions with important gifts. But he had to stop there; my mother was against frivolous things, she was an independent and emancipated woman.

I remember, the two of them discussed things a lot, as equals, man to man, woman to woman. It is the agreed custom everywhere to live very separate lives, roles that cannot be interchanged.

Everyone knew that my mother Ardo was very daring; she spoke with the men and smoked in public. Aunt Xaliima—I don't know if you remember this—would get very angry and would hide the packets of cigarettes. My mother did not take it to heart, she was solid and firm like the earth.

Aunt Xaliima once got very angry with me—I was older by then and it was just before I left—and she said: You will become a smoker like your mother! She must have deemed it a terrible insult.

My mother was right never to doubt her sister-in-law's affection because it was Aunt Xaliima who always took care of us. Like a guardian angel.

We were too small, Axad, to understand my mother who wept every day, who didn't get out of bed and whose eyes had purple circles around them, my mother who didn't wash herself anymore, who didn't eat anymore, who didn't go out anymore. She stayed in bed huddled up like a fetus, and I used to slide my head between her breast and her thighs to absorb her smell, infinitely. But having me close made her feel worse, she couldn't shake herself out of it. But Aunt Xaliima insisted that I continue all the same, she got angry: Go to your mother, who knows, maybe if she sees you she may recover, and with her directness she ended up burdening me with a big responsibility. Could I save my mother?

Every day men in spectacles came and everyone kept quiet when they began to examine her, everyone was worried, but my mother didn't even notice them, because by then she had lost interest in the things of this world.

Abbaayo, no one ever wanted to tell me why my mother died. We all fled from that crackling fire, everybody, absolutely everybody. Now that I am an adult, I think that what killed her was the pain she felt for those nine men shot on the beach without a trial, those nine men one of whom had a heart-shaped birthmark right in the middle of his forehead.

But why hate, thereby perpetuating the pain? Ardo was right, what was truly terrible about the war was that it had created this blind hatred among us, hatred among lonely people, scattered all over the world. She was right, Mogadishu, a large, cosmopolitan city in which we all lived: Somalis, Italians, Indians, Russians, Pakistanis, Yemenis, Chinese, Persians, Kenyans, Americans, and Indonesians. Ardo had said those words because she had sensed my underlying accusation needed to be unearthed. Earth was the element she knew.

Ardo had seen me stare at those earrings, earrings that I wanted back. She saw my heart that was immune to her pain and she realized that I was thinking of her guilt and of the *nabsi*. From whom had she received those eyes dripping blood? Liquid, like crimes that soil you. Collective sins to be expiated. One sad story was not enough to free me from the resentment that we breathed everywhere. The smell of dead flesh and of stagnant water.

It made me nauseous, you know? As soon as I drew near Termini station I smelled that same odor. It was different in the beginning, when I went there every day. I even hoped to meet you again. But Libeen told me you did not feel well, that it wasn't the right time. He kept you for himself. I only had a vague idea of where you lived. It was the constant moving that confused me. Too many people, too much news, too many moves. The men standing in front of the counter, it was a continuous greeting of people, recognizing each other, exchanging news right down to the last detail. It was in that place that I met my husband, just before it happened.

His small spectacles—the effect of that silver frame around the whites of his eyes—seemed like those of an intellectual who discusses the fate of a country. Did I think of the two of us as I had imagined my parents?

However, history does not repeat itself. At best our generation had produced men like Libeen or like Taageere. My husband was building barriers that divided men and the world in ever diminishing segments, getting smaller all the time. He moved around within those narrow, constricted spaces believing that he was comfortable. He left me, and he didn't finish his studies. He got married, he asked for political asylum in Holland, and he had four children. No, they don't work, neither he nor his wife.

Had he already shown signs of his indolent nature? I've asked myself that question. But it was when I began going out with him that it happened.

It was in the middle of the night when the telephone rang. There was nothing to be alarmed about as there were seven people living in the house who might receive a phone call and there was always someone calling from a place which was in a completely different time zone. However, that phone call was for me, and it didn't come from far away.

It was as if it were today, Axad, my dear. Libeen telling me about that ship that left Kismaayo for Mombasa loaded with passengers, so loaded that it couldn't make it with all of them. Aunt Xaliima always boasted that she knew how to swim, she told us about that river in the place where she grew up. She boasted about it, but if I had been there I would have said to her: Take care of yourself, I'll take care of the children. Those swollen legs of hers, could they make it?

I think the pain made me cling close to my husband. So close that I preferred to have Libeen hate me, to have him decide that he didn't want to speak to me anymore as long as I was with one of those who were responsible for his mother's death. That's why he was able to keep you away from me.

I was deeply in love with my husband. Maybe that's why I never wanted anyone else after he left.

* * *

I must tell you the rest of the story. I wanted to get rid of Ardo. So, I summoned up the courage that I did not have in the beginning. I managed not to answer her calls anymore. Those dangling eyes that obsessed me. At first the phone rang all the time, then less. Months had gone by and I had forgotten all about her.

Then, one day while I was on duty at the hospital, she arrived, brought in as an emergency, experiencing spasms. She was not screaming, poor thing, she was just afraid. Who knows if she deliberately came to the hospital where I work. How did she know when I was on duty? What's more, you know, you have no control over your labor pains. Her labor had started right then. But there was something that complicated the whole business, no small matter: the little girl that Ardo was carrying was upside down, her head near her mother's heart and her feet pointing downwards. In the past, they used to deliver children in that position, too;

nowadays, though, they prefer to operate because during a natural delivery the baby runs the risk of suffocating. So Ardo was in labor and she was weeping for these two sad reasons. She was sad that this baby too might not survive, and because she would not be able to push her out by herself. Ardo did not want them to open up her belly. But they had to open her up as this was an emergency, because this was before the date scheduled for her delivery and because her body had decided that the baby should be born before it was full term.

I saw Ardo's eyes, eyes that were expecting to see me. And do you know when I realized that everything is decreed?

I realized it when she said to me: Promise me you will be by my side in that moment, you must be careful with the baby's head, the baby's little head.

So I went along with her to the final ultrasound and—you won't believe this—the baby had turned around right at the very last moment. What could this be if not a miracle?

I took Ardo's baby in my hands. I washed away the blood, I placed her at her mother's breast. That baby was born washed, washed clean of all resentment. We had settled our debt with the *nabsi*.

The tiger eye brings together destinies. They say that this stone is the color of the earth and the stripes are golden yellow like the light. It is a stone that possesses great power because it harmonizes extremes and blends the energies of the sun with the earth. Its essence perhaps lies in the fusion.

That was the right moment to begin everything afresh. Like a road that, at the start, was the wrong one and that one must go down again. Everything from the beginning, building a life from the beginning. Can you re-stitch a web of existences that was constructed over two decades of life?

There are some knots that are loosened only when you reveal them. So, when I think back on it, I realize that that was the moment to ask her about the earrings. Ardo seemed so perfect with her baby in her arms. So perfect that only thanks to her could I free myself from the resentment that, for so long, had fueled my existence. Ardo stopped being my scapegoat. She explained everything to me in such a clear way.

Like a story that I had always known.

Many years ago, when she was still unmarried, Ardo went to work for an Italian lady and lived in her house. The lady had grown very fond of her since she brought back memories of Somalia, a land in which she had lived some very intense months. Ardo would cook *sambuusi* and the lady was filled with joy. She was a good person and treated Ardo well. All the same, Ardo was hoping for a better life, she wanted to explore other avenues, see the world, and find a husband. How could she do all this when she was closed up all day in an apartment? So, she had decided to leave the job, and they had separated on very affectionate terms. It was at this point that the earrings came into the picture, a parting gift. Before Ardo, another Somali girl had worked in that house. The lady spoke about her all the time, especially since the girl had disappeared from one moment to the next, without warning. Well, this girl had left several things behind, among which there were two gold earrings of the purest filigree. Embedded in the center was a tiger eye.

I didn't have the courage to confess my thoughts to her. Digging deep down inside myself I discovered that I was no longer so sure.

Were those earrings truly the same ones? My mother's tiger eyes?

The birth had filled me with joy. The next day I filled the bowl with warm water to wash her and check the stitches. It came quite naturally to me to first take that water in my hands and rinse my face. Then I bent toward the small mirror in the red frame that was over the wash basin and I did something I had not done in a long time. No, the mark did not go away.

In the following days I taught her how to take care of her baby girl. I rubbed her tiny body with oil and essences. I could feel the universe beating under the palm of my hands.

I was in pieces and my life had no meaning in her presence. I put my face close to her and she seemed to press her small fingers on the birthmark in the middle of my forehead.

She seems to turn your light on, Ardo used to say.

Ardo and I share a deep bond. I saw a lot of her before she left. I saw her daughter grow. Yes, I should go to see her. Who knows how beautiful she's become; by now she must be more than three years old.

7

TAAGEERE

YOU COME TO ME AND START asking questions. It's difficult for
me to believe you, do you understand? I've nothing against
you. But if you present yourself this way, how can I trust
you? The worst is that I had to figure it out for myself that
you work for them, that they sent you, otherwise you
wouldn't have told me. All right, all right, I didn't give you
enough time. You didn't want to scare me? One wrong word
and all those years of sacrifice go to waste, you block my
application for a passport. I didn't think you were a spy. My
friend, calm down. As I said to you, I have nothing against
you but rather against the people who mentioned my name.
People on my side, I'm sure. Deep down, those boys who say
they're my friends are all cowards. Am I letting my imagina-
tion run away with me? So then, why don't you help me
understand, for example, your relationship with the people
in Immigration. The role of interpreter is something I can
understand, and so is the fact that you don't make the de-

cisions, that your job is solely to communicate with me. I draw my own conclusions: if you work with them, you're on their side. No, I cannot imagine that it's possible to be on nobody's side. You do your job and that's it? But what kind of man would you be then? *Ninyow*, you should know where you stand. You're a mediator, that's what you told me. But tell me, when you're dealing with public housing, with political asylum, you really don't have any say in the matter? Working with the people in Immigration mustn't make you forget that you should help your own people. There's no line that separates us from our work on the one hand and our personal lives on the other: what we are is all one and the same. I don't agree, I don't think that the public and the private are two distinct things.

There, that's better: you must choose our side. You say that you're doing it for her good, that she's about to get her citizenship. But I need guarantees if you want me to speak about Maryam. That girl means a lot to me. No, not in the way you think. I already have a wife, a wife whom I recently married and who's expecting a baby. I should trust you out of a sense of brotherhood. People like you only pull out brotherhood when it suits them. You've been here longer than me, you work with them therefore you have to act in their favor. After all, you've only known about her disappearance for the last twenty days, why are you alarmed? This makes me nervous, it's the fault of those false friends who mentioned my name. I used to know Maryam but I'm not her brother or her father.

All right, if you can guarantee that this conversation is confidential, that you won't go and spill the beans to the *gaal* and if you empty your pockets and show me what you have in them, that you don't have tape recorders or microphones, then okay, I'll tell you what I know. You want to start from that evening, but why that one in particular? According to your information, that's the day she disappeared, that's what they told you.

What happened? Nothing unusual happened, only that there were too many people around, that's what. In my opinion, it's because of this silly habit of coming here to spend the summer, as if it were Mogadishu. As soon as it begins to get hot, whoever can, goes to visit a relative in some distant city. Some people even go round the world this way! In the past, I never asked myself where they found the money. Domenica was the one who made me think about it.

Domenica says having the money has nothing to do with it. She says it took her ten years to understand that Somalis are just not capable of putting money aside, or of settling down somewhere. That's what Domenica says. Maybe a family had a little extra money during that month in the summer so instead of buying new furniture, they decided to buy some plane tickets. Shouldn't life be lived day by day?

I'm saying this to you, but I'm sure you live in a nice house, right, my friend? You're a crafty one to answer me with a question. You want to know how long I've been here. Many years, but I am always ready to leave, I have my things packed in a bag. Actually, right now my wife should be sending me a visa for Italy. But I'm undecided, you know. I could be satisfied just taking the visa, but if I wait to get citizenship here, perhaps that would be even better.

Who's my wife? Oh, sorry, I thought I'd told you. My wife is called Domenica, she's Italian-Somali: Italian mother and Somali father.

She was also there the evening you're talking about. We had only just met! I know that wasn't many months ago; it was love at first sight, we got married immediately. I wanted to do things the right way, I married her so people wouldn't have the chance to say bad things about my woman.

That evening Domenica was taking footage for a film about us Somalis.

Have you seen that area? It's the right kind of place, with those tall, public housing buildings all in a circle, the yard in the middle full of dried-up grass and trees that look as if they will blow away from one moment to the next. In the summertime, people can't stay inside. The apartments are small and suffocating, there's not even any air conditioning. In the evening everyone comes down, dragging mattresses, pillows, and teapots. Then, everyone spends the night there, enjoying the cool air and chatting. In July it is truly very hot, you can hardly breathe.

It's all calm, all quiet, if it were not for certain characters. That crazy Saciid Saleebaan, for example, who cannot survive without his video camera. He hands it to some young kid and gets him to film him.

You're asking yourself why I say that he's crazy when I spend all night waiting for him at the police station. I'm not inconsistent, my friend. I'm beginning to realize that you know many, too many things to ask questions.

It's true, I waited at the station until they released him. I did so to spend time with Domenica, to keep her company. That was the second time that I had seen her and I was courting her. It worked faster than I thought it would! Domenica was at the police station because she and Saciid Saleebaan work together, they have to make a film about Somali refugees, something like that. Saciid Saleebaan has always had a passion for cameras. They met in Germany and she had come all the way here for that project, so she told me. I don't know how she can work with that madman; I've known Saciid Saleebaan forever, he was nuts even before the war. But Domenica finds him amusing, she says he's like that because he has suffered a lot. She says you have to admit that he has some original ideas. I'll show her original! I'm not jealous, it's a long story between me and Saciid Saleebaan's original ideas. Those beautiful ideas have made me lose a pile of money. And then, do you think that ridiculous idea of singing the Somali national anthem and yelling out crazy words is funny? The same national anthem that they played for us before every film with the blue flag flying, the Somali national anthem we had to sing at school before starting class, everyone lined up in the courtyard like soldiers. Some say that the anthem was composed by an Italian. That's all bullshit to me. And then, I'm proud of it, let me say so: *Soomaaliyeey toosoo, toosoo isku tiirsada ee, hadba kiina taag daranee, taageera weligiinee.* I think that it was by listening to the last verse that my father got the idea to call me Taageere. Otherwise he would never have thought of giving me a name that nobody else has.

Back to Saciid Saleebaan. He used to say, "Ladies and gentlemen," like in the shows, and he would begin to randomly list a number of countries: Australia, Canada, Sweden, Holland, Kenya, Italy. These are the countries where my people are dispersed, the people of the Horn of Africa, the only anarchic nation on the five continents, he would say.

He used to speak as they do on the newscasts, "It's hot, people have gathered in the courtyard with their mattresses, with cold drinks and tea. Everyone's outside enjoying the cool air, just as we did in Xamar when the heat became unbearable."

Meanwhile the young boys gathered round him and they were roaring with laughter. One of the ladies shouted out: Stop it, Saciid Saleebaan, stop playing around with that contraption. And he would start up again with "Ladies and gentlemen," just like a record.

This is the land of opportunity, the land of import-export, this is the land of racial integration, this is the land of multiculturalism!

Then, carried away with himself, he jumped up onto the stairs and pretended to be a rapper, calling us "brothers and sisters."

Listen up, brothers and sisters, we are gathered together on this summer night to shout out at the top of our lungs with you. Listen up, brothers and sisters, we are gathered here with you, but are we brothers and sisters? But who are you? Never saw you before!

That's exactly what he said, I swear. He picked up his video camera and went off huffing and puffing. Perhaps he got offended because everyone was laughing and some people were even getting annoyed. The thing is he fancies himself half American, that fool! What's more, I can't figure out whom he thinks that lovely video is for. Granted, nowadays people are in the habit of taking pictures of themselves all the time. People have always liked to take pictures of themselves, but once there was a certain elegance about it, you

had to comb your hair and put on nice clothes before you
had your picture taken. All the family together in front of
the camera. The children in order of height and in the center
the mother and the father looking very serious. Say cheese!

Saciid Saleebaan, on the other hand, acts like an American and then he's surprised when people get angry. Fortunately, Domenica was around to calm him down.

She was enjoying the evening. She chatted with me and
spent time with the girls. I think it's Domenica who does the
real work, the serious work, while Saciid only goofs around.
Why does she trust that madman? She continues to say that
it's out of respect for his idea, after all it was he who told
her "Let's make this film" at a time when Domenica was still
very confused. Many years ago. Filming has helped her reason calmly. And then, she is very loyal to people, you know,
that old-fashioned loyalty.

No doubt they will agree to show you the cassette,
they've got it back. That evening, the police confiscated it
when they arrived.

We want to know what really happened! they said.

But, I say, if it were only a case of understanding how
things went, why did they keep Saciid in jail all night?

The pictures, they said, will help us understand what the
heck you hoped to achieve with this demonstration.

They looked at the recording, and when they realized how
things had gone, they gave it back. But right now, the cassette
is in Italy. Domenica took all the material with her: You never
know, she told me. Do you think it could be useful?

You'd really like that video, my friend, I think you would
really like it.

Especially the beginning when the video camera was in
Domenica's hands. There she was with her video camera,
laughing and throwing her head back with all those auburn
curls of hers. I remembered her way of laughing, I had already seen her, we had had a conversation and I had liked
her. A lot.

"See you around" was her parting phrase but she had
left me nothing, not even a telephone number.

I don't use cell phones, she had said. Or was it an excuse for me? Did she want things to go gradually? Maybe, maybe. But I have to say, by then I had lost all hope of seeing her. I had searched for her for a long time. Obviously in all the wrong places. If only I had known that all I needed to do was ask Saciid Saleebaan.

Well, I had passed the tall buildings and I had entered the courtyard when I saw her, right there, surrounded by some old men. There, in the center, with her video camera. I almost ran up to her. I was running because of her. But no one noticed me because I usually stop to listen to the older people, and that's why they always acknowledge my presence with affection. They're happy because they repeat the same stories ten times over, always the same ones. So, if there's someone new to listen to them, they're happy to welcome them. And that evening they were all in a good mood, with the white plastic table out and the barbecue going, the coals in the middle of the yard, you can just imagine it. Perhaps it was the smoke that drew attention?

The fire was under control, I'm sure, and as I said, all I had to do was busy myself with something, to remain transparent. I didn't want Domenica to realize that I was there for her.

Boy, do you want to help your uncle? I had to take off all that tender goat meat and dip it in the marinade again: they used the word "marinata." The old folks really have Italian deep in their souls. I imagine what it must be like to learn a language as a child, when your head is free of cares, with room to fill it up with all the words you want.

My friend, I'm not digressing. If you don't like the way I'm explaining what happened, then take your questions somewhere else. I'm telling things in a logical way. You asked me about the video? The video isn't here, that's why I have to give you the details, exactly as it happened.

At the beginning there's this scene. Domenica must have been attracted by all those old folks to have stayed so long, and they were easily convinced, vain as they are. In front of the camera. Just think, then, what they thought when they found out that she was Taariikh's daughter. Sifting through their memories, all of them remembered him.

One especially: they had even been roommates when they studied together in Italy.

University roommates. They were friends, the two of them; otherwise Taariikh wouldn't have agreed to sleep with someone who suffered from *aerofagia*! They all laughed. I didn't understand every word because they were speaking Italian and the joke was for Domenica's benefit.

That's what the old folks do, they use difficult Italian words. I studied that language but not enough to understand *aerofagia*. Now I know it means excessive burping; Domenica explained it to me, she explained everything when we looked at the cassette again together.

I was telling you about Taariikh's ex-roommate. Proud as punch at the success of his word, he started off again as if the video camera and Domenica's face were one and the same thing. And he spoke about when he and Taariikh were students together at the University of Padua.

One day an Italian friend invited them to lunch at his house. They were two penniless African students and this Italian student instead had a house all his own! Wow, things were really different for these Italians: such a young student actually had a house all his own! They were surprised and, if truth be told, even a little pissed off because of that disproportionate difference. They swallowed their anger and went off quietly, on their best behavior, to the agreed-upon place on the agreed-upon day. Knock, knock—guess who was behind the front door? There was their friend, his father, mother, sister, and brothers—the entire family! So, instead of saying "my house," why didn't he say "our house"?

Have you ever spent time around old folks? It's always the same thing: one cracks a joke, the next claps, and everyone laughs. Then, whoever has a new story carries on.

I was watching Domenica but her eyes were too busy to notice me. Satisfied eyes. And the old folks vied with each other to make her happy.

You stole your father's eyes, they told her, and your head is the same shape as Cleopatra's!

They were drinking bottles of cold beer and they offered us fruit juice: You don't want to ruin yourself, do you, my boy?

Then, a couple with two children went by right in front of them, just in time for the old folks to start up again.

"That one married a *dhagax.*"

"What are you saying? Only someone like you could call a human being a stone!"

"Ah, but I can see that you're all laughing, and what's more, I call everything by its name."

"What does *dhagax* mean?" asked Domenica, and I, who couldn't wait to make myself known, immediately replied, "It's a rude way of referring to blacks who are not from our part of the world. However, I don't understand why it's offensive: stones are tough and beautiful." And I noticed—while Taariikh's old roommate slapped me on the back—I noticed that Domenica took her eyes off the camera and was looking at me, as if to say, "So it's really you, then."

I told you to be patient. This story also has to do with Maryam.

I'll continue, then. While we were there, me with the skewers over the barbecue, the ex-roommate passing out drinks, and the rest sitting around, someone else began to speak, someone who remembered Taariikh even though he had studied in Bologna instead of Padua. And this character, the one from Bologna, said he went to visit his father's grave three years ago. First, he took a plane to Kenya, then from Nairobi to Kismaayo, there and back. On his way back he stopped in Kenya, he needed a break. And, on that occasion, he went to a place where there were lots of Western tourists, a place where he met a Masai. What was the Masai doing?

He was selling knickknacks, said the old Bolognese man in Italian. For me it was a new word that needed translating, because the difficult words were the ones that made Domenica laugh. That's why I got her to explain them all to me when we looked at the video again together, months later. Watching it reminded us of the lucky beginning of our coming together.

Knickknacks. The Masai had never left Kenya, but through meeting many foreigners, he had learned many languages. Since the Masai told clever stories, the old Bolognese man asked him to go to the bar with him, so they could continue talking. But no, the Masai was not allowed to go into the bar where the foreign tourists went. So the ex-Bolognese, putting himself out, went to speak to the owner of the bar, who gave his consent, since he was only really interested in getting his money. They were chatting about life and other complicated matters when the Masai said an unforgettable phrase: They expropriated me. Yes, the Masai actually used the word "expropriated." What about Bologna? Bologna started laughing, saying to him: But expropriated what, if you don't even own two cows? Then that tall, thin scarecrow of a black said: No, they expropriated my soul. He could have chosen to continue living like a nomad, but it was much more worthwhile for him to walk those three miles every day to sell his knickknacks. The ex-Bolognese student, moved by the Masai's sense of being uprooted, something he shared most profoundly, bought some knickknacks as souvenir gifts for his daughter. In exchange for the tortoiseshell hair combs and the necklaces made of small colored stones, he left him an even ten dollars. The Masai was very, very happy. He had never seen a full ten dollars; he had seen one, two, three dollars at the very most. The Masai, having recovered his pride, even went as far as to say that from that day on, the ex-Bolognese student could have all the knickknacks he wanted.

I remember by heart all the conversations we had that evening. I've watched those recordings over and over again with Domenica, at least ten times. Domenica didn't realize that I was there from the very beginning, to help the old folks. So she stopped the video every time I appeared on-screen and she laughed—how she laughed—at my face with my mouth wide open. Stories: listening to stories and telling them is what I like best.

I was there up until Alberto the Italian-Somali arrived. How his friends teased him!

"He's started treating his mother well because he's afraid of going to hell!"

"It's true, isn't it, Alberto, that it was the Jehovah Witnesses who made you change?"

And he pretended to get upset and so that became their game, his refusing to go along with the joke.

That was when I left because I could see that Domenica was still busy, and after all, I had eaten two pieces of roasted goat meat and I didn't want it to seem as if I were scrounging. They offered, but it's rude to refuse, isn't it? All right, I'll continue: I'm telling you just as it happened in the video, right?

I am wandering around the courtyard looking for my friends. I stop because Maryam calls me: Taageere! Yes, that was the moment I saw her. She's slightly touched in the head, poor thing, that's why she's still with her mother at twenty-seven years of age. But her mother doesn't seem to be worried, she thinks she's still a child. And she's beautiful with those Indian eyes of hers. Maryam was sitting there, dressed in her *guntiino* with a light blue handkerchief on her head, and she was calling me.

She was sitting there looking at the sky. She said she was moved because it was amazing that everything was the same. Just like it was in February and the monsoons were resting during the *Tangabili*. Not a breath of wind. And she said, one evening she had a terrible headache, one of those headaches that get you right here, in the temples, and that give you no peace. And while she said this, she pressed her forehead between her index and middle fingers in such a way that it seemed that she still had her headache and that she wanted to squeeze it away. And then she began to speak about her cousin. An angel. The heat was unrelenting and her cousin had begun to drag the mattresses out, like that, without any sheets. Bare mattresses.

And she had got a large jug, full of iced water. She could still feel the ice-cold cloth, her headache that suddenly went away.

Her cousin, an angel. She had been angry at the beginning because in the evening they tell lots of stories. And she wasn't even able to listen. The evening meal lasts so long. You sit on the mattresses and you eat dinner. The children do what they want.

It was wonderful like that, under the stars.

That crazy Maryam never says things in an ordinary way. She sits there, looks at the sky, and you never know what she'll say next.

It makes me want to weep. There I was and she was making me cry, that oddball, so I said goodbye to her and I went away, because sooner or later we would have met up again. *Ninyow,* who's ever seen a man crying?

That's it, that was the last time I saw her.

But why do you want to talk about that evening? It's difficult for me to re-create what happened. You know how it is, I lose my train of thought, lots of things spring to mind, so it's probably better if we go and sit down somewhere; come on, let's go this way.

See that building? When I arrived, I lived there. It's full of Somalis. It's like being in Somalia. The trouble is, you don't learn the language. They stick you in there, in a building full of Somalis who are arguing and solving their problems among themselves. Do you think that's right? It's to make you feel you're not alone, you're saying. Think what you like. I know your reasons: if we all learned to speak English properly, who would need you? You're hoping you can change professions; good, even if now you live in the fancy part of town, you know who your brothers are. You know what people who stay around here are like. Here everyone ends up badly. Take those two young girls. They're fourteen years old and look how they're dressed. You think I'm a bigot? It's not about nudity, my brother, you're wrong. The thing is, you don't know whom you're speaking to, you don't know me. What I'm talking about is limits. In this country girls wear miniskirts for school uniforms, they have sex at thirteen. Their limits are different, they have no meaning for us, just like ours have none for them.

That's why when I talk about those two young girls, I say: They have mixed up their limits, their behavior doesn't conform to anyone's. They're damaged goods.

I don't deny that I have my preferences. But rigid, I'm not rigid. For example, I like Maryam's way of doing things. How did I describe it? She wears the *guntiino* and the *garbasaar* the way our women do. And I like Domenica even if you rarely see her wearing a skirt. She's Italian-Somali; she understands the differences. And she covers herself, maybe also out of respect, she doesn't go around showing her legs.

They say we don't integrate. Now they have even cut the welfare checks, but people still don't have the slightest inclination to go and break their backs in a factory. Sure, I go. You know what they all think, right? They think I'm crazy. Crazy! Because I couldn't care less about the welfare money! What I like is waking up in the morning with something to do. I know, assembling pieces of machinery is boring work, tiring work. That's why every now and then I go missing. You know everything, right, my friend? I can't hide anything from you! I feel like I'm talking to a wily policeman who manipulates conversations.

I was talking to you about welfare.

It's a vicious circle. The kids pretend they go to school and instead they stay home. If you don't have anything to do, boredom is just around the corner. And you know, here it's full of Jamaicans. What do you mean, what do the Jamaicans have to do with it? Try and say that word out loud and see what happens. Go on. Say "Jamaican" out loud. Last year it was a running battle. But they've calmed down, we showed them that we are a people with a war going on back home. Now, when they see one of us, they give us weed for free. No, not to me—I said one of us just as an example. In the general sense. My friend, you cleaned up so well that you could almost pass for a *gaal.*

But you must know, they must have called on you many times for matters of this kind. Cases of adolescents who smoke hashish, who don't go to school. The thing is, here everyone speaks about adolescence as if it were a disease and the problem ends up being just that. We spent those critical years like this. They helped you resolve your problems with burning metal.

The trouble is that kids raised here do not know what discipline is. They come with their mothers who do not know how to control them. Yes, that's true, our mothers raised us on their own. But in our country it was different. There were so many of us. And my father often came home. He would come home and enter the courtyard. Everyone around him. And he was strong and his mustache gave him an air of authority. He looked you in the eye, like this, without even touching you, and: Don't you disobey your mother, he would say. I remember my circumcision. We were shaking with fear. We ran off. That was normal. At seven years of age, the holy man comes, they say chop, it's all over in a minute, but everyone knows it hurts. It bleeds a lot. So we hid behind the bushes. And I could see my father, he was coming toward us, with his mustache. We came out before he found us. Very slowly, shaking his head, without saying a word. We didn't step out of line.

Fathers come and go, that's true, but here, let me say it again, here it's different. Take that young boy, the one we said hello to earlier. Poor thing, he's just come out of jail. He drove his mother crazy. And she took care of him with a leather whip until he bled. It took her a while, but at a certain point his mother realized on her own that things couldn't go on like that. The fact is that here you can't lay your hands on kids; here if you whip your child, you'll end up in jail. The kid soon found out that he could blackmail his mother: Touch me and I'll have you locked up, locked up, he told her, snorting defiantly. So the poor woman didn't know what to do. What did she do? She called the boy's father, who at the time was finishing up some business in the United Arab Emirates. The father came as fast as he could and, as soon as he got all the necessary documents, he dragged his son back with him to wrap up the business he had left unfinished. The first thing he did was send him to a Koranic school, hoping the religious instruction would straighten him out. And now? Look at that good-for-nothing, he roams around with his gang, he breaks into cars, and he already has a child from a young white girl. A little while back he was with an older woman. A woman who already had three children. Did he want to be a father to someone else's children? In my opinion, he wasn't even remotely thinking about being a father, he was looking for a mother. A stepmother who taught him lots of things he shouldn't have learned. Like smoking grass. Not surprising under those circumstances. The thing is, here they immediately accuse us of rape. If you touch a woman on the breast, like this, on the breast. He touched a girl on the breast and she accused him of rape.

This country ruins people. But I'm about to leave, I've found a place. As soon as they give me my passport, I'm joining my wife in Italy. That way I will be able to live with her, raise our son, and finally see my first child who now must be nine years old.

But this will only happen if you don't ruin everything, cooking up who knows what.

It took me a long time to find a new wife. A wife I liked. Because I continued to think about Shukri and my child, I compared every woman to her. How she carried herself, her almond-shaped eyes, and her breath that smelled of sweet milk: that was Shukri, unique.

Only Domenica was something different, another world, another purity. I thought: With this woman I can get a new start. With her, I stopped thinking of the past and started seeing things differently, finding ways to start over. Now she's in Italy and she's expecting my child. I was the one who sent her there. I asked her to meet my sister. She has this freedom to move in and out, to cross borders, truly a great gift that I don't envy but I feel I share with her.

I met her outside a wedding party when I had given up all idea of getting married again. I don't like the women I meet here. I was thinking of this and reluctantly I let myself be taken along to a wedding party. I could have said: No, I'm fed up with these things, I'm not interested. Have you ever been there, outside one of those parties? That evening I went, a friend took me. There was some *jaat* to chew. Have you seen the eyes of the people who chew *jaat*? Red eyes.

We were all over on one side watching the women go in.
Does this bother them? Not at all, they go there just for that!
They know that there is a herd of men just waiting to see
a bare armpit. It's not out of frustration; young men stand
outside parties because it's a social occasion. The girls dance
and have someone videotape them. Then the cassettes are
sold. They go there to be videotaped and to talk about the
other girls.

Look at what that one's wearing, isn't that the same *diric*
she wore last time? Huh, those jewels—they told me they
aren't even hers, poor thing, she borrowed them, she's had
to sell everything because of her son! No, she never knew
how to dance, she has a backside as big as a house, but it
doesn't do her any good. At long last, she's uncovered her
head, but I'm telling you, that's a *baruuko,* that isn't her hair,
if you look closely you can see the join; the women in her
family are all half bald!

It's all chatter chatter, gossiping tongues at work; they
have a grand time and they know that the others are saying
exactly the same things about them, but who cares, that's
what it's all about. A game that would bore me, to be honest. Usually I go because the others go, but lucky for me
that I went that evening, otherwise I would never have met
Domenica.

There I was, sitting on one side and then I see this young
woman come out. She goes and stands three feet from me
and she begins to talk.

I know you're thinking, what everyone else is thinking,
she says. I'm not thinking anything, I reply. And she goes
on, like someone talking to herself, and she says that she is
a serious woman, most certainly more serious than all those
women who are at that party, all made-up and perfumed in
search of a husband who will choose them by watching the
cassette. She's fed up with this story that mulatto women are
all trash. I tell her that what I know is that mulatto women
are famous for their beauty, not for being trash. Because you
are all racists, she says, being light-skinned must necessarily
be beautiful. It was different talking to Domenica, it wasn't

like being with other women, Domenica is used to speaking to men, in that certain way.

All right, all right, I'll tell you about Maryam, but why are you in such a hurry? I'm getting there.

Maryam didn't like these parties, everyone knew that. Pity she was a bit odd, poor thing.

They say that for a while her mother was very worried about her. There were lots of men who were asking for her hand, and every time they knocked on her door, Maryam would have a fit, really scary. She would lock herself in the bathroom and threaten to slit her wrists. These fits of hers damaged her reputation. Her mother protected her a lot, don't ask me why, I don't know. She's certainly hiding something. There are rumors.

It's difficult to refuse an arranged marriage. At times it's the woman herself who's looking for a match, especially if she's already been married. Can that work here? You tell me—with the kind of work you do, you should know.

I think of my sisters. They stayed at home, they didn't need to find a husband. My father would find them one. How do you know that they didn't choose the man they loved? For my sister Caasha it was different, she herself says it was for love. There were two of them who came asking for her as a bride. The first time she was eleven years old. So my father threw them out of the house. They waited. At sixteen she made her choice. She chose the older one because she reasoned this way: With the younger one I will most certainly argue more, better an older man because he will treat me better and with more patience. She reasoned this way, that she didn't want to have arguments every day over little things, that she preferred an attentive man who wouldn't be hanging around her all day. And that's the way it went. In your opinion that's not choosing. Then how do you explain all the time she spent waiting? Eight years going from one country to another, even from one continent to another, with four small children. Poor Caasha. I tried to send her some money to help her, but she saved most of it, with the sole objective of having that husband of hers join them.

And the difficulties she went through. Her second daughter had problems with her heart. She used to go back and forth to the hospital. According to you, this is not love?

Well, sure, you're right, it's not just the place that changes people. You could meet certain lowlife girls even in Mogadishu. Once, the daughter of an aunt came to our house as a guest for a few days. She did nothing in the kitchen, she didn't help the girls, she spent all her time sitting with us boys trying to be funny. Everyone hated her. Eventually she got the idea of sitting outside. There was a cement bench near our front door. Everyone was allowed to sit there: the men, the ladies to chat, the young girls to show themselves off, everyone, while they kept an eye on the little ones running around. The strange thing was that this girl sat outside on her own, with nobody next to her, and worse, she began to speak with a man from the neighborhood. She was an embarrassment to us all, a girl who starts talking to a man going by! My mother sent her packing! Do you see? My sisters never dared speak to a man who wasn't one of us. Here instead that's quite normal. The thing is that people who are in exile for a long time end up going mad.

Some time ago, for example. My cousin Cabdallah and I were at home with two friends, we were playing cards and the television was on. Sure, the place was a mess. His little son was running all over the room throwing things around. He was annoyed because he didn't like the program we were watching on TV. And Cabdallah wasn't taking any notice of him, he was too absorbed in his game of cards. Every now and then, he would take a swipe at him, as if he were swatting away a fly. It was because of his swiping and because the little boy was running around that he ended up bumping into his father's lighted cigarette. Just imagine it! Screaming at the top of his lungs, this kid who's burned himself on a cigarette. He was just calming down, and we were recovering from the fright, when we heard the key in the lock. Well, we were sitting quietly on the sofa when the door opened and his wife came in yelling. She's a full-grown woman, Sucdi, she must be twenty-four years old. Well, this full-grown woman goes up to him and grabs him. The two other young men were frozen by the counterattack, frozen in their seats, they didn't move. I took a deep breath and launched myself, I grabbed Cabdallah by his belt and pushed away his wife, who had given him a deep scratch on his cheek. The wound was bleeding.

When Cabdallah saw that blood was dripping from all over his face, he went crazy, he took hold of a chair and yelled at her: Get out of here, woman, get out of here, I don't want to see you ever again. The little boy ran after his mother, hugging her backside and crying: Don't hurt my mom, don't hurt my mom. That's children for you, they always take the mother's side. Is it because they know that women are weaker?

Seeing that Cabdallah was so furious, Sucdi ran off with her son, took the elevator down and then who knows where. Did she hear her son screaming because of the burn? No, I don't think so. Maybe someone had told her about it. You know what people are like, they like to stir things up. But I'm not sure, and then Sucdi has always liked to fight and now that she's an adult she's certainly not going to change.

Well, two days go by and while I'm on my way to work, I meet her in front of the building. She was crying, desperately, she didn't know where to go.

Taageere, I haven't got anybody, I'm alone with the child, she pleaded in the middle of the road.

She made me feel so sorry for her.

So I thought of going to Maryam and her mother to ask if they could put her up. They lived in a big house with four rooms and there were only the two of them. I was sure they would agree. But I would never have believed that that devil of a woman . . . Now, listen to me carefully; listen to what Sucdi is about to do.

Sucdi, all smiles, settles in with the child at Maryam's house. A day goes by and I go down into the basement to do my wash. In my building you have to stand in line because there are only a few machines for all the people who live there. Well, as I was saying, I am there waiting for a machine to free up, when I hear some noise on the stairs. I go outside, I look around carefully so as not to let myself be seen, and do you know what I see? I see the two of them on the stairs: Sucdi in front and Cabdallah behind. Hump, hump, hump, hump. Sucdi catches sight of me, lets out a squeak, and pulls down her dress.

I go back to my washing machines, angry at not having understood the situation. Did Sucdi want to make peace with Cabdallah right away?

On the fourth day Maryam calls me. She was very upset because "it's hard to know what Sucdi wants. She went out yesterday leaving the child asleep, 'I'm coming right back,' Sucdi told me. And instead, here we are. I wasn't even able to take him to school because he goes to school in another neighborhood that's far away and I don't even know the address."

Maryam was at home alone with the child, his mother wasn't there, she had gone out to lunch with her friends. Maryam didn't know which way to turn, she needed help. Some *sambuusi* people had ordered from her needed to be delivered to a party. Waiting for Sucdi to come back, it had gotten late, at this point Maryam couldn't carry all that food and the child on the bus. I said I would go straight over to help her and she began to tell me other things, that she knew that Sucdi still loved her husband but that this was not the way to behave. Because Cabdallah comes over to their house on the sly and continues to make love to her there. They even found some condoms in the garbage, shameful stuff, disgusting things that should be kept hidden.

Maryam's mother had told Sucdi that she was happy that things had worked out and that it would be a good thing for her to go back to her husband with the child. Sucdi had answered: OK, I'm going over to see if everything is all right at home, and she didn't come back. Maryam was worried because the child kept asking her lots of questions and she didn't know what to tell him. I said to her: Tell him his mother will come back and then they will go back home together. But she was still very worried and told me to hurry up.

It's true, Maryam and I were very close. Is this why they sent you to speak to me? My friend, you mustn't believe what people say: between me and that girl there's only friendship, pure friendship. I have always treated her with the utmost respect. Her mother had trouble preserving her reputation, that's what. Because of the rumors, stuff from long ago.

It seems that there are *jinni*, devils whom only the children in Saudi Arabia can see. Maryam's father worked in Riyadh, he was a guard in a hospital. They say he was a big womanizer. His wife lived in Mogadishu; they lived separate lives, he in one place, she in another. However, the years went by and even though she was able to live comfortably with the money her husband sent her, Maryam's mother wanted to have more children.

So she had decided to join her husband in Riyadh to enjoy what every married woman has a right to enjoy. When she moved there, naturally she took her daughter Maryam with her. By then she had been in Saudi Arabia for two years but still the children did not come. But you mustn't be in a hurry if fate is on your side, and so Maryam's mother waited hopefully. Suddenly she was taken ill and they took her to the hospital for a big operation. I think it was something to do with her ovaries, or her womb, something like that, and after the operation she stayed in the hospital for many days while Maryam was at home alone with her father. But that womanizer was really consumed with lust, he just couldn't stop himself. He would go around to the brothels with the child in the car. He would load the prostitutes on board and would spend his evening with the little girl asleep on the back seat.

When her mother came back, Maryam told her a lot of things. But her mother didn't say a word because she didn't know how to react and she didn't have a cent to her name. She was worried because they had told her she couldn't have any more children. Her husband could even send her away saying what use was a sterile wife to him.

Perhaps that was when Maryam got that look in her eyes. A few months after the operation, she and her mother returned to Mogadishu, to the home of her paternal grandmother. That was the house destined for them. And in that same house lived Xirsi, my very best friend, that's why I used to see a lot of her.

And as I told you, I've known her since I was small.

There are other opinions regarding her madness. Not that she's crazy, no. She has a vacant gaze and speaks to herself, as if there were a spirit that she has to respond to. Some say that Maryam's mother didn't get on with her mother-in-law. It seems that her mother-in-law mixed potions and that she put something in her food to give her the evil eye. Perhaps she miscalculated the amounts, who knows. She made a mistake and hurt her granddaughter instead of her daughter-in-law. You must believe me, I'm not trying to trick you, not me! You found out that Maryam paid for my ticket? No, I'm not hiding anything from you, trust me, my friend, but I can't explain everything in five minutes.

Let's go back to the telephone call. I went out right away and rushed over to Maryam's house. Even before I got out of the elevator I could hear the shouts. I recognized them, they were coming from Sucdi, that crazy woman. When she had gone in, she hadn't even closed the door.

The first thing I did was look for the little one. He was totally engrossed in front of the television, as if his ears were sealed and nothing was happening. Sucdi was in the kitchen with a stick in her hand.

Maryam: that girl always surprises me. She was keeping totally still in a corner and she was crying.

Sucdi was yelling at the top of her lungs. Since there had been nobody at our house, she had spent the whole night looking for Cabdallah, without finding him. "And what about you, where were you, you sod, yes, you," but she was raving because I had been at home all by myself. I told her to calm down, and you know what she yelled at me? That it was all a plot, we were all plotting against her, but that—fortunately—a neighbor had just told her the truth: someone had called Cabdallah to tell him to go and get his child.

So I looked at Maryam and I asked her: *Abbaayo,* were you the one who called Cabdallah? But she kept on crying, she didn't answer me, who knows why not. So the situation was getting worse.

At that point Sucdi rushed into the bathroom; she opened the cupboard over the washbasin and took out a packet of condoms. "Taageere, this woman is a devil! You protect her, but from today I can swear to this: She's the one who's having it off with my husband, dirty bitch!"

I wanted to say to her: You were the one who bought those condoms, but Maryam was putting me in an awkward situation, don't you see?

Never in my entire life have I seen anyone take so many insults without reacting. She even made me doubt her. I was there hanging on to Sucdi and begging Maryam to answer her. But it was useless, I had to throw her out with all my strength. Then, after she calmed down, I took the child out to her. I think she went right back to her house. She and Cabdallah love each other very much even though they shouldn't live together.

From that day on I have always asked myself why Maryam didn't react. Perhaps that's her nature, and that's it.

Ah, sorry, I forgot one thing. Hearing all that dramatic yelling somebody had called the police. Two policemen arrived, one was black, an African American. I told him everything was fine. Sucdi had already gone and Maryam was calming down. But he, the black man, insisted on coming in. He saw Maryam with her swollen face and ran his hand over her cheek. She let him do it. Everything OK? he asked, and Maryam nodded without saying a word. So he gave her a piece of paper, a piece of paper with his name on it, I think, and he said to her: If you need anything, ask for me. But am I just imagining all this, what I'm saying? Because everything happened so quickly, perhaps I imagined something that wasn't there.

You still believe that I'm trying to lead you astray, to put you off track. Not true, my friend, I'm telling you again, I don't know where she ended up. What? She was seen crossing the border? You're only telling me now? But was she alone? My brother, you tell me to tell you everything but you hide what you know from me. You think she'll lose her rights if she leaves the country? There, I knew it, you all are not sure that it was her.

No, I don't think she had a boyfriend. She's not someone who gets involved in things. In the morning she goes to her English class and then goes home. She has very few friends, she spends her afternoons with her cousins and then there are her mother's friends. Sure, our situation was different. But I told you, we knew each other from before, it's a long story.

I'd prefer not to talk about it, it's too painful. There's no love story between us, it's not what you think.

I'll have to dig into the recesses of my memory, because I wanted to forget everything, you see?

I'm talking about ten years ago. In fact, Maryam was married once. Actually, if truth be told, she still is. Her husband is called Xassan, he's an old wheeling-and-dealing shopkeeper who paid her weight in gold. The matter was arranged without the women knowing anything about it, directly between Maryam's father and Xassan. Those two men are the same age. I can't tell you too much about that time; it was her cousin Xirsi who told me all about it. It appears that, once she found out, Maryam refused to eat for many days. Her mother hadn't had the strength to intervene and she was trying to convince her to resign herself. Only Xirsi . . . perhaps because he was the only one who was so fond of her. They were like brother and sister, those two. Xirsi put up a lot of resistance to the marriage, he took it out on the men: You're all butchers, bushboys who think they can sell their female camels. But Xirsi was too young to be taken into consideration. Nobody listened to him, and during the wedding period he refused to show up out of protest.

I was telling you about Xirsi, he's the secret that unites us. Xirsi, my very dearest friend.

Finally Maryam resigned herself. However, she was biding her time in silence.

She married and got pregnant almost immediately. She was very young, sixteen perhaps. I remember that we went to see her when she had the baby. She was a wonderful child and Maryam had already lined her lashes with *indhokuul*. Sure she was happy about the baby. But she didn't have time to enjoy her, poor thing. It was destiny. When she died she was beginning to take her first steps. I try not to remember certain things, you know. If we remembered all the sadness in the world we wouldn't be able to survive.

I have also forgotten all the rest. The armed militias had occupied the city. We were all together; I was accompanying Xirsi and Maryam, who were on the run from her husband. I agreed with my friend's plan. He wanted to take advantage of the confusion to free his cousin. We were on our way to the house of some relatives who were about to leave. They had planned a very long journey, a journey toward the south, out of the city, toward the south, toward the border with Kenya. And they were in agreement with my friend's plan and I was following in my wife Shukri's tracks; she had just had our baby.

We arrived at the house from which they were about to leave. We were to be on the move in a very short while. And we had just arrived when Maryam realized that she hadn't brought her baby's photo. Could something of no practical value be worth so much? For her it was clearly the most important thing, otherwise how could you explain her hysteria, her shrieking lament: Aah, my photo, aah, my photo.

So, Xirsi said to me: Come with me, my friend, I can't take this lament anymore. We'll just go and come right back.

We left to get the photo. Then, on our way back it happened. They were shooting haphazardly from the truck, dha dha dha dha dhah. Xirsi died soon after, I was unharmed.

This is the secret that binds us.

I have never told anyone why Xirsi and I were in the middle of the road at that very moment. I have told nobody, I only told a girl I met a few days later. It was thanks to that girl that I began to speak again. Her name is Barni, full of light, she's my wife Domenica's cousin. Now they've been reunited in Italy. It isn't Maryam's fault that Xirsi died. But she can't get it out of her mind.

What do they say about the *jinni*? *Jinni* and the evil eye mask other things, my friend.

It's not true that they recommended other suitors for her to marry. I said that to throw you off track.

Maryam's father could not accept the fact that his daughter would play such a trick on his friend, a man of his own age to whom he had given her. He did everything possible to make her go back to old Xassan. However, Maryam had found a way to escape the past. Her hysteria became her shield. She didn't want to go back to old Xassan and she had to prevent them from forcing her to do so. I'm not saying that she pretends to be crazy, she just puts it on a bit, that's all. There's a very thin dividing line. It's not a pretense, but it's a letting oneself go, a kind of controlled craziness, let's say. She's thrown lots of tantrums. Like the time she locked herself in the bathroom and threatened to throw herself out. You should have seen her with her legs out of the window. People yelling. I came over, her mother had called me: Taageere, you are the only one who can make her see sense.

I felt calm, though. I knew that she had no intention of really throwing herself out.

I stood outside the bathroom talking to her: Maryam, calm down, this time you've gone too far, open the door for me.

This scene had been going on for some time and I was beginning to feel a little bit scared that, by going on and on pretending, she might really be tempted to go ahead with it in the end.

Right at that moment the police arrived. Only one police car and—speak of the devil—do you remember that policeman I told you about? The one who came the day Sucdi had accused Maryam of having it off with her husband? A mountain of a man, this black policeman was one and the same. And I noticed that he had a two-way radio—in fact, it could also have been a telephone—and that he was standing exactly under Maryam. If she had decided to throw herself down at that very moment, the two of them would have been squashed flat. I saw that policeman and I went up to him. I told him of my fears, my fear of the uncontrollable. I was just moving away when—who knows, maybe I was imagining things. Because it seemed to me—you know—it seemed to me that Maryam's voice was coming right out of that two-way radio.

The guy was gentle and Maryam had struck him in a special way. He went up to the top floor and then lowered himself down from the roof on a rope. Like a hero in the movies. A black hero, a solid mass of living muscle, take that! Well, they would never have accepted that black man into Maryam's family, and maybe that's exactly why she wanted him.

What do I know about old Xassan?

He, too, did everything he could to get Maryam back. I don't know if he tried to convince her himself. That dirty old man has the persuasive powers of a slippery snake. Of a rattlesnake, that's what he has. It's what he uses to buy people. But it had no effect on Maryam. Now he's leaving her in peace: after the lesson I gave him he'll think twice before . . .

However, it was Maryam who, through her own determination, changed things.

I was telling you about when Xirsi and I left her.

Maryam waited for us to return with the photo. She got over her fit of nerves, she calmed down. She waited as long as necessary, then, seeing that we didn't come back, she left with the others in a convoy, in a truck going south. She only found out about Xirsi's death when she reached Kenya.

I don't know what her reaction was. All that I know is her mother joined her a little later and they both managed to leave for America, where they were granted political asylum. But it took a long time. No, she didn't request asylum under a false name. You know that—why do you ask me these trick questions? Her name is Maryam and that's the name you see on her papers. You're asking yourself why she isn't registered as married?

Ninyow, here they give you a form to fill out and you write down what you need to, married or not married. What risk are you running? There's no office where it can be checked out, is there? Should Maryam have put herself in a trap of her own accord?

You won my trust only yesterday but I'm beginning to question my judgment. Are you sure the only reason you're looking for her is because of her papers? Because, you know, they are in order.

I see that you are well informed. It's true, I admit it. I left Kenya thanks to her. She paid for everything herself, the ticket to Italy and then the one here to America. Where did she get the money? That I don't know, how could I know? What? No, I am quite sure that she couldn't have stolen it from the old man. They didn't even meet! He went directly to Italy! He comes to America on business? But what do I know of that devil? Maybe, maybe. But he's never shown up here. What? That's outrageous: Maryam's mother ran Xassan's agency here in America! All intrigues, my friend, I have nothing to do with this, don't get me involved. But tell me, just out of curiosity, what does this agency deal in? Remittances to be sent back to Somalia. Geez, all that's left for you to do is accuse me of being a runner! A runner for the dirty old man! This story is pure fantasy—do you honestly think Maryam . . . Look, I say, you don't know whom you're talking about. Do you honestly think that Maryam and her little old mother would steal Xassan's money?

I, my friend, do not believe this story! I just don't believe it! Listen, why don't you go to Maryam's mother and ask her all these questions? You can't go because she's not here in this country anymore?

Hold on, you're telling me a whole string of things all at once to confuse me!

What I do know is that Maryam had access to an account which was opened by old Xassan when they were married. It was an account for her, but he checked the money that went in and out. It must have been from there that she got the money to pay for my ticket. Surely you won't find something illegal in this, too, I hope? I tell you Maryam did it for that photo, out of her love for her baby and for Xirsi. From then on I have never abandoned her.

What happened between me and old Xassan? Nothing, what could have happened? He now lives in Italy, he has his phone center and doesn't bother me, I put him right, I taught him a good lesson. He accused me of intimidation? No, my friend, you can't fool me with your words. Nobody loves old Xassan. That's why nobody complained when I gave him a beating. I don't think he was ashamed of talking about it. Everyone saw him the next day, he had no teeth. He asked for it, he went around saying bad things about me, he really asked for it. If you go around saying bad things about someone, you know that sooner or later he'll come looking for you.

I've lived in Italy, too. A complicated and unfortunate story. Maybe that country brings me bad luck? My wife Shukri was in Kenya when I was living in Rome, and she arrived there just as I left the country. Now Shukri and Domenica live there, with my nine-year-old son and with the one who's about to be born.

I had to leave, I was barely getting by. I had a good setup but it wasn't going to last forever. I was staying with some relatives, an uncle and aunt of mine who live in Rome, Diriiye Yuusuf and his wife, Safiya. They never had children. But they remained married for many years. It seems that the problem lies with her, but he has never even thought of repudiating her, he loves her the way she is. At one point Safiya even told him to take a second wife to have some children but he refused. That man is very generous and they are both very kind. They had me stay for many months and then helped me come to America. I felt at ease with them. They never made me feel I was a burden, it was like being at home. During those months, after the war broke out, there were many of us in Italy. It was there that we hoped we would get help. The older people knew Italian, and even before the war many girls had gone to Italy to be *boyeeso*. They would save up enough money to build a house in Somalia. With the war, there were too many of them. And this time they came with men and children, no joke. The Somali community tried to lend a hand, but it wasn't enough.

For many years no one wanted to go to Italy any longer. Now, of course they go, because of the boats. They've discovered the sea route. The Somalis pursue all routes. That's the way my little sister Luul got there. Diriiye Yuusuf and his wife continue to move on her behalf, they went to get her in Sicily and they had her stay at the beginning. Then they must have had a disagreement, from what Domenica told me.

Domenica left for Italy because I sent her to meet Luul. She hadn't been back for a long time, almost ten years, I think. It must have been strange for her. What's more, while she was looking for my sister, she ran into her cousin Barni, whom she was very close to as a child. The plot thickens: Barni, too, was looking for Luul but for a different reason. So they set off together, Domenica and her cousin, to look for my sister. And guess where they found her? She was at Shukri's house, my ex-wife. She was staying with her because Shukri was the only person in Italy who knew her, who loved her from when she was a child. Now Domenica is with Barni and Luul lives with Shukri. It appears that they see each other often and that they are all very good friends. Women are really incredible. What is there left for me to do but try to join them? They tell me it's impossible to bring Luul here. Whoever lands in Italy has to stay there, because of a new law, the fingerprinting law. What a curse. In that country they don't give you anything, no welfare. When I was there, there was no work, and when there was, what terrible work it was!

Where did I work? In a meatpacking plant, I don't know what to call it, a place where they kill rabbits. It was a nightmare: a metal conveyor belt with the rabbits hanging from it with a hook through their brains. The conveyor belt went around, this dead animal would arrive, and I had to skin it and take out its guts. It was a hard job and my hands were raw and then there was that violent killing of animals, all that blood after having lived through the war. At night I dreamed of rabbits everywhere with their heads skinned. Every so often I would take one home to my uncle and aunt, to roast in the oven. From that time on I have never eaten a rabbit again. Can you believe that?

At that time everybody had to go through Italy. Now though, nobody wants to stay, and yet there are four women there who mean a lot to me. What other choice do I have but to go back and begin skinning rabbits again? Maybe with Domenica's help I'll find a better job! And I still remember my Italian!

Several days ago there was a Sicilian guy with us. We were sitting on a wall, me, the Sicilian, a Vietnamese friend of mine, and a Jamaican. Then along came an Indian, an old man, not a young one. The others were smoking a joint. The others, not me. And the old Indian sat down with us, saying that he was going to stay a while to chat. We all said to him: Get out of here, if the police come, you're old, they'll think you're the pusher!

And he said: No, no, I can run. Instead, he took out twenty dollars and asked the Jamaican to go and buy him some smokes. The Jamaican, complaining, said to him: All right, I'll roll you a joint, but I want to see if you can smoke it all by yourself!

The old Indian, all happy, sat down and took the first drag. We were ready to burst with laughter and, I swear, I've never seen anything like it. First his feet, then his legs began to twist. Like someone doing a break-dance. His whole head was turning, it was making his neck, his face rotate. And his eyes! Never seen such eyes. I looked at the Sicilian and I said to him: Look at his *occhi* (eyes)! He was shocked because he didn't know that I spoke Italian and he answered right away: You're nuts! And I: *Waffanculu* (fuck off) and so on. But I won. In the end I knew more Italian swear words than he did.

You want to know about that evening.

Well, after the barbecue and the tea, I was finally able to sit down happily and talk to Domenica; I was dreaming, rocked by her eyes. Suddenly five cars full of policemen arrive, with those sirens going that make that deafening noise. We were sitting quietly enjoying the evening and they arrived with all that racket.

Then one of the guys who was there went forward, one of your colleagues, one who does the same kind of work you do—what do you call yourselves, mediators?—and says with the air of someone who solves problems: I'll speak to them!

They talked things over for a long time. I saw that he was slowly deflating, like a ball losing air. Then he came over to us. Everyone gathered tightly around him.

What do they want? asked the people.

They're saying "unauthorized gathering." I explained to them that we're here just to spend the evening.

And what did they answer?

That these are the rules and that if we want to live in this country we have to abide by them. For them, this is an unauthorized gathering!

At that point, Saciid Saleebaan, who was standing behind his camera not saying a word, jumped to his feet yelling: Excellent mediation! And everyone around him began to clap.

After that, Saciid Saleebaan took hold of his video camera to film the confused people who were going back inside.

This is the land of multiculturalism!

I think it all happened in that moment of great confusion. People were yelling and mattresses were being pulled from one side to the other. And there was that same black man that I told you about. With a huge motorbike: he looked like a cowboy. Maryam? Dressed like I'd never seen her, with cotton pants and a light blue T-shirt. She couldn't get onto the bike in her *diric,* right?

Who knows if they organized everything from start to finish. But I'm certain that now she's fine and that she'll show up again soon. So, do you think they went over the border?

8

DOMENICA

DEAR DOCTOR:

While taking this opportunity to thank you for having
worked with me to find a solution, I want to assure you that
I will endeavor to narrate the events in the most linear way
possible, thereby providing you with a clear and detailed de-
scription of my psychological and physical condition.

Let me tell you that I have deeply appreciated your will-
ingness to work with me. I am sure that this decision will
help me rebuild the complex existential path that will en-
able me to assume with integrity the responsibility of motherhood that lies ahead.

It is much easier for me to narrate the events in writing since my relationship with words is still an emotional
and fragmented one. It's not unusual for me to digress or to
follow the thread of a thought that ends up folding back on
itself.

As you have helped me understand, this is not unusual in people who come from a history of migration. Even if I am not—technically—an immigrant, I fully understand your remarks about Domenica having lived through estrangements and readjustments that are typical of immigrants.

The family tree that you suggested I draw took me days to prepare, surprising even me with its complexity. I don't deny that such a wide-reaching tree is essentially a feeble attempt to reclaim family ties that I feared were too tenuous. I share your interpretation of my tree as a mirror of historical-personal voids that need to be filled.

At this point I will end my introductory remarks. I hope that writing down my story will help me become that whole, adult person that I long to be.

According to my birth certificate I am Domenica Ta-ariikh, born in Mogadishu in 1970. As my name would suggest, my father is Somali and my mother Italian. I am therefore part of that small group of Italian-Somalis whose fathers, not mothers, are Somalis.

This was the reason why for years I only had my father's citizenship, even though the new Italian family law also allowed for the transmitting of nationality through the maternal side.

At that time, the fact that my father did not request Italian citizenship for me was a matter of pride for him. He so deeply desired to prove that his choice of a European wife did not necessarily mean that he was not committed to the cause of the national reconstruction of Somalia.

In reality, being solely Somali implied not having access to the Italian school in Mogadishu because of an agreement between the two governments. It also meant not participating in the life of the Italian community, which was made up, for the most part, of mulattos like me.

This small community used to meet at the Casa d'Italia (House of Italy), later renamed the Circolo Italiano (Italian Club), in order to dispel any possible suspicion of nostalgia for neocolonialism.

I do not deny that during my childhood I had the most conflicting feelings for that armored fortress where I imagined there was an abundance of delights and forbidden luxuries.

As a child I attended Xaawa Taka Elementary School, one of the largest in the downtown area. Xaawa Taka, a heroine of the Somali independence movement, was famous for having convinced women to finance the League of Young Somalis through the sale of their jewels. This gave a vital impulse to the struggle for autonomy. The statue in her honor portrayed her vigorously projecting herself forward with an arrow in her chest. I never understood how she was killed.

The school was beautiful, full of light, and there were fifty children in each class. The teachers were in their twenties. The large number of children and the recent transcription of the Somali language involved mass mobilization. Anyone who possessed a rudimentary knowledge of the new national writing system had to participate in its diffusion.

The alphabetization campaign went hand in hand with the widespread program of vaccination, especially against TB, which at the time was claiming many victims. Standing in line to be vaccinated, we spent a long time outside the classroom in our white and blue uniforms. The vaccine was normally injected in the forearm, so all the children of my generation share the same distinctive oval scar.

When school let out, a buzzing swarm of children bought things from the small vendors who used to gather there for that purpose. There were stalls selling notebooks and pencils, but we were much more interested in the little colored coolers containing the Popsicles in tin molds, or in the trays of milk candy.

One afternoon, taking advantage of the lighted coals left over from dinner, I made my own candies with milk and caramelized sugar. The satisfaction of making them was not comparable to the pleasure that I experienced when I bought them for a few *kumi* outside my school. While my cousins and I were waiting to be picked up, it was that delicious sweetness that kept us company.

At school some children belonged to the Fiori d'ottobre (October Flowers), the children's chorus that celebrated the success of our revolution by singing the praises of the president during official ceremonies. They were the envy of everybody because they often went off during school hours. Rumor had it that they participated in magnificent banquets. My cousin Libeen was a member of the October Flowers, and he was a major contributor to the spreading of the fantastic tales that were circulating about the group.

When we were about five, my cousin Barni and I began attending the classes that Sister Ernestina held for the Sacred Heart youth program. Second only to the cathedral, the Sacred Heart church was one of the only two Catholic churches in the city. Looking through recent images of Mogadishu it is not unusual to come across the ruins of what used to be the cathedral, a clear indication for the Italians of the extent of the damage done to the buildings in the capital.

Since the level of instruction in the Somali schools was rather lacking, my father Taariikh and his brother Sharmaarke, who had received instruction in Italian, decided to offer their daughters that same opportunity.

In Sister Ernestina's class we were all more or less the same age, all daughters of men who had studied in Europe. The classroom where we studied was rather dark, and the nun wrote letters and syllables on the blackboard that we had to read aloud and then copy down in a notebook. Among those words I have a particular recollection of the sound "ap-ple": its smell evoked the memory of my rare Italian holidays. Thanks to Sister Ernestina, we learned the first rudiments of the written language that otherwise would have been limited to those rigid letters contained in the squares of the pages in our notebooks.

The garden of the church was very well maintained, and there was a big children's slide that we couldn't wait to use since a metal slide was very unusual in those days.

Sister Ernestina and our parents had a tacit agreement that during our classes she was not to mix syllables and religion since our fathers were Muslims and what they feared most was that we might grow up estranged like the *ciyaal missioni*.

I am writing down this epithet because it has been for me the source of many questions in these past years, in fact, while *ciyaal* is the collective Somali word meaning children, *missioni* is clearly an Italian word. When I was little, it was not unusual for someone to ask me, in absolute good faith, if I was *missioni*, with neither I, nor the person asking, understanding the underlying meaning of that word.

Discriminated against by racial laws, the Italian-Somalis of the previous generations were raised mostly by missionaries, completely isolated from the rest of the population. That is why that term had a negative connotation, tied as it was to the idea of a denied paternity.

Growing up, Barni and I began attending the Sacred Heart youth group, especially in July and August, when the schools were closed and the humid monsoons, loaded with rain, forced us inside for longer than we were accustomed to.

That was the time when we learned to embroider with colored thread, tracing the flowery patterns on the cloth in chain stitch, a stitch that I was good at, and to fill in the background in Brocatello stitch, the stitch that only Barni could do well.

I think I have feelings of cautious affection for Sister Ernestina, who was still a missionary of her generation with many barriers and not a few preconceived ideas.

Once, a sort of yellow-black bumblebee flew in and started buzzing angrily above our heads. This event, apart from causing a major distraction, generated lots of laughter, since the poor bumblebee kept banging against the windowpanes, and than started moving around again as if drunk. What's more, that same little insect was the object of cruel persecution on the part of us children, who found its bright colors and its voluminous body covering particularly attractive. Usually, after capturing one, we would tie a colored thread to its leg and then observe its daring acrobatics, chanting all the while a nursery rhyme that went *Diley-kasey diley-kasey*.

That day, in front of Sister Ernestina, we limited ourselves to laughing, and yet we couldn't avoid being scolded. I will never forget the day the bumblebee entered our classroom: the nun said it was the devil who had sent it and that we were just like all the other Somalis, lazy and disinclined to work.

That night I dreamt of the baby Jesus observing us from his cradle of straw right above the blackboard. I dreamt of a baby Jesus with strangely red eyes who began to walk with a blank expression and who was looking for me in the dark, while I, in a state of panic, hid behind the bushes. In my dream I clearly saw my cousins passing by and I tried unsuccessfully to get Barni's attention, while the baby Jesus continued heading toward me, only me. That nightmare haunted me for years, and whenever it reoccurred I stayed awake all night, terrified.

This anguished dream caused me to look at the baby Jesus up there in front of us with a certain apprehension during class time, to the point that I even stopped copying the letters from the blackboard out of fear of raising my head. I was able to hide my fears for a few days, thanks to Barni's complicity—she quickly showed me the words when the teacher turned the other way.

My behavior could not go unnoticed, and Sister Ernestina began to reprimand me frequently, threatening to tell my parents that I was refusing to learn.

That's why I decided to reveal the reason for my behavior, telling her about my dream in detail, details that she immediately interpreted as a clear exhortation to convert.

The baby Jesus with his blank stare was the excuse Sister Ernestina produced when my mother asked for an explanation of why she had started to teach us catechism. It had been her wish to comfort me that had led her to teach us the gospel, and since she was simply telling us stories, she considered her behavior entirely acceptable.

I think the reason why my mother stopped trusting Sister Ernestina was a small but nevertheless quite important detail which I could not fully comprehend because of my age. This small detail had to do with our biblical drawings that were kept hidden in the classroom closet, so that our parents wouldn't notice anything. The matter became public knowledge because of me, because I couldn't stand the stress of being deceitful and, once home, I told my mother everything.

Our fathers were so indignant at this matter that for a period of time we attended the Somali school almost exclusively, with the flag-raising every morning, the white and blue uniforms, the hymns and patriotic singing.

I was a well-behaved child and, all in all, I was one of the privileged few. But being among the privileged few had some negative consequences: in fact it was from among the "favorites" that the teacher picked the class monitors. Needless to say, I hated that role, it was always painful for me, and never afforded me any of those privileges commonly enjoyed by those in a position of power.

Usually, the teacher took off the strap from one of our book bags and when we were too rowdy forced us all to put our heads down on our desks. Those who lifted their heads were hit with the strap. When the teacher left the classroom, she picked a monitor among the best-behaved pupils to maintain discipline. Almost everyone loved being picked, first because they would be certainly exempted from any punishment and second because, if they knew what they were doing, they could command the respect and goodwill of many children.

Naturally, you could not refuse to be a class monitor; if you did, the teacher had two solutions depending on her mood at the time. Either you immediately joined the ranks of the punishable pupils or, in the worst-case scenario, refusing meant punishment for the whole class. We had to remain in the garden without moving, our arms stretched out under the sun. After a few minutes our arms began to hurt a lot, but we could not move, nor could we lower them, lest we be hit with the strap. In the end, the anger of the group was completely directed against the class monitor who had sacrificed everyone to gain the respect of a few possible culprits.

My childhood home was a charming rectangular building with whitewashed walls. The whiteness of the wall was
broken up by the bright green of the doorway and the fuch-
sia color of the bougainvillea that burst forth irreverently.
Next to it, like an inseparable sister, grew a verbena plant
that smelled like a squashed bug. Every day I picked a little
bunch of flowers as a centerpiece for our table; I sprayed
perfume on it, and delivered it joyfully into my mother's
hands.

Flowers were my passion, even the mistreated hibiscus
bushes around the building belonging to Uncle Foodcadde's
family. Their large home seemed to be ready to welcome
anyone who might want to stop there: besides the immedi-
ate family members, meaning my uncle, his wife Xaliima,
and their children, there was a constant stream of relatives
and friends.

Our homes were part of the same compound with a
shared flower garden that Yuusuf, the custodian, made a
point of protecting at nightfall. He boasted that he knew
how to love plants and the secrets of their births and deaths.

Jealous of my passion, I vied with him for the task of
taking care of the flowers. The conflict erupted because of
the mistreated hibiscus. My cousin Libeen used to rip off the
corolla to lick the nectar and then threw it away, without a
second thought for so much wasted beauty. Fuming, I would
follow him to prevent him from perpetrating that crime, and
in so doing, I fueled his desire to spite me. This didn't bother
Yuusuf: plants, in his opinion, existed for our benefit and so
we were free to do whatever we wanted with them.

My aunt and uncle's house, enclosed on all sides by
hibiscus plants, was the place where Barni lived until her
mother's death and the same place she returned to after we
had left.

The circumstances surrounding Barni's mother's death
were never made completely clear. The only certain thing
is that it was a tragic incident that could have killed several
people, a fire that burned half the house down, that start-

ed in the middle of the night. If it hadn't been for Yuusuf's watchfulness, no one would have survived.

The fire took half of the building, miraculously sparing the hibiscus hedge. Almost nothing was left of Barni's mother, asleep in the flames. She died in the middle of one of the summers I spent in Italy, and it radically changed our lives.

Soon after that, Barni moved in with us and that is how we ended up spending the following three years as twin sisters, sleeping in the same room, holding hands. Barni, who was a pillar of strength for me, suffered from nightmares for a long time. This is what happened in the following three years—the last years before I moved to Italy.

In Mogadishu, my mother worked at the Italian Cultural Center and was mainly in contact with people who spoke her own language. In those days this was a common occurrence, even outside such institutions, since all educated people spoke Italian. Somali is a language with a syntax and a way of organizing thoughts that is quite different from Italian. Learning it could be a long process and not a very gratifying one.

The popularity of Italian, and the difficulty of learning a language that had not yet been codified, are, I think, the two reasons that prevented my mother from learning Somali well even though, years later, she confessed to me that she understood much more than she let on.

My father, on the other hand, was practically bilingual and didn't make any effort to encourage his wife's feeble attempts to learn Somali. Not understanding became for her a sort of hiding place into which she could retreat every time the challenges of living there and of interacting with people prevented her from coming out of her shell.

The numerous domestic tasks that she had to solve by herself meant that, as I got older, my role as interpreter became more and more demanding, until I turned into a great dissimulator, ready to please the series of adult interlocutors that I had to regularly deal with.

I lived translation as an entertainment sometimes, but more often with a strong sense of responsibility, especially when I had to tone down harshness, to hide negative feelings. I was dealing with blunt utterances that sprung unfiltered from the soul. Voices that were entrusted to me to ferry across without the speaker making any effort to adapt them to the receiver.

I acquired a profound knowledge of the human soul thanks to this daily exercise that trained me to understand the deepest recesses of the adult mind, and I became an anxious child, always worried about the possible repercussions of badly relayed words.

Before I learned to refine my dual role, though, I had several accidents along the way. For instance, this incident happened during a period in which I had acquired the very bad habit of listening furtively to the grown-ups' conversations: I eavesdropped and deliberately reported back. I even tried to have my mother back up my spying. I went to her and asked if, when I translated, I could relate things exactly as I had heard them. She nodded without questioning my mysterious projects too much. I left satisfied and already plotting tricks: I could translate the sentences I had heard, even if no one asked me to do so.

An opportunity came up right away. One evening my cousins and I, after eating together as usual, had run out of new stories to tell each other. That is when Libeen began asking me questions about my mother. I was proud of the feelings—a mixture of fascination and awe—that my cousin had toward my mother. The fact that she only communicated with me allowed me to fuel that awe.

My mother, her silky hair hanging down to her waist, her skin diaphanous, almost transparent, was considered a real beauty by everyone. So many times people told me that I had been unlucky not to have inherited her beauty, but rather plenty of color and those curls that got tangled from my father!

So, that evening, following Libeen's questions on that fascinating topic, the other cousins also found the courage to indulge their curiosity. The poor wretched souls took a deep breath before asking me if the fabulous creature had ever uttered a word about them. Did my mother have an opinion about those insignificant children? I searched and delved into my memory until I remembered a certain day when my mother had told a young aunt that those cousins would have been really good-looking children if only their ears didn't stick out so much. Only too happy to have found the information they were requesting, I repeated the second part of my mother's statement to them, saying that I had heard her say that they had enormous sticking-out ears.

This act of bravado of mine caused quite a diplomatic disaster in the family, since my cousins reported the whole thing in tears to Aunt Xaliima, who immediately summoned me to her. I still remember her stern face at the top of the stairs, her expression as she looked at me while stroking her little boys' heads. She told me I was the most ungrateful child she had ever met, that not only did I roam around there until "midsnights" but now I had even humiliated her children. I shrank back more and more until Barni intervened on my behalf, saying that I had only translated some words. Hearing this, Aunt Xaliima got even madder and, pointing to the crushed expressions of her children, yelled at me to go home immediately to explain to my mother that certain things should not be said, not even in jest.

My only comfort was Barni's hugs. She tried to remind me how brusque Aunt Xaliima appeared to be, but what a softy she really was.

In my ten years in Mogadishu I had the chance to visit Italy four times. The first trip is too deeply buried in my early years for me to remember anything about it. But what I remember most about the other departures are the endless preparations. Entire days spent with my mother shopping, searching for all kinds of presents for her family and friends. They were veritable expeditions among the souvenir sellers at the Lido, among the shoemakers in Bondheere, and the goldsmiths of the tamarind tree market.

We traveled loaded with amber necklaces, leather bags, clay critters, filigree bracelets, brightly colored fabrics, and we always carried with us long lists made by those who stayed behind: lists of size 6 jeans, patent leather sandals, a toy car for each little boy, little dolls for the girls, a checkered shirt, green pine bubble bath.

The airfare was rather expensive and, along with all the excessive expectations generated by our trips, it was one of the main deterrents to their being repeated. Being an emigrant in both directions is quite exhausting, especially for those who, like us, lived in economic circumstances that necessitated daily sacrifices.

In order to make the most of our trip, my mother and I spent the whole summer in Italy. Our visits were a succession of days dedicated to re-establishing lost ties, to renewing relationships that distance had weakened.

The things I appreciated about Italy are all the things that today, as a mother, I consider abhorrent, but that for a child remain marvelous, like the supermarkets filled with packaged snacks, the cartoons on TV, and the amusement park rides.

My maternal relatives had never been to Mogadishu, and since they could not understand the healthy lifestyle I lived there, they scolded my mother, who didn't worry at all about my being transfixed in front of the TV for hours.

Luckily, we spent the two months of our holiday mainly in an old farmhouse where I, along with my cousins, this time all Italian, could roam freely in the surrounding fields. What I remember in particular about those weeks, apart from the bellyfuls of blackberries and the fireflies that every child falls in love with, are the long hikes we took to reach the little church on top of the hill. I would visit it like a devout follower because of the aura of Franciscan mysticism that the place exuded.

In my mind, the countryside is linked to a fervent Catholic religiosity, fueled by my love for long walks through the woods in order to reach the safe haven of the sanctuaries.

For my part, as a child I always experienced religion in a passionate way. I tried to overcome the sense of guilt that I

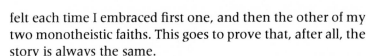

felt each time I embraced first one, and then the other of my two monotheistic faiths. This goes to prove that, after all, the story is always the same.

My mother was, and I imagine still is, a practicing Catholic; after all, she named me Domenica (Sunday), and she attended church every Sunday even in Mogadishu, where she certainly was not forced to do so by circumstances. Today I am convinced that her reason for not learning Somali, and her religious belief, were both attempts to protect her identity, to somehow preserve it in the middle of that confusion. I, instead, continued to switch from one to the other: I studied the Koran, I observed Ramadan for a few hours with my cousins, and, at the same time, I accompanied my mother to mass.

What terrified me most, returning from my Italian holidays, was finding myself reduced to the state of a linguistic tabula rasa. I do not know if this is a well-known phenomenon or if it is simply related to my nature, but it so happened that, after a two-month absence, it took me almost a week to regain the use of the Somali language.

I experienced this inability to communicate as a serious mutilation, especially because it meant that my linguistic competence was cut in half. It prevented me from emitting comprehensible sounds, but it did not spare me from understanding people who were cursing my amnesia.

I still remember the day I returned to Mogadishu for the penultimate time. My father came to get us in his Fiat 131. Barni did not accompany him, as she usually did. At that point I did not yet know that her mother had recently died. An aunt had taken her out of town for a few weeks to help her recover from the shock. The half-burned-down home kept reminding her of the fire.

The absence of my cousin, the person I wanted to see even more than my own father, immediately put me in a bad mood. Did I perhaps sense that something terrible had happened? It must have been this intuition that made my mind travel elsewhere, so far away that it distanced me from my own body. I was immersed in gloomy thoughts when, as I put my bag in the trunk, I burned my calf on the hot exhaust pipe.

I didn't even complain, and since there was no way of treating the burn, I arrived home with my leg still smoking. As you entered the compound, our building was in front of Foodcadde's, so I only learned later about the damage caused by the fire.

My cousins rushed to welcome me and, noticing the bright red circle on my calf, asked me what had happened.

Had Barni been there, not only would I have been happier, but I would have been able to rely on her linguistic support, since she was the only one among all the cousins who spoke Italian. It was Barni who gave me protection each time I returned, it was she who helped me slip quickly back into the other language. In her absence, I had to manage by myself while feeling very embarrassed. My cousins lined up looking at me in amusement while I mimed the dramatic scene in which, inadvertently, I had pressed my leg against the red hot exhaust pipe. The show went on for quite some time until the delight of the little ones was interrupted by the voice of Libeen, who, seeing me in that state and even before he said hello to me, exclaimed worriedly: Did you forget your Somali again?

Apart from the transition periods, during the first nine years of my life I think I was completely bilingual. I enjoyed the privilege of alternating between different languages and interlocutors. Those brief periods of amnesia, however, were premonitions of a far worse disease that was to manifest itself soon after, and that would rob me of one of my voices for a long time.

But all this happened only after Barni had named my second soul, leaving a permanent sign on my very name. She named me Axad, Sunday, like the Arabic root of the number one.

I wish to share with you one last matter relating to my childhood. Currently it is a topic widely debated by many women in the West, so I have been turning it over in my mind for a long time. If this were not the case, then maybe the story I am about to tell you would not have assumed such importance for me. During my ponderings, I have come to realize that there is something that escapes your Western understanding: incommunicable details.

Here, in Italy, the body is considered untouchable, pain intolerable, decay abominable. But this inviolability disregards respect for that body, the imminence of that pain, the cure for that decay. Is the breakdown of the human body distressing because it makes us think of death? Fragility is so much a part of us.

Barni has talked to me at length about the women she takes care of during their deliveries. So many women say that, in that moment, they experience the sensation of dying. And yet, I am sure, death is something different; it is ceasing to be, it is not protracted awareness, it is not the opposite of pleasure. In giving birth, what you feel is the laceration that splits the earth, it is separation that sucks you back, up to that highest point, as if your soul experienced, for an instant, the privileged sensation of infinity, a blinding insight. As if space and time diverged very slightly, only for an instant, a glimpse of eternity. What I mean to say is that learning to accept pain can be very pleasurable.

Is it because we try to hide death that everything becomes so unbearable? I talked to my Somali friends who take care of the elderly. I asked them about caring for a body in the state it is in when it is falling to pieces. Washing, handling, treating, oiling, nourishing, massaging, marking it, for me means loving that body, recognizing its sacredness.

But let's return to the episode I wanted to share with you.

At this point, Barni and I were living under the same roof. Not that we saw each other more than before, but the physical proximity at night made our relationship even closer. Ours was an elective sisterhood so the complete sharing of spaces, objects, clothes, and food was a deliberate choice that was not random.

We were about six or seven years old when all our cousins went through the initiation ritual. Being excluded from the celebration was made more bearable by our shared exclusion. It was almost sunset when we entered Uncle Foodcadde's house holding hands. We had spent the day like many others except for the fact that we couldn't join our cousins because of their "commitment." I clearly remember Libeen standing at the top of the stairs proudly showing us his purple-red penis with the foreskin removed. The little girls instead were lying down all dressed up in their best clothes on Persian carpets in the drawing room that was normally off-limits to us. They were smiling slightly and looked proud as if the initiation had welcomed them into an inner circle of mysteries that we could not understand. I don't deny that we felt a strange, annoying envy mixed with shame.

Aunt Xaliima reinforced this feeling by not missing the opportunity to remind us to tell those wicked parents of mine that they had had been irresponsible in not giving their consent for the "Sunna circumcision." In her opinion the "Sunna" was a symbolic ritual that would have kept our clitorises whole and that would guarantee that purity necessary for us to be considered marriageable women. Barni and I were too young to understand and we kept on demanding that we be allowed to join the group of the infibulated girls, causing furious arguments. My mother and my father's categorical veto and the opinion expressed by Barni's parents when they were alive is what saved us.

It was, however, a day of celebration when many goats were killed and their meat cooked for the guests and for the poor. All of us children took part in the ceremony: the butcher dug a deep hole in the yard, slit the goats' throats, their lives slowly dripping away as they kicked their heels less and less. We felt sorry for those poor animals, and at the same time, we knew that if we wanted to eat meat this was something that had to be done.

On ordinary days, the chicken vendor went from door to door. He kept the birds tied up in a straw basket, and whenever he found a client, he slit their throats and plucked them right there on the spot. You cannot imagine the surprise when, some time later, I discovered that my Italian classmates were completely unaware of what happened to the animals whose meat they ate. While rereading this paragraph, I realize that some logical connections might at first seem obscure; I therefore ask you to please keep on reading because I cannot clarify the purpose of so much reasoning before telling you about certain events that are inseparable from the whole story.

I was about nine when my mother decided to return to Italy. She did not tell me right away, perhaps out of fear of heart-wrenching goodbyes. There was no closure, no time for the reflection that the occasion called for. So, the separation was not processed, the mourning was not observed. Instead, a languor took hold of me as if I had been betrayed. Things weren't so bad at first; it was very similar to the summers I had already experienced. The sense of permanence only came later. I cannot give you the reason for our sudden move, I am not sure if even my mother was aware of it at the beginning. Her lack of awareness would explain why she left so many of her things in Somalia just like someone who is thinking of returning might do.

At first, the source of my anguish was Barni's absence, and my profound solitude. I who was accustomed to sharing spaces with dozens of children, suddenly found myself in a silent house. Visitors were a rare and unusual occurrence. My classmates, who had been together since first grade, seemed to disappear at the end of the school day.

In class I was welcomed with lively curiosity at first, but soon I was relegated to the anonymous group of "all the other children." I know that this can seem like something positive to you, and yet, on closer observation, the anonymity I felt was, I believe, the main cause for the amnesia that obscured the next nine years of my life. Being half Somali became an enormous headache for which I always had to "justify" my linguistic competence and my skin color, without enjoying anything in return. I was already accustomed to this kind of question, but in reverse. However, in Mogadishu it was more a case of being aware of the difference rather than isolating it.

When I was a child my cousins considered me as white as milk, but seeing me again after the war, the first thing everyone noticed was that I looked much darker than they remembered. Since it is quite improbable that the winter sun in Italy had a stronger effect than the constant equatorial rays, it becomes apparent that it is the surrounding context that modifies the perception of reality.

The move to Italy implied the complete erasure of my short past. In my attempt to protect myself from melancholy recollections, my memory began a strenuous fight with the past, and proceeded to systematically wipe out much of my previous knowledge.

Barni continued to write to me for many years, without ever giving up. I almost felt annoyed by her letters; I did not read them and I hid them, unopened, in my drawer.

I wanted to get rid of Barni's image and I did so with a vehemence that I didn't realize I possessed. Perhaps she expected it. This is the only way I can explain the tenacity, devoid of resentment, with which she continued to look for me. Can a deep tie of affection be so boundless that it remains selfless, without expectations? Years later, when I was able to talk to her about those years, I understood that Barni had sensed many things that I myself had been unaware of. I saw that, deep down, she knew that her presence would never leave me. I kept meeting her in my dreams and I kept conversing with the heart-shaped birthmark in the middle of her forehead. It was as if I had in front of me the reflected image of the two of us as children in front of a mirror. I wondered what it must be like to be completely white or completely black; Barni laughed out loud and answered that one doesn't feel any different, that I needed to continue to be the way I was, beautiful in my lightness.

In my adolescent years, there wasn't much left of that light that I exuded. This growing isolation was fed by, and in turn fed, my mother's ever more frequent crises. I tried to soothe her pain, I protected her, and in so doing I became an accomplice in her sickness, preventing her from seeking out for herself the key to overcoming her grief. Today I know that in order to come out of the darkness we need to believe in our own strength. For many years my father tried, or perhaps pretended, to maintain a relationship, showing up now and then unexpectedly, and behaving as if he had been there all the time. He tried to be responsible and my mother quickly forgot how we lived when he wasn't there, feeding on his vain promises.

Most of the time, though, it was just the two of us, alone.

By the time I finished middle school I already believed life was so unbearable that it wasn't worth living. I remember that period because that's when the problem with the cutting started. The cracks resurfaced along with the memories, and I needed a way to control them.

I nurtured the conviction that my mother's suffering originated in my estrangement, in the distance between us that she feared, in the absences I evoked. I began to consider myself an evil person who inflicts undeserved torment on the person she loves the most, forgetting that the roots of her pain were not in me, but in the man she had chosen to love. I tried to gain her favor by dedicating my life completely to her happiness: I excelled in school, I cooked for her, I kept the house clean, I only had well-behaved friends, I studied the piano. I wanted her to embrace me, to take me in her arms, to cradle me like she did when I was a child, but it was me, rather, who embraced her, held her in my arms and cradled her.

I began to work my body with persistence, proceeding to the complete removal of all the gestures, the behaviors, the smells, the colors, that she might recognize as not similar to her own. I wanted to ward off the danger that other people's comments on my Somali origins could cause her to falter.

I do not know if my mother was aware of these efforts. Today, I realize that she felt guilty about her fear that I did not belong to her. Above all, she was terrified of losing me, of seeing me sucked back by forces that she had no control over.

In fact, that is exactly what happened.

My mother hated mixing the dough with her bare hands, she did not mix ingredients, she simply juxtaposed them, keeping them separate. She detested sliminess, oils, everything that was greasy, slippery. This aversion of hers was obsessive, as if it were the mirror image of what separated us.

Was it because I felt eccentric and undefined that I began to torture my skin? Did I perhaps believe that with the blade I could cut off the ambiguity of my essence?

You, doctor, will help me understand.

I can tell you that cutting became almost a morbid pleasure; I used to buy the blades at the supermarket, planning the time and place where I would use them. They were, for the most part, linear wounds, clean cuts from which I watched the blood flow, incisions that I reviewed meticulously until I drew a web of thin threads on my skin.

Was it perhaps to make a statement that I cut myself with such rage? Aren't initiation rites meant to mark a presence? I do not know if I will be able to explain to you and to myself the origin of those lacerations. My ultimate goal is to provide you with all the possible information in order to avoid a future relapse. I will discuss this matter again later, but not before I tell you how I ended up in the diaspora with the others.

When I turned sixteen my mother no longer concerned herself with me. She applied to go to work abroad and left the house at my complete disposal, so that I could finish my education. She felt I was mature enough to take care of myself.

So, after the limitations of the previous years, which were tied to my sense of responsibility toward her, I moved on to a freedom I had difficulty handling. I waited anxiously for her to come back on vacation, and I began to act obsessively, wearing the impeccable clothes she liked me to wear, trying to keep up the house in that almost aseptic atmosphere she liked. I thought that in order to avoid getting lost, I should keep the compass pointed toward those Catholic models used by her own mother to educate her a generation before.

It was a mimesis.

My boyfriend was a polite and serious classmate with whom I studied in the afternoons, I went out to the movies and had dinner with him on Sundays, with all of his family. My mother was enthusiastic about him, and they both communicated by winking at each other when I said something unintelligible (which still happened). Too bad the situation was completely anomalous, because I lived by myself and had a black father. This notwithstanding, our relationship seemed to last over the years, and at the end of high school we began to think about whether we should get married right away or if it would be better to wait until we had finished college. We decided to take some more time, hoping to better define some variables. Destiny, however, had other things in store for me.

Soon after my mother's departure, I felt the need to seek out Barni. Her old letters lay intact in a drawer, the news I had about her was limited to the meager information passed on by my father during his visits, and to a recent photograph that she had the farsightedness to mail to me with no return address.

I received this photograph soon before my mother's move, without yet imagining what a strong influence this was to have on my feelings. Barni had grown up in my absence, I had grown up in hers. And yet she was my sister, my second soul, she made me whole. Without her, hadn't I lost my way?

These developing thoughts grew stronger with my mother's distance, and about a year later Barni and I began an intense correspondence, enlivened by a weekly five-minute phone call in which we proved to ourselves that our seven-year separation had not weakened our bond. Barni had suffered, but had patiently accepted my silence. Con-

vinced of our reciprocal affection, she had waited for me to
stitch our torn edges back together again.

* * *

In the summer of 1990, my father showed up again. I
was on break from my university exams so I had a chance
to spend more time than usual with him. He was kind and
unusually full of good intentions: he seemed to be genu-
inely determined to change his way of life. He stated how
important it was for him to mend our relationship and told
me he very much wished for my mother and me to go back
to Mogadishu for a visit. He downplayed the disintegrating
political situation. My mother believed him and decided to
give him a chance: our trip was planned for the Christmas
holidays, and, after buying the tickets well in advance, everyone went back to where they had come from.

Except, as I had imagined, my father was once again
swallowed up by his world and became basically unreach-
able. He rarely called, hardly ever gave a sign of life, or of
what had seemed to be his intended plan.

His unreliability plunged my mother into a deep cri-
sis. She called me every night from Tunisia, where she was
working then, formulating a thousand different hypotheses,
the same ones she had grappled with for years, about the
presence of other wives, other lovers, other lives. Consumed
by his absence, she couldn't resign herself to living an independent life, and she inexorably fell into the traps he set for
her. Thus defeated, she would, once again, begin complaining about the unreliability of Somalis and about the cruelty
of men in general.

As the date of the trip grew closer, the idea of my going
alone began to take shape. Why was my mother coming? A
European in a country on the brink of collapse, looking for
an ephemeral man? It would be better if I left on my own. I
had a different perspective, he was my father, and we would
finally be able to understand where we stood.

"We," she and I: the first person plural was a given in
these situations. My mother habitually used "we" when
talking about the two of us, as if we were one essence, one

will, one person. Most of the time I felt flattered by this, I was suffused with her presence, I recognized myself as an extension of her. I accepted acting on behalf of our plural identity without questioning too much whether what I was doing was really what I wanted to do. That's why I agreed to serve as the dutiful advance party for my mother because I desired to act as a filter for her again, once and forever.

I arrived in Mogadishu on the last scheduled flight in December 1990. As always, decorously dressed and, following my mother's advice, carrying a collection of generic presents for the unknown relatives. I hadn't been back for eleven years and I felt the emotion sticking to my skin like the humid and brackish air of the city. But I didn't even have the time to see it again. Suddenly, a whirlwind of events, a cousin who drags me out of the airport and rushes me to the Italian embassy. The war was raging and I should never have left Italy. Everything happened so quickly and I was in such a state of shock that I still struggle to recall events. I'm missing some links as if those three days, from the day of my arrival to the day of my departure, were a hurried slide show that goes by too fast. Flashing images, like the armed adolescents, the swollen dead bodies, distraught women, and, in the end, my cousin by my side—in his composed stillness—slowly sipping a Fanta orange drink.

Libeen, victorious in his composure, had a more prominent jaw than I remembered, but he still exhibited the same calm habit that everyone admired as he took his time sipping his drink, making all the other children die with envy. Libeen didn't leave me for a minute, and his devotion was rewarded with a place next to me on the direct flight to Rome. I felt like a stupid package that doesn't even get opened and is returned to the sender a little bit dirtier and somewhat crumpled.

The flight was jam-packed with all kinds of people. There were Italians who had always been in Mogadishu, living off the earnings from a company or from some other dealings.

There was the occasional privileged Somali, there were the overpaid professors involved in technical cooperation, and next to me was Libeen. I didn't say a word during the entire flight, and the landing went smoothly eight hours later. People on the plane were so laden with belongings and with mixed emotions that I felt as if I were crushed aboard one of those jam-packed ships that they were showing on television at that time. The pathetic flow of refugees poured onto the conveyor belt from which they apprehensively grabbed their luggage, the scant remains of a lifetime, and then proceeded toward the exit. I remained motionless, looking at the conveyor belt. My luggage had been among the first to arrive and was going round and round. In those days more than one plane had brought the Italians back to safely. Each time a new flight arrived, the crowd of waiting relatives reappeared at the exits of the airport's international terminal. Suddenly, among the dust cloud created by the relatives who had arrived all dressed up to welcome their dear ones who had escaped the collapse of Somalia, I had a vision.

She was there, her face properly grief-stricken, and dressed for the occasion. She was talking to another woman her age, no doubt telling her how worried she was for her only daughter, who had escaped the carnage—leaving out the circumstances that had taken me to Mogadishu at such an inappropriate moment.

In that instant, in that place, for the first time I felt resentment swelling up inside me, as if those few days in the city of my birth had saturated me with the poison that was permeating the air.

I spoke, after all those hours of silence on the plane; I spoke, asking my cousin to go out and wait for me in a café: my mother would certainly not recognize him after all those years. I went to the restroom, I cried my eyes out, I pulled at my hair in rage, and it was then that I started cutting myself again with my nail scissors. That day I stopped shedding tears. After that, I was only able to cry again many years later, when my cousin Libeen silently decided that we needed to part. The restroom, luckily, was deserted, so I had time to regain my composure, blot my cuts with tissues, and wrap my hands in the scarf that had held back my hair. I managed to stop crying; I rinsed my face and emerged from the bathroom almost an hour later. The conveyor belt was still going round and round carrying my luggage filled with ridiculous frivolities. As I hoped, my mother had left. I went out and I found a distressed Libeen, after which we looked for a hotel without him asking me any questions.

This event marks the beginning of my existence as a war refugee, even if I had found myself in the war zone purely by chance and only for a few days. As a refugee I followed the flow of a diaspora that was only marginally connected to me. I internalized its makeup, the absence of a vision, its lack of goals. I wandered around between Europe and the United States for almost ten years, following the trends that drove the masses of young people my age from one continent to the next, from a worse welfare system to a better one. I survived. Feeling lost, I moved from the house of one relative to that of another, searching for protection and warmth, always with a half-unpacked bag, a life spent amassing anecdotes and ways to survive. Temporary situations that succeeded one another for years. I became a polyglot; I exhumed my Somali and the ancient proclivity for the nomadic life. I reconnected the threads and strengthened them.

That was my furrow, that was my destiny.

So, if I met Taageere, if I listened to what he had to tell me, it certainly wasn't by chance, but because that was what was meant to happen at that point in my life. Perhaps, if it had happened a few years earlier, I would never have agreed to marry him, I would not have conceived a child, I would not have come searching for his sister. But at that point, the plea that came from him, someone who embodies the very essence of bewilderment, was precious and soothing. I had to return to Italy because it was the place where I could put all the pieces back together again. After that I could leave again, but first I had to fix the things that I had left unfinished.

Was that the end of a dark chapter?

When I decided to follow Libeen and ignore my mother, I stopped talking. I cannot quite explain why my cousin took care of me with such devotion from the first moment. Sure, I had grown up with him and the others for ten years. Delving into his memory, he would certainly have remembered how as a child I already used silence as a weapon. If there was something I needed to fight against, I deliberately lost my voice. And yet, just as easily as I lost it, I also got it back. Mine was not a traumatic silence; it was a conscious, voluntary silence. This time there was something else along with this silence, something far more difficult to understand. The cuts were resurfacing.

They were the trauma of the unfulfilled return, the impossibility of meeting my father and the awareness that my mother and I were two separate beings. I completely lost my sense of direction, I stopped sleeping, and I began to wander around unlikely places in the middle of the night. When I was resting, sitting on a bench or a wall, I used to pull the blades out of my pockets and make deep cuts. Libeen tried to find a remedy for so much suffering. He took care of me, he watched over me. I believe it was his feeling of presumed omnipotence that prevented him from sharing my worries. Did he really think he could solve everything by himself?

One night I was stopped by the police. My normal appearance starkly belied my mental state. They imagined I had been the victim of an assault and they took me to the emergency room. Their main worry was not my cuts: they were superficial and could be taken care of with a few stitches.

No, what they found very upsetting was my unnecessarily defensive attitude, my excessive feelings of aversion toward them. They tried to stop me and I ran away, they caught up with me and I kept them at a distance with wild kicks, they asked me some questions and I spat in their faces. Finally, in a state of exhaustion, I consented to answer—with a challenge. The idea came to me after I overheard them expressing concern that I might not speak Italian.

I pulled out my pen and I began to answer their questions on paper. I wrote in my narrow handwriting, intentionally using rare and unusual words. As you know, it is a game that I find seductive every time. I use difficult words, I employ convoluted sentences. I especially do it when I start talking, because I want to demonstrate how far I can stretch my language. I want everyone to know, beyond the shadow of a doubt, that this language belongs to me. It is my childhood babbling, it is the plural subject that raised me, it is the name of my essence, it is my mother.

I was writing on the hood of a car, my letters dense and complicated, and while I was doing so, the sleeve of my shirt rode up a little, showing clearly the tight threads of the web I had carved on my skin.

The policemen were watching me and that is when they saw my purplish cuts; they saw my complicated writing and decided I needed to see a psychiatrist. But I was still too entangled in those marks to let them take care of me. I did not break my silence, and I waited for Libeen to come and get me. The ensuing days went by without my noticing them. Objects and minutes had no meaning; I remained motionless for an indefinite amount of time, bent over in a corner of the room staring at my groin. I was waiting for Libeen to come back, to try and nourish me, to pretend to bring me good news, to force me to get into the tub to wash away all that torment. That emotional state, that sleepless torpor, was something I had never experienced before. Was it my mother's illness that was taking hold of my body? It took many years for it to leave me completely, for it to dissolve, slowly, always keeping a warning light on in my heart. I lived. I let myself live. I followed my older cousin without asking too many questions. Too much mourning, too many interruptions.

I stayed in Rome with him for about a month and I was not even capable of meeting Barni. Today I am certain that Libeen, in some way, prevented me from doing so. Did he fear that the strong tie that connected me to Barni would take me away from him? Did he want me all to himself?

Or was he perhaps worried that this reunion would further damage me?

I remained entangled with Libeen for many years. Not even from this vantage point can I explain the nature of our relationship. An intricate entanglement that was never a real relationship, man and woman, fiancé and fiancée: that's not what we were. And yet there was no space left for other relationships. It was inexpressible tension, repressed desire, chaste closeness. I wrapped myself in his presence, I felt welcomed.

We left and we went to a land to which neither of us belonged.

In my memory, first of all, is the color of the sky, a smoky gray, then the six-lane thruways, constantly illuminated by the yellow anti-fog lights. The horizon seemed to expand along those strips of land snatched from the sea, neat squares protected by a sophisticated system of dikes and dunes, barricaded against the advancing tide.

These were the Netherlands where half the land is below sea level, where, instead of the old windmills, there are now pumps to drain the land, where the two regions from which Holland gets its name have a population density that is immediately apparent. There are townhouses and neighborhoods filled with tall buildings lacking cohesiveness.

It's a monotonous scene, flat land that goes on and on, canals like pulsating arteries and bike riders bending low against the easterly wind, like the poplars on the side of the road. So many faces and, every now and then, an anonymous patchwork of vistas and signs. What was the honey-sweet appeal that attracted so much humanity to that environment? I lived in those places looking for answers. I stayed by Libeen's side loving him with a dependent love, the love of an unconsummated sin. I asked myself about people being separated and finding each other again and I shunned an unspeakable truth. The truth about my father Taariikh's body, lost at war, and never found.

I am almost at the climax of my story. The family tree, that very intricate tree that I drew for you, was nothing but the symbol of an absence, an absence that I have never been able to put into words. A mourning I have avoided all these years. Uncle Foodcadde was the last one in my family to see my father, Taariikh. What is left of him are only stories and conjectures.

My Aunt Xaliima died in a shipwreck along with dozens of relatives while she was trying to reach the coast of Kenya by sea. I think it was the most devastating tragedy, especially because it was the first one that hit our family. I wonder how Libeen managed to hide it from me. Uncle Foodcadde, who had remained in Mogadishu to make sure everyone found a way to get out, tried to rejoin his brother. Overcome by grief because of the drownings, he was trying at least to save the lives of those he still had. He managed to find Taariikh once again, but my father didn't want to be saved. He found out about the shipwreck and he left armed, searching for scapegoats against whom he could unleash all of his impotent rage. Taariikh got lost in the fighting.

For many years I dreamed about his coming back. I even hoped to hear from someone who might have buried his body, but that has never happened. For a long time my father remained taboo. He hovered over us, but neither Libeen nor I could say his name. He remained inside of me like an obsession that has never left me. Of course, my mother found out about it. Was this the reason why I could not talk to her for so long? I did not want Taariikh's death to be acknowledged. No doubt my mother looked for me, with great difficulty, because she knew nothing of the diaspora. For many years I managed to avoid hearing her voice. Only the occasional postcard. It was because of that unmentionable fear that she might pronounce the name of that deprivation, that she would say his name using the plural "we," as if it were a matter that concerned us both, indissolubly.

The birth of my son has finally filled that void. His name is Taariikh, like my father's, so that the story can be regenerated. It will be a good omen.

Maybe my husband Taageere will join us, or maybe he won't. I don't worry about it. I want him to be the one to decide his own future. I have learned at my own expense that excessive concern kills people's souls. This is what happened to my mother. Without me she would have done just fine. I burned her with excessive love. It must not be so; that I now know. Love must be separate, it must not be a protection. Now I have a being who needs me.

I can continue to work. Luckily, I have a profession I learned in Holland. I will never stop being grateful to Libeen for this. My dream remains that of making a documentary about the Somali diaspora, and in the meantime knowing how to edit and shoot a movie allows me to find plenty of work, with a flexible schedule.

There is only one question that needs to be addressed. It is the reason why I originally talked to you about the initiation rites, the inviolability of the body, the lacerations. Will I be able to make you understand why I have decided to have my son circumcised? I know you disapprove, and I must confess that I have taken into consideration many opinions that are contrary to mine. As I told you, in Somalia circumcision takes place during childhood; it is a collective ceremony with a social purpose. A rite that affirms the belonging of an individual to a group. I don't mean to lecture, I am just saying this to remind you: the procedure has a hygienic as well as an aesthetic function and it cannot be likened to female infibulation, which is truly a mutilation. When little Taariikh was born, obviously I also asked the pediatrician's advice. I didn't tell him I was thinking of having the procedure done because I first wanted to hear his opinion. I do not deny that his violently negative opinion shocked me deeply, making me seriously question the effects that such an ordeal would have on a small child. I also asked the doctor if what everybody says is true, if it's true that when we are little and our flesh is soft the pain is less intense. He answered indignantly that this commonly held belief is entirely based on the inability of the newborn to express an opinion. How can we be absolutely sure that such a trauma will not have a long-term effect on his psyche?

Well, I wanted to take into account all the different points of view in order to come to an informed decision. I debated the question at length; I spent long sleepless nights. In the end, if I have decided to do what I have decided to do, it was to avoid standing in the way of my son's right to belong. I had to mark his belonging on his body.

With my Taariikh I use those Italian words that spontaneously spring from my mouth. Wouldn't different languages coming from the same mother overload him? A mother cannot run the risk of being split in two. Couldn't referring to the same thing with a different name each time cause a child to be schizophrenic? It is because of this profound concern that I have decided to speak my mother tongue to him. My mother tongue, as I keep telling everyone, is Italian, because there is no other that I speak with such ease.

I am sure that when he gets a little older Barni and I will teach him Somali. Circumcision, in the meantime, marks his belonging to this story. I think I have come to the end.

Thanking you profusely for your kind attention, I send you my warmest regards.

DOMENICA TAARIIKH

9

EPILOGUE—BARNI

THE SUMMER VACATION HAS BEGUN. Little Taariikh is one year old now; we decided to travel by car in case we felt like stopping to see someone else. Uncle Foodcadde is very excited, he's already called three times to find out if we are really coming soon. Many years have gone by. When I think of us, a constellation takes shape in my mind that links each of us to the other and guides us at the same time. We close the suitcases; we're hardly taking anything, we've tried to squeeze everything into a few bags so we can move around more easily.

We have to take little Taariikh on a trip so he can meet Uncle Foodcadde.

It's time to establish ties that strengthen without suffocating. Where is everyone? We find each single star, we retrieve the thread of the story. The story is still entangled in the confrontations, but we shall find the way out, I don't doubt it.

If we take off this immobilizing mask, if we can free our-selves from the shell in which everything is familiar, if we can strip off the film that isolates us from the people we live with, if we let our surfaces be scratched, something in-side will spring back to life. We are weary of fighting our personal war, weary of always being the same, irrevocably separated from the context.

In all the countries I have visited I was welcomed as if in my own house. I always thanked people for the hospitality I received and I was always scolded: Don't say thank you, it's what's due to you, if you say thank you it implies that the act of offering hospitality itself was not reward enough for your host. I explained: Thanking someone for me means ac-knowledging someone's generosity, not taking it for granted, being ready to accept the rules of the people welcoming me. Not expecting anything. This was what hospitality meant for the nomads, I'm sure. Give to those in need, receive if you are in need, simply, without expectations. Expectations kill generosity.

What shall we do then? The poet with the burnt hip said: *I have not fought during these last few days, my sword lies on the ground, I sought inspiration in the Milky Way. If what you ex-pect is a reading of the stars, your wait will be appeased. Follow me.*

We travel north, Domenica Axad, little Taariikh, and I. We have to take the child on a pilgrimage. Uncle Foodcadde is very excited, how excited he is! He always says we mustn't fret, we mustn't worry about the hard work that he does, thank heavens our dear old uncle manages to keep his mind busy. I have a brain that works, he tells us, I keep up with the news, every day I read the Italian newspaper, *La Repubblica,* I listen to the BBC and Al-Jazirah in the hope that things will change. I get by. You should see the other people my age here, with all the free time they have, they don't know what to do, they lose their minds. I keep myself busy. Uncle Foodcadde is on his own, a widower, but he's never thought of taking another wife. I'm old, he says. Perhaps his life could have some meaning again. He tells us that he doesn't have the courage to go back home without being able to offer something to the needy people there. Foodcadde is not the kind of person who hands out five euros left and right, he thinks it's degrading.

So he prefers to do that tough job, allowing his mind to empty itself a little, to clear itself. It's not just his problem. If I think of all Domenica Axad's muddled thinking . . . Thank goodness she's gotten better since the baby was born. Otherwise, she was running the risk of causing her brain to short-circuit, that poor brain of hers. The psychologist helped her solve a lot of problems. By writing her that long letter, by reconstructing her story, Domenica Axad was able to loosen a lot of knots. She had even been afraid that they wanted to take away her baby just because she had had him circumcised. Actually, no one had noticed. In the end, if I think about it, we all have congested brains.

More than thirty years have gone by since our independence; our name was respected, our flag flew high in the wind, in our home we lacked for nothing, there were vessels for the water, jugs for the milk, and utensils for the hearth. The blow that devastated us is no small thing, but we have not yet touched the bottom. Therefore, what shall we do next?

We carry our home with us, our home can travel. It's not fixed walls that make a home out of the place where we live.

In our home, Domenica Axad, little Taariikh, and I find comfort and protection, we lay down foundations in order to have the strength to fight every day. It's no longer possible to remain isolated; we seek to adapt and to rebuild our path. Through living together, we can share the greater part of our pain. A mother alone is no longer enough for her children, no one knows that better than Domenica Axad and me. Our mothers suffered from too much loneliness. Together we will make it, children should be raised together. Only by doing that, many absences will become irrelevant; it's by helping babies be born that I overcame death. I'm not in a hurry, I place my trust in destiny. The man I loved went somewhere else, but it will happen again, I will love again.

If the father does not follow the straight and narrow, our beacon will be the beauty of women. Wedding parties, love between

young people, harmonious clothes. Somalis all, I ask you a question,
Is "amooraati" like getting married?

In the final analysis, it's much easier for us women. Isn't it true that we lead the same lives no matter where we are? Isn't it true that we continue to look after, to take care of someone? Men feel useless, their names generate conflict, and they no longer play the role of decision-makers. Let's leave them without power, and let's stop protecting them, living weak lives has never produced good results.

Uncle Foodcadde has spent many years in exile.

When Domenica Axad and I, his brothers' only two daughters, arrive in the small village where he lives, he is overcome with emotion. He greets us from the thirteenth floor of the building he lives in and he welcomes us with a king's banquet that cost him more than his weekly check.

Domenica Axad films the scene from below. Foodcadde appears like a tiny spot on the balcony, in my arms I have little Taariikh, who's trying to get hold of the camera. We go up in the elevator, our uncle hugs us, laughing out loud with joy, he clasps his little nephew to his chest, and he says to Domenica Axad: Go on, film this meeting of generations. He sits in a flowered armchair and holds a new cell phone in his hand, just like a modern businessman.

The television is on even though no one is taking any notice of the images flashing across the screen, and believe it or not, there's even a documentary on about the savanna, with lions in the foreground.

Meanwhile Foodcadde discusses the BBC news with a friend: Now you can't even trust that source, they're all obsessed with bloodlines.

When he's not working, Uncle Foodcadde doesn't know how to pass the time so he goes to the mosque; he feels good there, he feels clean.

Faith, however, cannot make the nostalgia go away.

News travels around and the telephone keeps on ringing. They even call from Somalia: Foodcadde, you're the family elder, we must avenge a murder, let's gather the camels and put an end to the feuds. So, has history come to a standstill?

The thumb has no nail, the palm is covered in hairs, the hips and legs are not in harmony. Rings in noses, shaved eyebrows, what kind of beauty is this? Today it is the wife who repudiates the husband! Somalis all, I ask you a question, what does "sebareeyt" mean?

It means that if a man abandons his wife and he doesn't provide for his son, he cannot expect her to just wait, wait to get old, or let herself be covered in insults, when she doesn't remain faithful to the man who has abandoned her. It's lucky that there are still some understanding *wadaad* who for five hundred euros are willing to preside over an intercontinental telephone repudiation; Islam is taking on the fathers' responsibility.

There are even people who have the audacity to say that it's their mothers' fault if these children who are scattered throughout the world misbehave, without even taking into consideration their fathers who have washed their hands of them. The mother does what she can, what kind of an example is a man who cannot even run his own life? We still are overly concerned with appearances, we point fingers at the rings in noses, at the bare bellies; we don't want to get near the abyss, no one is able to fill it. Children to take care of you in old age: if we have them for this reason, it's not worth it; let's try not to go against the current, the place in which they grow up will make them stronger.

The killing of the innocent, your people's hatred, the spilling of blood, the catastrophes before us. Each one of us tries to explain the causes in his own way and corrects his neighbor.

Since we have no experts, let the tumor that is sprouting on your nose be removed the way you deem best!

At Utrecht station we met Gaandi, who was passing through. The timetable only gave the departure times, not the arrival times. In the Netherlands we were the only people who were meeting someone who was arriving. Gaandi was in Europe to raise funds; he had chosen to live in Somalia where his skills were needed. Gaandi recognized us: It's you, the daughters of my old friends. How lucky we were to meet him and to find out what we hadn't heard about, what nobody had bothered to tell us.

Gaandi had seen Uncle Taariikh for the last time. Taariikh had blood on his face and was bringing in the wounded to be treated. That last time he had found a minute to stop and talk to his friend. Taariikh felt he was too old to flee, if that was the fruit, the rotten, fallen fruit, he could not let everything there just go bad. Taariikh did not feel like starting all over again, he wanted to make himself useful in his own land for the time he had left to live.

He had stayed behind for an entire evening to talk to his friend Gaandi, talking about their childhood and the years of teaching on the banks of the River Giuba. He talked about a man who treated him like a son and who gave him *kiniini* for malaria. That was the man who had taught him to filter the water using an earthenware jug, and to fish in the village where they did not eat meat. The schoolhouse was a hut and they used state-issued notebooks. Taariikh couldn't handle leading that kind of life anymore and the man responsible for that area looked at him sarcastically, saying that in that village there had already been a young boy before him who wanted to get ahead.

Taariikh had talked of these memories. He had washed off the blood from his body and had said goodbye to Gaandi with the parting phrase that there was nothing quite like the village where he had been born, in a valley surrounded by mountains, with a bubbling stream. For him, water was life. Perhaps that's what he was looking for when he disappeared.

Times are bad, famine has struck us, the lambs are dying of hunger, let's help each other while we wait for things to get better. On the move during the night, there are shouts, there are screams, the water vessels are badly secured, how dangerous the situation is, how dark is the period that I have awoken in! Soomaalay dhamaantaa, I ask this question, what's this life of hardship all about?

On our way back, we came to a decision. Bit by bit, crossing borders, bit by bit coming back. Little Taariikh snugly between us. For a second we almost had doubts. Who knows if Domenica's mother lives in the same house? For sure, Domenica's mother knew nothing about her grandchild. Domenica's mother had been waiting for her daughter for many, too many years. Water is life, water washes away. Domenica rings her mother's doorbell with little Taariikh in her arms. Domenica is crying so much that she can hardly breathe. It's a good sign. Believe me, this time it's a good sign.

Chase away the bad omens, good has never hurt anyone, the story goes on, this morning the poem is good, you must separate and correct, the year we are in, the years that have gone by, everyone passes on things in his own way, if I do not hit upon the truth, if I simply pass it by, let the men of culture correct me.

GLOSSARY

Proper names and Somali words are transcribed according to the Somali writing system.

aabbe: Father, dad

abbaayadey: My sister

abbaayo: Sister (also a term of endearment)

Allahu Akbar: Praise be to God

amiin: Amen

amooraati: People in love
(from Italian *innamorati*)

aroos: Marriage

bajiiye: Garbanzo bean balls

barbaroni: Peppers
(from Italian *peperoni*)

bariimo luuliyooo: July 1
(from Italian *primo luglio*)

baruuko: Wig
(from Italian *parrucca*)

berri: Tomorrow

bismillaahi: In the name of God!

bluug: Blue
(from Italian *blù*)

boyeeso: Feminine of *boy,* derived from the name used for household help in British colonies *buraambur:* — Female poetry genre

Cali Dhareerow, — Drooling Ali,
xaggee u jeeddaa: — where are you going?

catar: — Type of perfume from the Orient

cillaan: — Henna used to paint nails, the palms of hands, or feet.

ciyaal: — Kids, sons and daughters, children; *ciyaal maamo:* mama's boy

ciyaal missioni: — Children of mixed blood who were being raised in the Catholic schools

dadqalato: — Cannibals

dalbooley: — A woman with knock knees

defreddi:
(from Italian *tè freddo*) — Iced tea

dhagax: — Stone, rock

diley-kasey: — A refrain that I might have invented

diric: — Woman's loose dress made of thin fabric, with wide sleeves

draddorio:
(from Italian *trattoria*) — Neighborhood restaurant

dumaashi: — Sister-in-law

elfis: — A hairstyle like Elvis Presley's ducktail hairdo

farmashiiyo:
(from Italian *farmacia*) — Pharmacy

fasakh: — To annul someone's marriage

fasoleeti:
(from Italian *fazzoletto*) — Headscarf

gaal: — White, non-Muslim

gabareymaanyo: — Mermaid

gambar: — Stool

garbasaar: — Very light woman's shawl used to cover head and shoulders

god(ka):	The hole, the trench
goonooyin: (from Italian *gonne*)	Skirts
guntiino:	A long cotton shift tied at the shoulder and pulled in at the waist
haa:	Yes
haye:	Yes, okay (used as a greeting)
huwa ya huwa:	Rhyme used to lull children to sleep, rocking them on one's knees; lullaby
iid:	Celebration (normally used for Islamic religious holidays)
ilbax:	Civil, urban
indho-kuul:	Kaja— black powder used to paint the outline of the eyes (kohl)
iska-dhal:	Mixed, born of mixed-heritage parents
istekiini: (from Italian *stecchino*)	Toothpick
jaat:	A plant used as a stimulant
jabaati: (from Italian *ciabatte*)	Slippers
jareer:	Kinky hair
jinni:	Devil, demon
kabushiini: (from Italian *cappuccino*)	Cappuccino
kafey: (from Italian *caffè*)	Coffee color, chestnut, brown
khaniis:	Male homosexual
khansiir:	Pig
kiniini: (from Italian *chinino*)	Quinine (medication used to fight malaria). The word has since been used as a synonym for any kind of pill.
kumi:	A coin worth one-tenth of a Somali shilling

mashallah:	Thank God
missioni:	Children of mixed blood who were being raised in the Catholic schools
nabsi:	Divine punishment, nemesis
nin(yow):	Oh man
ootkac:	Dried meat stored in butter
qalbi(geyga):	My soul, my feeling, my heart
raamo:	Dreadlock
rummay:	Twig of the *cadey* plant used as a toothbrush
salaam calaykum:	Peace be with you!
salli:	Small mat used for prayers
sambuusi:	Puff pastry triangles filled with spiced minced meat
sebareeyt:	Separate, split
seytuun:	Guava fruit
shaash:	Silk scarf used by married women to cover their heads
sharmuuto:	Prostitute
shayddaan:	Satan, devil, demon
sida:	So, thus
Soomaalay dhamaantaa:	"Somalis to you all," first line of the last poem of *Qabyo 1*, a theatrical piece written and acted by Maxamuud Cabdullahi Ciise, also known as Sangub, in 1998
Soomaali baan ahay:	"I am Somali," 1977 poem by Cabdul-qaadir Xirsi Siyaad, also known as "Yam-yam"

Soomaaliyeey toosoo, toosoo isku tiirsada ee, hadba kina taag daranee, taageera weligiinee:	Somalis, wake up, lean on each other, help the weakest, always support each other (initial words of the Somali national anthem)
suugo: (from Italian *sugo*)	Pasta sauce
tangabili: (from Swahili)	Dry season between the two monsoon seasons
tartiib:	Slowly, unhurriedly, little by little
tusbax:	Muslim rosary
ummuliso:	Midwife, obstetrician
uunsi:	A mixture of incense, resins, and fragrant sticks to be burned
wadaad:	Muslim religious man, holy man
waddani:	Patriotic
walaal:	Brother
Xamar waa lagu xumeeyay:	"Mogadishu, You Were Devastated," a 1991–92 song by Axmed Naaji

CRISTINA ALI FARAH

was born in Verona, Italy. She grew up in Mogadishu, but fled to Rome when the civil war erupted. She has written several books of poetry and is active in promoting African literature in Italy. *Madre piccola* has been shortlisted for the Vittorini Literary Prize.